PRAISE FOR TAMMY L. GRACE

"*A Season of Hope* is a perfect holiday read! Warm wonderful and gentle tale reflecting small town romance at its best."
— *Jeanie, review of A Season for Hope: A Christmas Novella*

"This book is a clean, simple romance with a background story very similar to the works of Debbie Macomber. If you like Macomber's books you will like this one. The main character, Hope and her son Jake are on a road trip when their car breaks down, thus starts the story. A holiday tale filled with dogs, holiday fun, and the joy of giving will warm your heart."
— *Avid Mystery Reader, review of A Season for Hope: A Christmas Novella*

"This book was just as enchanting as the others. Hardships with the love of a special group of friends. I recommend the series as a must read. I loved every exciting moment. A new author for me. She's fabulous."
—*Maggie!, review of Pieces of Home: A Hometown Harbor Novel (Book 4)*

"Tammy is an amazing author, she reminds me of Debbie Macomber… Delightful, heartwarming...just down to earth."
— *Plee, review of A Promise of Home: A Hometown Harbor Novel (Book 3)*

"This was an entertaining and relaxing novel. Tammy Grace has a simple yet compelling way of drawing the reader into the lives of her characters. It was a pleasure to read a story that didn't rely on theatrical tricks, unrealistic events or steamy sex scenes to fill up the pages. Her characters and plot were strong enough to hold the reader's interest."
—*MrsQ125, review of Finding Home: A Hometown Harbor Novel (Book 1)*

"This is a beautifully written story of loss, grief, forgiveness and healing. I believe anyone could relate to the situations and feelings represented here. This is a read that will stay with you long after you've completed the book."
—*Cassidy Hop, review of Finally Home: A Hometown Harbor Novel (Book 5)*

Killer Music and Deadly Connection are award-winning novels, earning the 2016 & 2017 Mystery Gold Medal by the Global E-Book Awards

"Killer Music is a clever and well-crafted whodunit. The vivid and colorful characters shine as the author gradually reveals their hidden secrets—an absorbing page-turning read."
— *Jason Deas, bestselling author of Pushed and Birdsongs*

"I could not put this book down! It was so well written & a suspenseful read! This is definitely a 5-star story! I'm hoping there will be a sequel!"
—*Colleen, review of Killer Music*

"This is the best book yet by this author. The plot was well crafted with an unanticipated ending. I like to try to leap ahead and see if I can accurately guess the outcome. I was able to predict some of the plot but not the actual details which made reading the last several chapters quite engrossing."

—*0001PW, review of Deadly Connection*

KILLER MUSIC

A COOPER HARRINGTON DETECTIVE NOVEL

TAMMY L. GRACE

LONE MOUNTAIN PRESS

Killer Music
A novel by
Tammy L. Grace

Killer Music is a work of fiction. Names, characters, places and incidents either are products of the author's imagination or are used fictitiously. Any resemblance to actual events, locales, entities, or persons, living or dead, is entirely coincidental.

www.tammylgrace.com
Facebook: https://www.facebook.com/tammylgrace.books
Twitter: @TammyLGrace

Published in the United States by Lone Mountain Press, Nevada

ISBN 978-1-9455912-7-3 (paperback)
SECOND EDITION
ISBN 978-0-9912434-7-1 (eBook)
FIRST EDITION
Cover design by Elizabeth Mackey Graphic Design
Printed in the United States of America

ALSO BY TAMMY L. GRACE

Remember to subscribe to Tammy's exclusive group of readers for your gift, only available to readers on her mailing list. **Sign up at www. tammylgrace.com. Follow this link to subscribe at https://wp.me/ P9umIy-e** and you'll receive the exclusive interview she did with all the canine characters in her Hometown Harbor Series.

Follow Tammy on Facebook by liking her page. You may also follow Tammy on book retailers or at BookBub by clicking on the follow button.

~This one's for my dad~
The best detective and most dedicated public servant I'll ever know,
who taught me integrity and character

"The true test of a man's character is what he does when no one is
watching."
— John Wooden

KILLER MUSIC

A COOPER HARRINGTON DETECTIVE NOVEL

Book 1

1

A heavy pounding rattled the door of the penthouse hotel suite and roused Grayson Taylor early Friday morning. His heart hammering, he jumped from the bed, disoriented, but prompted by the banging, he rushed to the door. He looked through the peephole and rubbed his eyes. Pressing his eye to the door again, he studied the man on the other side.

He tiptoed back to the bedroom and told Pamela to stay in the room and not come out. His heart rate steadied as thoughts of the past swirled in his head. Still confused, but less startled, he answered the door. "Andy, what brings you by?"

"I just came by to tell you what a rotten son of a bitch you are," shouted the irate man in jeans, a t-shirt, and a ball cap.

Grayson peeked into the quiet hallway and opened the door wider, motioning Andy inside, leading him to the couch in front of the huge window showcasing the Nashville skyline. "What's this all about? I haven't seen you for years."

Andy refused to sit, instead pacing with his fists clenched, "Yeah, that's why I'm here. Abby would kill me if she knew I was here, but you need to know something."

"What's Abby got to do with this? I haven't seen your sister since high school. And how did you know I was here?"

"Well, Gray, we regular folks have friends too and one of mine happens to work here and told me I could find you in the penthouse. No surprise, since you're such a big shot," yelled Andy.

"What do you want, Andy? And, keep your voice down."

"Don't tell me what to do," he spat. "You've always thought you were better than us and I'm sick of watching Abby struggle while you live your life without a care in the world, getting richer and richer."

"What do you mean?"

"I mean Abby's working two jobs to support your son and you don't give a shit."

"What in the hell are you talking about, Andy? Are you drunk or something?"

"No, I'm not drunk, you asshole. Remember when you got Abby pregnant when she was seventeen and solved it all by giving her money for an abortion? Ring a bell, Gray?"

Gray went pale, "Yes, I do remember and I'm not proud of it."

"Well, unlike you, Abby didn't feel right killing a baby because he was an inconvenience. So, for the last seventeen years our family has worked hard to help Abby and her son. He wants to go to college when he graduates next year, so Abby's been working two jobs to help save money. They live in an apartment out by the airport and she has a job at a school and works at a pizza place at night. I'm sick of watching her suffer, and knowing you have no worries pisses me off."

Gray's knees wobbled. He sat on the couch. "Andy, you have to believe me, I had no idea. I've always regretted what happened with Abby and the baby, but she made it clear she didn't want to see me ever again. So, I stayed away."

"I'm sure she still doesn't want to see you Gray, but I don't think it's fair. Taylor's a great kid. He's smart and responsible and a good son. He deserves more."

"Taylor? She named him Taylor?"

"Yes, and he looks just like you," he said with contempt. "So, maybe you can find a way to help him. She's too proud to ask or take anything, but like I said, Taylor deserves a future. I'm sure you'll be at the party tomorrow night out at Silverwood, won't you?"

"Yes, I will. All the record companies will be there. It's one of the main reasons I made the trip to Nashville. Why?"

"Well, Taylor works at Silverwood during the summer, so you'll see him at the party. Maybe when you see him you'll decide to step up and be a man. Call me when you do," said Andy, as he thrust a card at Gray.

They both turned as they heard a loud knock on the door and a voice said, "Mr. Taylor, Nashville Police, please open the door."

Andy followed Gray to the door as Gray opened it, "Officer?"

"Mr. Taylor, we've had a report of a domestic disturbance. Is there a problem?"

"I'm sorry, officer. We got carried away, there's no problem. We're fine," he said, as he patted Andy on the back.

"Is that right, sir?" asked the officer of Andy.

"Yes, officer. Sorry to trouble you. I'll talk to you later, Gray. I'm late for work," said Andy, as he moved towards the hallway.

"Are you certain there's no problem, Mr. Taylor?"

"I'm sure; again, I'm sorry to trouble you and disturb the guests." Gray slipped a card from the table and passed it to Andy as he made his way to the door.

The officers agreed to let Andy leave after taking his name and contact numbers. As Gray was seeing Andy out, a woman stepped out of the bedroom in her robe. "Gray, what's going on?"

"Nothing, it's all fine. We'll be done in a minute and then we can get going."

She returned to the bedroom and the officers inquired as to her identity. Gray's head hung as he explained she was a secretary at the Nashville office of his recording company, Global Records. He told them he ran the Los Angeles office and was here for meetings and a gathering this weekend and Pamela had come over to work on some spreadsheets. He finished giving the officers his contact information and reluctantly gave them Pamela's information. The officers wished him a good day and left.

As they rode the elevator down they both smirked and one said, "I bet you a Cronut they weren't working on spreadsheets. How dumb does he think we are?" They shook their heads as they checked in with the manager and reported everything was fine before leaving.

Gray shut the door and sank to the couch, with his head in his hands. He had a son. He couldn't believe Abby had never told him or contacted him. How was he going to explain this to his wife, Emily? Speaking of explaining things, he had to end it with Pamela. He knew those cops didn't believe his lame spreadsheet story, which illustrated how low he had sunk.

Not only was he willing to compromise the values his parents had instilled in him by going along with corporate ploys to take advantage of unknowing artists, he'd become an adulterer. It sickened him as he reflected on how far he'd strayed from his roots. Somehow in the last year he'd even convinced himself it was no big deal to see Pamela when he was in town. He had justified it based on his emotionless marriage and enjoyed being with Pamela, who made him feel special and important. His parents would be so ashamed if they knew what his life had become.

He knew this wasn't fair to Emily or his daughter, Hannah. Looking at the clock he decided he better get Pamela moving and tell her he was done with their relationship. He only saw her when he was in Nashville, which was usually every six weeks. He hoped she wouldn't be too upset, but in reality their relationship was only about sex. They never went anywhere together for fear of being recognized. How much fun could it be for her?

He braced himself and went into the bedroom. Pamela was already dressed and gathering her things. "I need to get to work," she said.

"Before you go, I need to talk for a minute," he motioned her to the sofa. "I think we need to stop this. It's not fair to you and I can't keep doing this to my wife."

She gasped and began to cry. "What's going on Gray? Everything was fine last night." She blubbered as she held a tissue to her nose. "What did that man say to you?"

"He had nothing to do with it. I can't do this anymore. You need a real boyfriend, and I have a wife and family. It's not right. I'm sorry. I don't want to upset you. I just can't see you anymore," he said, as he patted her hand.

She pulled her hand away. "I'm not some piece of trash you can use and throw away, Gray," she said, anger rising in her voice. "It doesn't work that way."

"I'm truly sorry, Pamela. It's over."

"I can't believe you're doing this to me, you selfish bastard. Don't you think this is over, not for a minute," she said, tiny bubbles of saliva escaping from her lips. She snatched her purse and stomped through the suite, black tracks of mascara etched down her face.

Gray didn't know what to do. He heard her heels click across the tile and the door slam. Before he had time to consider his next move, his cell phone rang. He saw it was Emily calling from her parents' house in Kentucky.

He took a deep breath. "Hi, honey. How's it going?"

"Not so good. Dad had a bad night. I'm not sure he's going to pull through," she said, her voice cracking.

"I'm sorry, baby. I've got a couple of things to finish up here, but could be there Sunday morning."

"That would be good, Gray. I'm trying to be positive for Mom, but I don't think he's going to make it."

"How's Hannah?"

"She's okay. She's been occupied with the horses and hasn't been to the hospital. I don't think it's wise for her to see him like this."

"I was supposed to have brunch with Mom and Dad on Sunday, but I'll let them know what's going on with your dad. Bowling Green is only an hour away and I can be there first thing on Sunday. We'll figure things out. Give Hannah a kiss for me and I'll talk to y'all soon. Love you, Em."

As Gray disconnected he knew he'd made a mistake ever getting involved with Pamela. He clasped his forehead probing the carpet for answers, as he contemplated the news of his son with Abby. He wasn't sure what he was going to do, but Andy had a point about providing for Taylor. Resting his elbow on the arm of the couch, he saw it was after nine.

He forced himself to shower and shave and while studying the mirror, he formulated a plan. He had until two o'clock when he was meeting with the CEO of Global Records, Mel Lewis. The dread of anticipation boiled in his stomach as he considered his plan to tell Mel he was leaving the company and starting his own independent label. Mel would be furious, but Gray was eager to get away from the corporate world that seemed to bring only misery to his life these days.

Gray swallowed a few bites of dry toast from room service and changed into a suit. He poured a cup of coffee and dialed Andy's cell phone. He told Andy he'd been thinking about Taylor and Abby and wanted to know where they lived. Andy warned him again not to contact Abby and Gray promised he wouldn't. Gray said he wanted to drive by and see where they lived and figure out how to help. Andy told him the apartment complex was on Glastonbury Road, near the airport. He jotted down the information and called a cab.

He directed the driver and as the city passed by, his predicament weighed upon him. A part of him was excited to get a chance to see Taylor tomorrow night, but another part of him was scared to death. He hated to do this to Emily right now. She was in Bowling Green visiting her parents, due to her father's failing health. She didn't need another problem and he knew she would be shocked to learn he had a son. Despite the distance he suffered in his marriage, he loved Emily and for the life of him he couldn't figure out why he'd been such a fool to have an affair with Pamela. He knew he couldn't tell her about his indiscretion right now, on top of everything else.

His thoughts were broken by the driver announcing they had arrived. Abby's apartment complex looked clean, but worn. The thought of her living here and working day and night, brought on a stab of agony in his heart. He would have helped her; she had to know that. He scanned the area noting the fast food joints, graffiti laden walls, and the crowds gathered at the bus stops, and felt only shame and guilt.

He and Emily lived in a beautiful house on the beach in Malibu. Hannah went to a private school, had a horse, took lessons for everything, and lacked for nothing. He made millions of dollars and spared no expense on Emily or Hannah. They enjoyed a wealthy lifestyle and if he let himself walk in Andy or Abby's shoes, he knew it wasn't fair.

He racked his brain for a way to help Taylor. Maybe he could provide an anonymous scholarship, if Abby was set on Taylor never knowing him. He wanted to make provisions for him. He asked the driver to turn around and take him back downtown. On the way back, he called his attorney.

"Hey, Steve, sorry to bother you. I'm away in Nashville on

business and received some rather surprising news. It seems I have a son by the name of Taylor Nelson. It happened when I was in high school. Anyway, I'd like you to start working on the paperwork to make sure I provide for him. I'd like to set up some kind of fund for college and I'll be providing for him in my will. I'll work with you when I get back to L.A. next week, but want you to start on some options. And, Steve, I haven't told Emily yet. I'll be doing so in the next few days. I'll text you the details and talk to you next week."

As soon as hung up he texted Steve a message and asked him to set up an anonymous scholarship for Taylor and transfer $400,000 into it immediately. He passed along Abby's name and their address. He received the acknowledgement back from Steve and leaned against the seat with relief in making the first right move of many he planned.

As some of the twisting in his stomach waned, he decided to stop for lunch before his meeting at Global Records. He didn't want to upset Mel and was thankful for everything he had done for him, but he couldn't keep justifying his actions all for the good of the company and his bank account. He wanted to be a better example for Hannah and now for Taylor.

He had reservations at the Bluebird Café tonight and was looking forward to listening to some new artists he planned to sign to his independent label. He hoped the day would end on a better note.

2

Cooper glanced at his watch as Myrtle poured his coffee. It was early Friday morning and as was tradition for the last twenty years, he was meeting his best friend and Nashville's Chief of Detectives, Ben Mason, for breakfast. Coop, as he was known to everyone, met Ben when they were both attending Vanderbilt Law School. Although they couldn't be more unalike in looks, with Ben short, stocky, and balding, and Coop tall and lanky, with a full head of dark hair, they were closer than brothers.

Peg's Pancakes was already teeming with customers, the sweet aroma of syrup punctuated by the cacophony of spoons swirled against mugs of hot coffee. Coop's hands, with nails bitten to the quick, reached for the sugar shaker. As he stirred the stream of white crystals into his second cup of the morning, Ben walked through the door.

Ben slid into the vinyl covered booth and Myrtle appeared and poured his coffee. "How're my two favorite guys on this sweltering morning?"

"Hey, Myrtle, how ya doin'?" asked Ben.

She glanced at the door admitting another group of diners.

"Busier than a one-eyed cat watching two rat holes. What'll it be today, the usual?"

"Works for me," said Coop.

"Sounds good," said Ben.

"Back in a jiffy," said Myrtle, topping off Coop's coffee as she hustled to the kitchen.

"So, how's your week been?" asked Coop.

"Not too bad. Been dealing with a string of burglaries, but I think we have a good lead and should wrap it up today. What about you?"

"Keeping busy. I'm finishing up some work for a corporate client on some background checks and doing polygraphs. Nothing too exciting in the life of a private investigator this week," said Coop, as he saw Myrtle rounding the corner with two enormous plates.

Myrtle delivered their breakfasts and the two dug into stacks of warm, fluffy pancakes, along with bacon and eggs. "Y'all enjoy," she said, leaving the check with the plates and a box to go.

Coop wiped some sticky syrup from his mouth and continued, "I'm stuck going to a soiree tomorrow night with Shelby. Her office has tickets for the rising stars in country music party out at Silverwood, which means dressing up and listening to a bunch of phonies all night."

"Too bad for you. Jen and I are going to watch the Sounds play tomorrow night. The boys are on a camping trip with friends and we have the night free. I was going to see if you wanted to come."

"Oh, man. You're killing me. I'd much rather go watch a baseball game than go to some stupid party, but I already promised Shelby and she's excited. Beau Branson's supposed to be there and she's eager to meet him," said Coop, rolling his eyes.

"Next time. So, this Shelby… is she more than a flavor of the month for you?"

Coop looked up and shrugged. "She's nice and cute, but we don't have much in common. I promised I'd go to this thing. It's only our second date. I can't seem to find the right woman." He paused and speared a wedge of pancake. "You lucked out with Jen."

Two uniformed patrol officers seated near Coop and Ben jumped up from their table, threw some money down and hurried past other patrons. On their way, one of them saw Ben and said, "Morning, Chief. We gotta run, there's some kind of domestic disturbance at the penthouse at the Loews."

"Be safe," warned Ben. He hated domestic calls, since they could deteriorate into dangerous and unpredictable situations for the officers.

Ben and Coop finished their breakfast and left their usual generous tip for Myrtle before heading to their cars. Coop stood to reveal his snarky t-shirt of the day, which read "I'd rather be a SMARTASS than a DUMBASS."

Ben laughed and said, "New shirt? I don't remember that one."

"Thanks for noticing. It came in the mail yesterday. I think it's a perfect addition to my collection."

As they stepped outside, the heft of the June morning air was like a soggy hot blanket. Coop saw Gus, his golden retriever, poke his head out of the window of his Jeep he had parked under the canopy of a beech tree. Ben was parked next to Coop and gave Gus a thorough petting before getting in his car. "See you next Friday. Have fun at your party tomorrow," said Ben, with a hint of a snicker.

"Don't remind me. Think of me while you're drinking beer and watching the game. I envy you, you know." Coop waved as he hopped in his vintage metallic green Jeep.

Coop pulled up to his office, only about a mile from Peg's

Pancakes. As he parked around back of the renovated three-story home that served as the office of Harrington and Associates, he noticed the lawn needed trimming. He'd remind Annabelle to call the kid to take care of the lawn. Gus hopped out and waited for Coop by the back door, anxious for air conditioning. The welcoming aroma of fresh coffee greeted them, signaling Annabelle was already hard at work.

"Morning, AB, we're here," shouted Coop.

"Hey, Coop," said a sweet voice coming from the front of the house. Gus ran through the house and found Annabelle at her desk. She bent down to pet Gus and rub his ears, "Hey, Gus, how's my favorite doggie?" Gus relished the attention, tongue hanging out, with a slight smile on his face. He made a beeline for his fancy water fountain bowl the moment her hand left his neck.

Coop, holding a fresh cup of coffee, sauntered to the reception area, where Annabelle's large antique desk sat atop shiny oak flooring. "Could you call that kid who mows the lawn and tell him to get on it? It looks pretty bad." He set the box from Peg's Pancakes on the desk.

"Sure, I'm just finishing up your background reports. I wanted you to be able to deliver them today. I'll call him after I wrap these up. How was Ben this morning?"

"He's fabulous. He gets to go to a baseball game tomorrow," he said, his tone laden with sarcasm.

"Oh, bummer. Maybe you'll have a good time at the party." She popped open the box. "Oh, yum, thanks for my breakfast," she said, eyeing the pancakes smothered with peaches and whipped cream.

"I know I need to have a better attitude about Shelby. Now I know how Uncle John must have felt with Aunt Camille dragging him to all those parties and fundraisers. She lives for that stuff, too. I'm not into those things."

"Well, that's been Camille's whole life. It's all she knows. She's a sweetie."

The sound of lapping water ended and Gus plopped down at Annabelle's feet, positioning himself so the breeze from the vent wafted over him. "Traitor," Coop said as he left Gus and went to his door. His office consisted of a large space with brick walls, like most of the rest of the house. A cozy fireplace dominated one wall where the addition of a sofa and chairs made for a casual conversation area. The rest of the room held an oversized desk and conference table, plus a couple of leather chairs, one of which Gus claimed as his own. The office emitted a masculine vibe, done in dark wood with forest green carpeting and accents. It had been his uncle's office until his death last year.

Coop had grown up in rural Nevada and had a typical middle class life with his parents and one brother. When he decided to attend Vanderbilt, his dad's brother, John, and his wife, Camille, had insisted Coop live with them. Coop went from ordinary surroundings to genteel affluence with one plane ride across the country.

Aunt Camille was part of the history of Belle Meade, Tennessee, and came from generations of old family money. She and Uncle John lived in a beautiful mansion on Jackson Boulevard. The home was situated on ten acres surrounded by wooded land and boasted a pool and pool house along with a tennis court. She had grown up with horses and although she never rode now, she still maintained the stables, which housed a handful of her most favorite steeds. Aunt Camille had never worked, but kept busy with luncheons, teas, church, clubs, and charity events.

John Harrington had retired as a police detective when Coop was a senior in college. After retirement, John opened a private investigation company on 17th Avenue, close to Vanderbilt. Coop starting working for his uncle during the summer and continued part-time while attending law school. Coop loved his uncle and discovered his own knack for investigative work.

During his sophomore year, his mother abandoned his father for a much younger man and never looked back. Since then she'd bounced from man to man and still hadn't settled down. The infrequent contact that ensued degenerated into no communication, unless, of course, she needed something. That was the same year Coop first experienced trouble sleeping. Doctors chalked it up to stress caused by school and his parents, but the symptoms never diminished and years later he was deemed a chronic insomniac.

Despite Coop's efforts to convince his father to move to Tennessee, he stayed in Nevada. He had never remarried, and to Coop's knowledge, never dated much. Coop's brother lived near his dad and had blessed him with a whole herd of grandchildren, which kept the old man occupied. After he graduated, he had no desire to return to Nevada and face the home he realized had only a veneer of happiness. When he passed the bar he decided to stay and work full time for his uncle and incorporated a variety of legal services into the company.

Uncle John had died last year and left Harrington and Associates to Coop. Coop employed Annabelle, his friend from college, who had been with Uncle John since she graduated, and two young investigators, Madison and Ross. They each had an office on one side of the reception area. As was his uncle's habit, Coop took on one or two law students as interns, but with their graduation in May, their shared office remained empty. Although Annabelle was a top tier graduate of Vanderbilt Law, she was not interested in passing the bar and was content to manage the office and act as Coop's paralegal. She also appreciated the relaxed atmosphere of the office, delighted to trade corporate suits and pantyhose for jeans and sandals.

Coop looked forward to coming to work each day and cherished happy memories of the time spent with his uncle, learning the finer points of investigative work. His aunt and uncle didn't have any children and treated Coop as a son. In fact, Coop still lived at the mansion. They wanted him to stay after graduating and although concern for his dad tore at him, he enjoyed them both so much he elected to stay. His dad urged him to be happy and had visited often, but with time the visits dwindled, until in recent years they didn't exist at all.

Now here he was, forty-something and still living with his aunt. It worked for him and he was used to the comforts it offered. He knew Aunt Camille was lonely without his uncle and no children of her own. Whenever he thought about getting his own place, he justified staying, for her sake.

Madison and Ross arrived around ten o'clock. They were working on a couple of divorce cases, which involved some snooping and surveillance work at night. While Coop was doing his best to clear his desk of stacks of papers beginning to resemble the famous Italian tower, he heard the whir of the lawnmower. Annabelle came in with several envelopes of reports ready to be delivered and wedged them under the base of his telephone, next to the ever present bowl of peanut M&M's. "Thanks, AB. I see our juvenile delinquent has arrived to mow the lawn."

"Yes, Justin said he forgot." She opened the armoire and removed a polo shirt and plopped it on top of Coop's phone.

"I knew better than to have made this deal with him to start with, but thought it would give him something to do and keep him out of mischief." Coop helped Justin when he got in a bit of trouble and in exchange Justin was supposed to mow the grass and take care of the outside areas all summer.

"He seemed genuine and got right over here after I called. I think he'll be okay."

"Keep your eye on him. I'm going to head downtown with these reports. She tapped the collared shirt with her finger. "I know. I'll change before I leave." He didn't dare ignore the dress code Annabelle insisted upon when he attended meetings with clients. His "wiseassery" as she called it, wasn't appropriate. He dug in his heels on the issue of shorts in the summer, but lost the battle when it came to his clever t-shirts.

He put on the fresh polo and hollered, "I'll see you after lunch. I'll leave Gus, since it's so hot out today," he said, as he headed for the back door.

3

_____

C oop pulled up to the gate at Silverwood on Saturday night, behind a line of sleek limousines. Silverwood was a gorgeous botanical garden, boasting over one hundred acres and housing an historic limestone mansion that had been inhabited by a wealthy Nashville family for decades, until it was turned into an art museum. It was a popular venue for both elegant and casual events.

Coop's turn came and he inched the car forward. "Hey, Eula Mae, how you doing tonight?" he asked, as he handed his tickets to the wisp of a woman, with her gray hair coiffed to perfection. Eula Mae was a longtime friend of Aunt Camille's and worked the ticket booth for various events.

"Just peachy, Coop. It's a busy night with lots of limos comin' through. It's always so excitin'," she said, with her pink lipstick smile. "Go ahead and park in the lot and a shuttle will take y'all up to the mansion, if y'all don't want to walk. You two have fun," she said with a wink, straightening the signature green vest she wore over her spotless white blouse.

Coop drove on and parked in the lot closest to the mansion. Eula Mae was right about the limos. They were lined up circling the driveway and snaked all the way to the parking lot. Coop opened Shelby's door and they both agreed to walk and enjoy the gardens. Shelby wore a glittery champagne colored dress with a sheer wrap and sparkly high heels.

It was still quite warm, but not unbearable with the light breeze and the shade of the trees. Shelby squeezed Coop's hand, "Thank you for coming tonight. I know this isn't your thing, but I think you'll have fun. It's pretty here, anyway."

He shrugged. "You look beautiful, by the way. You sure you're okay to walk in those?" he asked, looking down at her heels that put her only a few inches shy of his six-foot two-inch frame.

"You look handsome tonight. I never see you in anything but shorts and those rude t-shirts," she said, taking in his charcoal suit, dress shirt and his thick dark hair set off with the slightest hint of gray at the temples. She stumbled and gripped his arm tighter. "I may have to take the shuttle back," she laughed," but, I'll make it up there. I'm a little nervous, since nobody else from the radio station is coming tonight. I might not know many people."

"We'll be fine. Don't worry about it. Besides, isn't Beau Branson the one you're really here to see?" His caramel eyes teased her with a wink.

She laughed again, "Yeah, I'm pretty jazzed to see him. We're in the middle of lining him up to come into the station so hopefully, I can talk to him for a minute."

The gardens were in full bloom and looked gorgeous. The mansion was decorated in tiny white lights and country music drifted through the air. As they entered the mansion, they were checked in by another attendant in a green vest and given several drink tokens. There were hors d'oeuvres stations set up throughout the three-story manor. A small stage was set up for performances on the first floor with a variety of seating options available throughout the mansion. Coop was glad it was finger foods and not a fancy sit down dinner, so he wouldn't be forced to spend the evening sandwiched between people he didn't know.

Shelby saw a few people she knew from other radio stations and while she visited, Coop went to retrieve drinks. They sat and shared a plate of tacos, sliders, and spring rolls. Shelby was too nervous to eat much and decided to mingle while Coop stayed and finished up the food.

Coop's phone vibrated. He saw a text from Ben with a picture of the baseball game and a message *'wish you were here and I bet you do too!'* Coop grinned as he put the phone back.

He decided to peruse the artwork and find Shelby. He made his way to the top floor and embarked on a tour of the galleries. After going through a few displays he happened upon a man who looked important, talking to a younger blonde woman, in a tight pink dress that left little to the imagination. She was crying and her face was a mess, streaked with tears and makeup. He overheard the man say, "Pull yourself together, Pamela. You need to move on."

The man was trying to console her, but his motions were hurried and impatient. The man looked up, startled when Coop entered the room. "Sorry," Coop said, "I was just looking at the artwork."

"No problem. I'm leaving," said the man, as he strode from the room.

"Are you all right?" asked Coop, looking at the woman. His eyes were drawn to the revealing neckline of her dress and the cleavage she advertised.

"I'll be fine. I need to find the ladies room," she said, clutching her purse and shuffling into the hall.

Coop thought it looked like a couple's tiff. He'd have to find Shelby and ask her if she knew the man. Coop continued looking at the paintings and made his way downstairs. He saw Shelby standing with a group of people and as he surveyed the group, he noticed the man from the art gallery. Coop walked up to Shelby and put his hand on her back.

Shelby introduced him to the people she was with. Coop paid minimal attention until she got to Grayson Taylor, the man he had seen upstairs. Coop played nice and acted interested in their music talk and told everyone he was pleased to meet them. As the conversation ended and they drifted to the next group he asked her, "What do you know about Grayson Taylor?"

"Not much, except he's an executive at Global Records. He runs the Los Angeles office, but he started here in Nashville. Why?"

"I saw him up on the third floor talking to some lady who was upset and crying."

"Oh, that's weird. Who was she?"

"I don't know. I heard him call her Pamela," he said scanning the crowd. "If I see her, I'll point her out to you. She's in a low-cut pink dress."

They continued wandering and found some dessert. As they were scouting a table, they heard a band begin to play and Beau Branson was announced. The applause was deafening as Beau took the stage and tipped his hat to the crowd. He sang his new hit single, "Tennessee Summer", and it was an obvious winner with the horde of fans. The crowd swayed in unison and sang along with the performer. When it ended, more screaming and applause followed.

Shelby wanted to go and try to meet him, so they inched their way towards the stage. She got his attention as someone shoved another drink in his hand. "Hello, Mr. Branson."

"You can call me Beau, sweetheart," he said.

"Okay, Beau. I'm Shelby Saunders and I'm with WNSH here in Nashville," she said handing him her card. "We'd love to have you on the show. Do y'all have some time while you're in Nashville?"

"For you, darlin', I'll make time. He pulled a card out of his pocket and gave it to Shelby. "Here's my card and my personal cell. You call me and we'll set up a date." He winked as he looked her up and down.

"Great," Shelby stammered. "Just fantastic. Thanks so much. I enjoyed your song tonight."

"Thanks, darlin'. See ya, Shelby," he said, giving her a kiss on her cheek. He tipped his glass up to finish the last of the amber liquid.

Shelby went over to Coop and tapped her feet in a happy dance. "He told me he'd come on the show. I'm so excited and they're going to be thrilled at the station."

Coop noticed Beau talking to another group of people with a fresh drink in his hand. As he glanced around the room he spotted Pamela and whispered to Shelby. "Past Beau's group, there's a lady in a pink dress, do you know her?" he said.

"No, I don't think so. I'll see if I can find out," she said, heading off to chat with more people. Coop decided to continue people watching and have some dessert while he waited for Shelby.

While eating a rich *crème brulée*, he noticed Grayson Taylor in a heated discussion with the man Shelby had introduced as Mel Lewis, the CEO of Global Records. They were in the corner under the staircase. Coop had a clear view of Mel, red faced and spitting as he yelled, "This isn't over, Gray. I'm not gonna let you get away with this." Grayson hung his head and shook it. Mel stormed off and went out the front door.

Shelby was back at the table and Coop slipped her a chocolate truffle he had saved. "Come with me, Coop. You need to meet some of the legislators upstairs."

Coop let Shelby guide him to another gathering on the second floor in one of the art galleries. Several people were listening to Senator Grant Wagner. He was one of the longest serving legislators and the reigning powerful Chairman of the Finance Committee. With his sights set on a higher political office, he had thrown his hat in the race for Governor of Tennessee. He was smiling a toothy grin and dispensing hand-shakes and campaign brochures. He flashed his flawless smile above his thick neck and clasped hands with Shelby and Coop. While gripping their hands, he added in a heavy drawl, "Ah look forward to your support in November." He introduced his Chief of Staff, Meredith Stevens, who smiled and handed them a bumper sticker and brochure.

In the next group they were introduced to the current Speaker of the House, a woman, Lois Evans. She shook hands with everyone and listened with genuine interest while she visited with people. When Shelby told her she was from WNSH, Ms. Evans commented she listened to the station every day on her way to her office. She was warm and friendly and both Shelby and Coop enjoyed visiting with her. She was accompa-nied by her teenaged daughter, who was excited to see the musicians. When Ms. Evans heard Coop's last name she asked if he was related to Camille and went on to tell him that her mother was great friends with his aunt. They made small talk for a few minutes and when the notes from the band drifted upstairs, said a hasty goodbye and headed downstairs.

Shelby was enjoying the music and performances and Coop decided to continue one of his favorite hobbies—observing. He was a natural and blended in anywhere as he enjoyed trying to figure out people and their stories. He was certain Pamela was not Grayson Taylor's wife and he was curious about the argu-ment he witnessed involving Mel Lewis. He decided to focus on Mr. Taylor—the lead character in his mind's novel.

The first thing Coop noticed was Grayson wasn't paying any attention to the musical performances. He was spending much of his time watching the servers and kept visiting the appetizer stations, but wasn't eating much. Mr. Taylor made a point of ignoring Pamela and if she was nearby, he changed course and disappeared. Mel returned to the party and was standing with several other music people, clapping along with the songs and from his stagger and red face, appeared to have cashed in all his drink tokens.

The last act was finishing up and Coop saw Grayson head upstairs. He decided to wander and follow him. Coop feigned interest in the paintings and purposely chose the rooms opposite the direction Grayson took. There were a few other people milling about, discussing the artistic methods and messages hidden in the paintings. Coop made his way through a couple of rooms and as he was stepping out into the hallway he saw Grayson move out to the terrace.

As Coop entered the next art collection, he came upon Beau Branson holding court with several female fans. The singer was staggering when he walked and slurring his words, but became more alert as he turned his head and followed Grayson's progress to the terrace.

Gray stepped onto the terrace, thankful to get away from everyone for a few minutes and think. He had recognized Taylor the instant he saw him at the appetizer station. He had watched him work and interact and noticed he was polite with the guests and kept busy, always working. He was tall with a welcoming smile. He also noticed he'd inherited Abby's beautiful deep blue eyes.

As he stepped out to the end of the terrace, he rested his hands on the low stone wall. He heard a murmur of voices coming from the tree and statuary garden adjacent to the terrace. He heard both a man's voice and a woman's, but didn't recognize either. The woman said, "What if they find out?" Followed by a man's stern voice, "That won't happen. We'll take care of it."

Gray didn't need to see or talk with anyone else. He moved

to the furthest end of the terrace, away from the garden entrance and rested against the stone ledge. He decided to send Emily a quick text to check in. He punched in a message—*Hi Em. Just wanted to check on you. Getting ready to leave the party soon. I need to talk to you tomorrow about some things. I've done some things in the past and I need to make some changes. I'll explain all tomorrow. Kiss Hannah, Love you, G.* He put the phone back in his pocket as he heard the door to the terrace bang open.

"Grayson Taylor! I thought I saw you slither by," said Beau, in a thundering tone.

"Beau, you sounded great tonight."

"Don't try to make nice with me. See how successful I am now, despite you and your dirty tricks. Don't think I've forgotten how you screwed me, you lying, cheating, son of a bitch," he yelled, his face inches away from Gray.

Gray winced at the heavy scent of whiskey on Beau's breath. "Hey, why don't we talk about this over some coffee?"

"I don't need to talk, you asshole. You need to listen. You cost me lots of money and held back my career when you stole my song. Do you really think you can get away with your shit?"

Gray remained calm and composed. "Beau, I know you're upset and I don't blame you. I'm sorry things didn't go your way back then, but look at you now, you—"

Beau yelled and cut him off, "Don't start, Gray. You conned me and you're gonna pay for it. I'll make sure you pay if it's the last thing I do."

Gray glanced through the glass doors and saw a crowd gathered inside gawking at them on the terrace. "Let's take a walk, Beau, come on," said Gray, motioning to the staircase that led down to the driveway.

"Don't walk away from me," yelled Beau, as he followed Gray down the stairs. They walked along the driveway amid the limos lined up like shiny jewels, as the beat of country music drifted out of the mansion.

After a lot of hollering on Beau's part and listening on Gray's, Beau stomped off into the sea of limos. Gray wanted to talk to Beau when he wasn't drunk and had calmed down. He tapped in a reminder to call Beau on Monday before slipping his cellphone back into his jacket pocket. Using the exterior staircase, Gray made his way back up to the terrace and eased back against the ledge.

Gray knew in his heart Global had screwed the young artist when Beau first approached them with a song. It was the kind of corporate antics that had recently pushed him to make his decision to leave. Gray had gone along with Global for over ten years. He'd done it for the money and promotions, but looking back he knew Beau wasn't the only young artist he'd help take advantage of for the benefit of the corporation, and ultimately his own bank account. He was done with the greed and allure of his position.

He knew he needed to right some wrongs and would start by telling Emily about Taylor and how he was making sure he was taken care of for college and beyond. He wanted Abby to allow him to have a relationship with his son, but suspected it would take some doing. Maybe Andy would be willing to help him. He only hoped Emily would forgive him and understand about Taylor and about him leaving Global. He'd tried to mention starting his own label before, but she always blew it off as an overreaction and didn't realize his seriousness. They'd have to make some adjustments, but in the long run he knew they'd be happier. They would move back to Nashville, near his beloved parents, and she'd be closer to her family.

He stood and reached for his phone again, turning at a quick scraping noise. It was the last sound Gray heard before he was struck on the head and toppled over the terrace, landing with a muted thud on the stone wall below. Gloved hands grabbed his lifeless body and rolled it under the mass of flowering shrubs along the cool limestone wall.

4

Coop was one of the first to notice Beau yelling out on the terrace. He was the typical rowdy drunk, but after watching for a few minutes, it looked like things were calming down. Coop left when he saw them walking down the stairs. He'd endured enough of the rich and famous for one night.

He went downstairs and found Shelby, snatched another bite of dessert for the ride home and guided her out of the mansion. As soon as they hit the steps, he loosened his tie and unbuttoned his shirt. She talked nonstop about how much fun she had and how connecting with the new artists would impress her boss. She was willing to walk to the parking lot, so they dodged another parade of limos as they made their way back to Camille's Mercedes sedan, where he chucked his suit jacket in the back seat.

Coop dropped Shelby off at her apartment in Green Hills and drove the short distance to Belle Meade. He saw the lights in his aunt's bedroom, so he tapped on the door and peeked in. She was propped up in bed reading a book, with Gus on the floor beside her.

"Hey, Aunt Camille, I'm home."

"Oh, good. Did you have fun?"

"It was interesting and the food was yummy. I saw Eula Mae at the gate," he said, yawning, as he petted Gus. "Oh, and we met Lois Evans, the Speaker of the House, and she said her mom's a friend of yours."

"Oh, yes. Lois is a charming girl and I've known her mom, Francene, forever. They're a wonderful family and Francene is mighty proud of her little girl."

"She seemed sincere. I'm all tuckered out, so I'm heading to bed. Good night," said Coop.

"Good night, Coop. Sweet dreams," said Camille, as Gus padded out and followed his master to his wing of the house.

Despite the white noise machine, blackout blinds, and lack of any distractions like a television in his room, sleep was elusive. Coop practiced his relaxation techniques, but didn't fall asleep until after three in the morning. Two hours later, his cell phone blared with the theme song from *Perry Mason*. He reached out in the darkness in an effort to silence the noise. He struggled to focus his eyes on the button below Ben's photo.

"This had better be good for this early on a Sunday morning," he answered.

"It's a suspicious death kind of good. What happened at that party last night? I'm on my way to Silverwood with a report of a dead body."

"What, who's dead?"

"I don't know yet. A gardener found a man's body in the bushes near the mansion this morning. I figured since you were a guest you could be of some help. Wanna meet me there?"

"Sure, I'll see you in a few," said Coop, scrambling out of bed.

He took a quick shower hoping the hot spray would be a substitute for sleep and threw on some jeans and his "Stupidity is not a Crime, So You're Free to Go" shirt. He found Camille in the kitchen pouring a cup of coffee. "My you're up early today, Coop."

"I know. Ben called and said they found a dead body at Silverwood. He wants me to meet him there. Sounds like it's someone from the party last night. I'm going to leave Gus here. I'll be back as soon as I can," he said, giving her a quick peck on the cheek.

"Oh, my, how exciting! Just like when John would rush out to a homicide. I'll watch Gus. Call me when you know something."

Coop grabbed a bottle of sweet tea, hopped in the Jeep, and headed down Belle Meade Boulevard for the short two mile drive. As he pulled up to the gate, he saw Ben's car heading up to the mansion. There was a young officer at the gate this morning and Coop scribbled his name and told him he was with Chief Mason. The officer consulted a list, made a note, and waved him through.

Coop drove up the path and instead of parking in the lot, went all the way up to the circular driveway of the mansion. Ben was standing outside and motioned to Coop when he saw his Jeep.

Ben was scribbling in his notepad, while talking to the first officers on the scene. Ben finished his conversation and stepped away to talk with Coop. "Well, we have a positive I.D. on the victim. His name's Grayson Taylor; he's a VP at Global Records and runs their Los Angeles operation."

"I saw him last night. He was in an argument out on the terrace with Beau Branson. Beau was pretty drunk and loud. They left together using the exterior staircase."

"It looks like Mr. Taylor took a dive off the terrace. We won't know for sure until the medical examiner completes her work, but that's our best guess. We're working on notifying next of kin. We're getting a guest list too. What time did you see Beau with him?"

"I'd guess around ten-thirty. We left shortly after I saw them and I was home by eleven-thirty. The place was crawling with people, mostly the music crowd, artists and labels, plus a few politicians and their groupies. The list will be massive."

"And, this will be a high profile case, with so many important people here last night. So, we'll have the pleasure of interviewing artists and politicians, two of my favorite species. Tell me anything else you noticed last night."

"Well, I first saw him talking with a young blond woman, wearing a pink dress. She was crying and upset and he was sort of consoling her, but ditched her when I walked in on them. Her name is Pamela, but I don't know anything else. Shelby was going to ask around, so she may know more."

Ben was writing some notes, "Good, okay, I can work with that."

"And, I noticed the victim talking with Mel Lewis, the CEO of Global. They were in a pretty heated discussion under the staircase earlier in the evening. Mel was steamed and walked out, but eventually came back because I saw him watching the performances later on."

Another detective came up to Ben, "Hey, boss, they have video on the art and the gate only, so we're getting it and will start going through it. It sounds like most people were using car services, so we'll start visiting all the limo companies we can pick up from video or other sources."

"Good work, Jimmy. Coop was here last night so he's sharing some observations with me. We'll see what the M.E. says, but Coop saw our victim alive around ten-thirty. As soon as we get the guest list, start going through it and cross reference it with cars and times. Pull his cell phone records and financials while you're at it. We're going to have to talk to Beau

Branson, Mel Lewis, and anybody named Pamela. Get some addresses on them."

"Any chance it was an accidental fall?" asked Coop.

"Always a chance, but I don't think so. There're some scuff marks on the terrace, so it looks like something happened, and I don't think he landed where he was found. I think someone tried to hide his body in all those shrubs. His head is a mess and there's blood on the stone wall, but I don't think he could have landed so conveniently, completed covered by the foliage. They're meticulous about their gardens here, which is why the gardener found him. He goes through the shrubs each morning to clean out any litter or debris and the body wasn't noticeable until he dug into the plants. From the looks of the dirt, he was positioned in the bushes. No footprints, other than the gardener's. Someone either took the time to brush the dirt over them or the gardener trampled any that were there."

"Ben, one other thing I noticed and this was only because I was people-watching and found Mr. Taylor interesting. His attention was focused on the serving staff and he kept visiting the appetizer stations. He'd always take a plate, but I never saw him eat much, so I'm not sure why, but something was odd."

Ben made another note as his cell phone chirped. He scribbled while talking and hung up. "That was on the wife, Emily. We talked to Los Angeles and they found out the wife is actually in Bowling Green visiting her parents. I've got to make the notification, so I think I'll drive up and do it in person."

"Sorry, Ben, I know that won't be easy. Give me a call when you get back," said Coop, as Jimmy ran up to them.

"Boss, we were running the victim through our database, just routine. He came up as a party to a disturbance at the Loews Friday morning. Officers responded and talked with him and another guy," he said, checking his notes. "Guy's name was Andy Nelson. They both said it was a misunderstanding. Also, they listed a Pamela Hargrove as another person who was in the hotel room with Mr. Taylor."

Coop's eyebrows arched up above his sleep deprived eyes, "That must have been the call Friday when we were at breakfast."

"Yeah, sounds like the right time. And now we have a name for Pamela in the pink dress. I'm going to find Kate and have her drive up with me to talk to the wife. I'll call you later, Coop."

Coop got back home and made some breakfast. He retold the story to Aunt Camille, who was riveted to her seat listening. "I don't think it sounds like the killer was a woman. It would take a lot of strength to move a dead body," she offered.

"Well, it takes some investigative work and Ben's one of the best, so I'm sure he'll get it figured out. He's going to call when he gets back from talking with the wife up in Bowling Green."

Aunt Camille decided she'd pay a visit to Eula Mae and see what she knew. Coop warned her not to share too much information, since he was sure Ben's team would be talking to Eula Mae as part of their investigation.

Coop watched some television and ended up nodding off with Gus's head in his lap. He was startled when his cell phone rang around noon. "Hi, Ben. How's it going?"

"Just getting back to town. We talked to the wife and she was in a state of shock. They've got a little girl about nine years old, it wasn't fun. We asked her about her activities last night, as a routine matter, and especially since she was so close to the crime scene. That really outraged her. She said she's planning to hire her own investigator to look into her husband's death. It took some time to calm her down and I ended up giving her your name as someone she could trust in Nashville. She'll be in touch, so I wanted to warn you."

"Oh, wow, well thanks for the referral. I'm not sure I'll be able to do anything more than you guys."

"I tried to explain that, but when I told her you attended the party last night, she got even more interested. I think she's used to having what she wants and immediate action, so she could be high maintenance."

"Understood. I'll let you know if she calls."

"I'm on my way to interview Beau now. I'll talk to you later, Coop."

5

—————

Coop decided he better call Shelby and tell her the news. She sounded groggy when she answered and he figured she'd gone out again after he dropped her off. He shared his morning discovery with her, which shocked her out of her slight hangover. While they were talking, she remembered she found out Pamela was a secretary at Global Records. Coop told her the police had learned her name and were going to talk with her and several other guests. She asked Coop to call her with any news.

As soon as he hung up from Shelby, his cell phone rang showing a transfer from his business number. "Harrington and Associates," he answered.

"I'm calling for Cooper Harrington, this is Emily Taylor."

"Hello, Mrs. Taylor. Please call me Coop."

"You probably know why I'm calling. I spoke with Chief Mason this morning and he gave me your name and number. I'd like to hire you to look into my husband's death."

"Well, Mrs. Taylor, I'd be happy to help you, but you do understand the police are actively working the case and in all likelihood will figure things out soon?"

"That's what Chief Mason told me, but I want someone dedicated to this full time. Tell me what you need from me. I want to know why my husband died."

Coop explained his fee schedule and she agreed to wire funds to him on Monday morning. She also shared what she knew about Gray's visit to Nashville and that he sent her a text last night telling her he wanted to talk and change some things. She was planning to stay in Bowling Green for at least the next week and gave Coop her contact information. He promised he would check in with her throughout the coming week and told her he would e-mail her an engagement contract for his services.

Coop used his home office, where his desk was almost as cluttered as the one at work, and filled out the contract and sent it to her. He sympathized with her, but thought she was wasting her money. He gave Ben a quick call and let him know he was officially on the case and working for Emily. Ben suggested Coop come down to the office and look at the information they had gathered. Ben hinted he'd be grateful if Coop would stop and pick up some sandwiches on the way.

Coop hollered at Gus and they took off to meet Ben at the West Precinct. Coop went through a drive-up and ordered several sandwiches and drinks. He and Gus arrived and were directed to a large room set up with a few cubicles and a giant whiteboard. Ben was seated at the conference table and waved when he saw Coop. Gus darted to Ben and received a long petting, with his head in Ben's lap. Ben called for Kate and Jimmy and they gathered at the table and dug into a late lunch. "Thanks for the grub, Coop," said Jimmy, with a mouthful, as he palmed a bite of sandwich for Gus, stationed under the table.

"No problem. So, what do you guys have so far?" asked Coop.

"Take a look at the murder board," said Ben, as he motioned to the oversized whiteboard encompassing one wall of the room. Coop noticed a timeline with the interval between the time Grayson was found and when he saw him arguing with Beau on the terrace. He considered a list of names on the right and photos, including Pamela Hargrove, Mel Lewis, Beau Branson, and Andy Nelson.

"Who's Andy Nelson?" asked Coop.

"He's the man who created the disturbance during our breakfast. He's a construction worker and has lived here all his life. He's got a clean record and according to the report, Mr. Taylor said there was no problem and the two of them had calmed down when the uniforms arrived. The report also confirmed Pamela was in the bedroom during the incident."

"I knew she wasn't his wife when I saw them fighting at the party."

"I interviewed Beau and his surprise seemed genuine when he learned Grayson was dead. He wasn't broken up about it and told me he squabbled with Grayson at the party. Apparently, Beau was mad at him for stealing a song of his when he first began his career. He wasn't sure of the time, but said he left Gray in the driveway and thought he went back up the stairs to the terrace. He said he left right after that with a few fans and they went downtown. We'll have to run down his alibi and confirm when he left."

The foursome finished their lunch. Ben directed Kate and Jimmy to check out Beau's alibi. "How about you come with me to pay a visit to Mel Lewis and Pamela Hargrove and see what we can learn?" Ben asked Coop.

"Sure, I'll leave Gus in your office." The dog followed Coop into the office and flopped onto his well-used bed Ben kept for him. Ben's squad was used to Gus and would see to his needs while they were gone. Just as Coop was content being an unpaid consultant to Ben's team, compensated with beer and donuts, Gus was always happy to tag along and get paid in dog treats, or the occasional sandwich.

They drove downtown to see Ms. Hargrove first. She lived in a luxury building on Church Street. They approached the lobby desk and Ben showed his credentials and asked for her apartment. The security guard phoned her and told her he was sending a detective up to see her.

They rode the elevator to the seventeenth floor and knocked on her door. She answered, looking much less glamorous than last night, dressed in exercise clothes with her hair pulled back. "Yes," she said.

"Ms. Hargrove, I'm Detective Mason and this is Mr. Harrington. We need to ask you a few questions about Grayson Taylor."

She rolled her eyes. "Come in. I don't know anything about it. The policemen came to the room and talked to Gray and the other guy, that's all I know."

"You're talking about Friday morning, ma'am?"

"Yes, that's right."

"We're actually here about Saturday night at Silverwood. The party you attended," said Ben.

"Oh," she raised her eyebrows. She glanced at Coop. "Say, you're the guy who asked me if I was okay, aren't you?" She eyed his shirt. "You look different now."

"Yes, ma'am that was me."

"When's the last time you saw Grayson Taylor?" asked Ben.

"Saturday, at the party. The last we talked was around nine, when Mr. Harrington saw us. I saw him again a little later, but didn't talk to him. Why? What's this about?"

"What's the nature of your relationship with Mr. Taylor?"

"I'm a secretary at Global Records here in Nashville. He runs our office in L.A., but when he's here I do some work for him."

"And, that's what you were doing in his hotel room Friday morning?"

Her face fell. "I was helping him get ready for a meeting."

"Ms. Hargrove, Mr. Taylor is dead and I need some truthful answers," said Ben. "Now."

Her eyes widened with shock. She went pale, "What? Gray's dead? When?"

"He was found early this morning. We're investigating his death now and we need the truth. What was the nature of your relationship?"

Tears pooled in her eyes. "We'd been seeing each other for the last year or so, when he came to Nashville."

Ben glanced at Coop and nodded. "Ms. Hargrove when I saw you with Mr. Taylor you were visibly upset. What was that about?" asked Coop.

She sniffed and got up to get a handful of tissues. "Gray told me Friday morning after the police left that it was over. He said I deserved a real boyfriend and he couldn't keep doing this to his wife." She blew her nose. "When I saw him at the party I tried to talk to him about it. I loved him; I didn't want to let him go. He was adamant that it had to end. He told me to pull myself together and move on."

"What time did you leave the party?"

"Oh, it was late. Probably around eleven-thirty or so. I took the car service with Mr. Lewis, so they'll have a record of the time."

"Which car service?" asked Ben.

"We use Executive Limos."

"Do you know of anyone who may have wanted to harm Mr. Taylor?" Ben asked, as he wrote in his black moleskin notebook.

She shook her head. "Not really. I mean the business is tough. He has to turn down artists now and then. I know Mr. Lewis was hopping mad at him Saturday night. He was pretty drunk but kept telling me Gray wasn't going to get away with it."

"With what?"

"I'm not sure. He kept rambling on about Gray screwing him over."

"Did the limo drop you here at your apartment?"

She dropped her eyes. "Yes…and Mr. Lewis. He spent a few hours here with me."

"Did he say any more about Mr. Taylor while he was here?" asked Ben.

She shook her head. "No, we didn't talk much. We had sex and he slept for a couple of hours and the car service took him home."

"What time was that?"

"I'd say about four o'clock this morning." Her chin puckered and tears flowed down her cheeks. "You must think I'm a real slut. Sleeping with Gray and Mel. It's just I want to be more than a secretary, you know."

Ben and Coop only nodded. "We appreciate your time. If you think of anything else, please give me a call," said Ben, handing her a card.

"How's his wife?" she asked.

"Distressed, as is his young daughter. She's hired Mr. Harrington to help with the investigation," Ben motioned to Coop.

"I'm so sorry," she wiped her nose again.

"We'll see ourselves out. I need to ask you to stay in Nashville. If you have to travel, I need to know about it beforehand."

Her skin, already pale, went a shade lighter. "Am I a suspect?"

"Not at the moment, but until this investigation is further along, I'm taking a look at everyone and will be verifying your information. Just routine."

Ben and Coop rose and made their way to the door, taking in the view from the balcony. Ben reached for the door and Coop turned back, "You have a lovely apartment."

She stared at him, a wad of tissues in her hand. "Yeah, thanks," she mumbled.

"We'll be in touch, Ms. Hargrove," said Ben, as he and Coop stepped into the hall.

They were silent as they waited for the elevator. They made their way to the lobby and Ben stopped and asked the security guard to connect him with his supervisor. He made a discreet call and led them to a door behind the desk.

Ben and Coop shook hands with a white-haired man wearing an expensive suit and silk tie. He agreed to provide the camera footage from the building and promised to messenger it over within a few hours. A quick glance at the log confirmed Pamela's account, noting a guest arriving with her and leaving at four in the morning.

Ben drove his blue Crown Victoria from the parking garage and aimed it for the precinct. Since Mel's estate wasn't far from Camille's, Coop decided to stop and pick up Gus and his Jeep so he could go home when they were done with the interview. The quiet streets of Sunday made for a quick ride. "So, it'll be interesting to see what Mr. Lewis has to tell us about last night."

"Yeah, I have a feeling our favorite secretary will call him before we arrive," said Coop.

"I wonder if Gray knew she was sleeping with the big boss."

"I don't know. We'll have to see what they were arguing about last night. Maybe it was Pamela. But, I did get the feeling Gray was done with her when I saw them talking in the gallery. He wasn't showing her much love."

Ben dropped Coop at the office where he ran in and retrieved Gus. They followed Ben as he swung his unmarked car into a driveway blocked by an elaborate gate and pressed the buzzer. A woman's voice answered, "Yes?"

"I'm Chief of Detectives, Ben Mason, Nashville Police. I need to see Mr. Lewis, please. I'm with an associate, Mr. Harrington; he's in the Jeep behind me."

"One moment," said the robotic voice.

A few minutes later they heard the buzz of the gate and it swung open. Ben drove up the tree-lined driveway and a large, stone estate came into view. He got out of his department issued sedan, its squeaky doors out of place next to the groomed house and yard. "Wow, a larger mansion than yours, Coop," quipped Ben.

Coop gave him a sideways glance as he surveyed the huge house, which he estimated to be twenty thousand square feet. He told Gus to stay as he left the side of his Jeep.

As Ben was beginning to lift the knocker in the shape of a musical note, the door opened and an older man in black tails greeted them. "Mr. Lewis is expecting you. He's out by the pool. Please follow me."

They left the marble rotunda of the entry and followed the butler through rooms dripping with opulence and wealth to a gorgeous outdoor living area and huge pool. They found the balding Mr. Lewis in swimming trunks with a towel around his shoulders, sipping a drink. Moments later a petite maid delivered a tray with lemonade, iced tea, bottles of beer, and frosty mugs.

"Gentlemen," he waved. "Please have a seat and help yourselves to a cold drink." He set his drink on the table. "I'm Mel Lewis," he said, extending his hand to Ben.

"Thanks, Ben Mason, Chief of Detectives and this is Coop Harrington, he's consulting on the case."

Coop shook hands and made himself an Arnold Palmer from the tray.

"Terrible business about Grayson. I take it that's why you're here?"

"Yes, sir. Tell me, how you learned about his death?" asked Ben.

"On Twitter."

Ben rolled his eyes at Coop. "Tell us about yesterday. What were you two arguing about at the party?"

Mel shook his head. "I probably overreacted."

"Mr. Lewis, I was at Silverwood last night and it looked like you were on the verge of exploding," added Coop.

"Yeah, I was hot. Gray came to see me Friday afternoon to tell me he was leaving Global and starting his own label. I couldn't believe it, not after all I'd done for him. I gave him the VP job out in L.A. and paid him a fortune. It didn't make any sense to me." He shook his head and took a hefty swallow of his drink. "I couldn't understand why he would betray me like that."

"Did you ask him?" asked Ben.

"Yeah. He said it was time for a change and he wanted to run his own company, his own way. I told him he basically had his own company out in L.A. to run, but that wasn't good enough. He told me he was tired of the big corporate stuff and wanted out."

"When was he going to leave?"

"Soon, too soon. He wanted to be out within a month. That infuriated me. It would be impossible to replace him and giving me four weeks was ridiculous. We've got things in the works now that only he knows about and Gray leaving would be a real hardship."

"When did you last see him?"

"At the party." He looked at Coop with a hint of recognition. "Now I remember you. Yeah, you were there with some hot girl from radio, right?"

Coop nodded. "Yes, sir. I was a guest."

Mel couldn't pinpoint the exact time he saw Gray, but admitted to the heated discussion under the staircase and said he saw him after their conversation, but they didn't speak again. He remembered leaving the party around eleven-thirty and used his car service.

"And, what time did you get home?" asked Ben.

"Well, my wife's out of town, so I stayed out and didn't get home here until after four this morning. Took a shower and went to bed, slept in later than usual."

"Where were you until four?"

"I need to keep this confidential," he whispered, his eyes darting around the patio. "I was with a lady friend."

"Name, address," said Ben, in a clipped tone.

"Pamela, she works at the office. She lives on Church Street."

"Did you know Pamela was also sleeping with Gray?" asked Ben.

Mel's cheeks reddened and his eyes went wide. "No, I don't believe it." He got up and paced around the table his flabby belly jiggling as he strode back and forth. "Who told you that?"

"You need to talk to Pamela," said Ben. "Now, just a few more questions. Take your seat, Mr. Lewis."

Mel continued to stomp around the pool and back to the table. He seized his glass and slugged the rest of the drink down and gave Ben a hard stare.

"Did you spend any time on the terrace at Silverwood last night?"

"Not much. I took a walk to cool off after talking to Gray and stepped out there, but not for long."

"Was anyone there when you were there?"

He thought and looked out at the pool. "No, I heard some voices on the other side of the trees towards the back of the house, but nobody was on the terrace."

"Can you think of anyone who'd want to harm Mr. Taylor?"

He shook his head. "I was pissed off, but I would never hurt Gray. I've got a temper, but I'm all bark. I know Beau was angry with Gray and I saw them head off together after Beau's song, but I can't believe he'd resort to killing him."

Ben passed him a card and told him to call if he thought of anything else that could be helpful. He let Mr. Lewis know the police would be searching Gray's office in Nashville and in Los

Angeles and would have a warrant to seize any pertinent items.

Mel nodded. "Not a problem. I'll make sure the staff knows to let you take anything you need. I was mad at Gray, but for selfish reasons. I don't know how I'm going to run things without him and now I don't even have a month to prepare." His eyes misted over and his head slumped down, his heavy chest folding onto his swollen midsection. He stared at his lap, mouth agape, resembling a forlorn turtle.

"We'll see ourselves out. I'm telling everyone I talk to, if you need to travel outside of Nashville, I need to know about it. We'll be verifying alibis and until the investigation is complete, I need everyone associated to stay in the area."

"I understand. I'll have to go to L.A. in the next few days. I've got a mess to deal with out there."

"Keep me informed," said Ben.

Coop hurried to swallow the rest of his drink and set the glass on the silver tray. They were ushered out by the butler.

"I don't think Mel knew Pamela was sleeping with Gray," said Coop, as they walked to the cars.

Ben nodded. "Yeah, the shock looked genuine. He was fuming."

"I think Mel was footing the bill for Pamela's view. I don't know many secretaries who can afford to live in that building. That's why she looked so sad when we left. I think she knows the jig is up and she's going to be out on the street."

"These damn music people are a nightmare. Their lives are like a soap opera."

"When will you have the autopsy results?"

"Tomorrow. Doc Lawrence said she'd do it today and have some preliminary stuff by morning. We need to talk to Andy Nelson and get his story and check back with Jimmy and Kate."

"You're going to have a huge list of people to go through from the party. It was packed last night. In addition to the music people and their entourages, you'll have the politicians and their lackeys."

"I know. I was hoping one of these interviews would pop and we'd have a clear motive, but so far, I'm not feeling sure about any of them. Maybe Andy will lead us somewhere."

Ben consulted his phone. "Andy lives out in Donelson. How about we stop for a bite to eat and head out there?"

"Aunt Camille will be cooking her Sunday supper. You'll have to put up with her questions, but her chicken and biscuits sound good to me."

"Yeah, I'm hungry. We'll eat fast and run out to see Andy."

They pulled up to Camille's and when they walked in smelled the mouthwatering scent of fried chicken and baked sugar. "Aunt Camille, I brought Ben for supper. We're working so we have to hurry," hollered Coop. Gus bounded through the house and into the kitchen. After twenty years, Coop still struggled to call the evening meal supper and the noon meal dinner, but Aunt Camille insisted.

"Oh, boys, I'm so glad you're here. I can't wait to hear about the case. I saw Eula Mae today, but she wasn't much help," said Camille, as she took a pan of biscuits out of the oven.

Ben sniffed out a peach pie on the counter and came up behind Camille and gave her a quick hug. "Smells delicious."

"Oh, y'all sit down. Everything's ready. Coop, get the sweet tea out and we'll dig in."

They gathered around the table to share a huge meal and were peppered with questions from Camille. "Do y'all have a cause of death yet? Any suspects? What about the wife, she's probably involved, right?"

Coop held up his hand. "We don't know much of anything right now. It's still early and we've been interviewing people all day and need to get out to Donelson to interview another person as soon as we're done here."

Ben added, "We won't have the autopsy results until tomorrow. The wife has hired your illustrious nephew to investigate and I don't believe she's involved."

"Oh, my. Well, you never know. I'll try to find out more for you boys tomorrow. I've got a hair and nail appointment at Bella's, so I'll get the scoop." She touched her wisps of white hair, barely disguising her pink scalp. She kept standing appointments at Bella's every other day to have her thin hair fluffed by an expert. She smiled as she shoveled out giant wedges of peach pie and topped each with a generous dollop of whipped cream.

Feeling stuffed, both Coop and Ben gave Camille a kiss on the cheek. "Thanks for supper, Aunt Camille. It was superb," said Coop, as he patted Gus on the head. "I'm going to take the Jeep and follow Ben out to Donelson. I'll see you when I get home."

"Gus and I will be waiting. Take care." She waved from the door and coaxed the dog inside when they drove away.

"Come on, Gus. We've got a mystery to solve." She buzzed for Mrs. Henderson, the housekeeper and weekday cook, who lived in the caretaker's cottage with her husband. He tended the gardens and did general handyman work around the estate. Mrs. Henderson would clean up Camille's kitchen and get things ready for Monday.

Camille retrieved her flowery notebook and Gus hopped up onto the chintz sofa in her sitting room and watched as she scanned the list she teased from her visit with Eula Mae. She began writing notes next to the name of each partygoer from last night. "Somebody on this list is a murderer, Gus." Her pale blue eyes twinkled with delight.

Gus sighed and plopped his chin on her leg, ready for a night of secret sleuthing.

6

Coop followed as Ben steered his land yacht to the suburb of Donelson. He and Coop park in front of a modest, but well-kept home and noticed an old pickup truck with faded letters advertising Nelson Construction.

Ben rang the bell and the door was opened by a man in jeans and a t-shirt. "We're looking for Andy Nelson. I'm Chief of Detectives Mason with the Nashville Police and this is my associate, Mr. Harrington," Ben said, as he held up his identification and badge.

The man opened the door wider and furrowed his brow. "I'm Andy, come on in." A baseball game blared from the television and Andy rushed for the remote to mute it. "What can I do for you?"

"We're here about Grayson Taylor," said Ben.

"Man, I thought we cleared it up with the officers who came to the hotel. We had a disagreement, but it wasn't a big deal. Did he complain?"

"No, nothing like that. Actually, Mr. Taylor is dead," said Ben, staring at Andy.

Andy's eyes went wide. "What? Gray's dead? How?"

"His body was found at Silverwood early this morning. When did you last see him?"

"Oh, man. I can't believe this," Andy shook his head.

"Mr. Nelson, when did you last see him?" asked Ben again.

"Uh, well that morning at the hotel. Friday morning."

"What were you arguing about?"

"Oh, man. I knew Gray from high school, here in Nashville. He and my sister dated. I, uh, I went to see him because I wanted him to help my sister and his son."

"So, Mr. Taylor had a son with your sister?"

Andy nodded. "Yeah, but she never told him. Taylor, that's his name, he's seventeen and wants to go to college. I found out from a friend of mine who's a maid at the hotel that he was in town and I went to tell him off and get him to help."

"So, does your sister know you did this?" asked Coop.

"No, no. She'd kill me." He gasped and continued, "I mean, not really. She didn't want any help from him or for Gray to know about Taylor."

"So, did Mr. Taylor agree to help?" asked Ben.

Andy nodded. "He called me later and asked where Abby lived. He promised he wouldn't contact her or Taylor, but wanted to see where they lived. He sounded sincere." He paused and raked his fingers through his dark hair. "Oh, shit. I told him Taylor would be working the party at Silverwood last night."

"Did Taylor say anything about Grayson?" asked Coop.

"No. I picked him up after work last night and he never said a word. Just talked about how busy they were and how much he got in tips. He was happy."

"So, you were at Silverwood last night?" asked Ben, getting out his notepad.

Andy nodded, "Yeah. I picked Taylor up around midnight. Abby had to work today, so I offered, so she could go to bed at a decent hour."

"What time did you arrive at Silverwood?" asked Ben.

"I was there early, close to eleven. I was out with some friends and didn't want to drive all the way home and turn around again, so I waited in the parking lot for him."

Ben continued to ask him about where he went and took down the name of his friends and the place they ate dinner. He also asked for Abby's contact information and verified that he had driven his truck to Silverwood, taking down the plate numbers.

"Oh, man, this is going to be hard for Abby and Taylor. Is there any way you could hold off talking to Taylor until my parents and I can be there to help Abby? She's gonna be so mad and probably sad, what a mess."

"Is there anyone you can think of who would want to harm Gray?" asked Ben.

Andy shook his head. "Not that I can think of. I was mad at him, but only wanted him to help Abby. She deserved that much, but he hasn't been in Nashville for a long time, so no, I can't think of anyone."

Ben's phone chirped and he excused himself. Coop continued chatting with Andy. "So, is Abby at work now?"

"No, she's home now. She worked this morning at the pizza place and she has her other job at the school tomorrow. She got off at three today."

"We're going to have to talk to her and Taylor, soon. I'm actually a private detective consulting on this case. I could offer my office as opposed to the police station and see if we could get your family there, so you could all talk in a neutral area. I'm sure it's going to be a difficult situation."

Andy nodded. "Yeah, I'm going to be in major trouble with Abby and my parents."

"Where do your parents live?"

"They have a condo off Hillsboro Pike. We finally convinced them to sell the old house a few years ago and buy a place they didn't have to worry about."

Ben came in from outside. "Coop, could I have a word? Excuse us for a minute, Mr. Nelson."

Andy sat in his recliner staring at the silent game on television as the two men walked outside.

"That was Kate. They're running down limos and alibis and so far the stories are checking out."

"I know Andy's timeline may put him at Silverwood when Grayson was killed, but I don't think he did it. He's concerned about his family. I offered to have a meeting at my office with all of them, knowing we have to question them, but hoping to diffuse some of the emotion."

"Yeah, we could make that work. You've got enough offices in your place to separate them. I'll have Kate and Jimmy meet us and we'll get Andy to help get his family there. Then we'll call it a night."

They knocked on Andy's door and suggested he contact his parents and explain the situation and have them meet at Coop's office, which wasn't too far from their condo. Coop offered to call Abby and tell her he was investigating a death at Silverwood and ask her to bring Taylor to his office.

Andy was still on the phone with his parents when Coop disconnected his cell call to Abby. "It took some convincing, and she may call Andy to verify, but she said she'd bring Taylor and leave now. I didn't reveal the victim, just told her I was working with the police on a death investigation and since Taylor was working last night, we need to interview him."

Ben nodded. "Kate and Jimmy are on the way. We better get a move on."

Andy hung up. "Well, I'm in the dog house for sure. But, Mom and Dad are on their way to your office. What a complete mess this is going to be."

Ben offered to drive Andy and he accepted without any hesitation. Coop followed Ben as they hurried to get to his office before Andy's parents arrived. Coop thought of speed limits as more of a suggestion than a rigid rule. His philosophy coupled with the assistance of Ben's red lights allowed them to make it to his office in ten minutes.

Coop ran in and turned on the lights and made sure the offices were presentable. He shoveled the stacks off his desk and stuffed them into the credenza and around the corner on the floor. Thankful for Annabelle's insistence that his conference table be kept clear of paperwork at all times, he looked around the office, satisfied it looked more organized. Kate and Jimmy arrived next and Ben set them up in Ross's office, which was much less cluttered than Madison's.

"Andy, let's go outside and direct your parents to park in the back and we'll get them set up in this smaller office," suggested Ben.

Andy's parents arrived and were ushered to Kate and Jimmy. Ben stashed Andy in Madison's office, who took after her boss when it came to clutter. He sat on the only chair cleared of paper. "We'll come and get you as soon as we need you."

Andy hung his head. "Okay, I'm sure she's going to be steamed. The whole story's going to come out and it could devastate Taylor. I'm sorry I ever went to see Gray."

Ben squeezed his shoulder. "It's going to be okay. It won't be a pleasant night, but everyone will get over it, especially when they realize you were trying to help." Ben left Andy with a magazine and shut the door.

A compact car pulled to the curb. "Coop, she's here," said Ben, as he poked his head into Coop's office.

"I think we shouldn't mention Andy's visit and approach this as a death investigation. Explain to Abby we need to question her son and then we'll talk to them together. See if she'll go for that, so we can get the best information from him, before the emotions of the evening take over," said Coop.

"I'll let you try that route and I'll stay out here with her. If there's something there, I don't want to question a juvenile without his parent. I'll do my best to explain the situation to her while you talk to Taylor. After that we'll get the family together to help them explain about Grayson."

Coop sighed. "Here goes nothing." He opened the door. "Ms. Nelson, I'm Coop Harrington. You must be Taylor," he said, shaking the young man's hand.

Abby's dark hair was pulled back in a ponytail and her vivid blue eyes were supported by dark circles. She looked worn out and Coop knew they were only going to add to her trouble.

"This is Chief of Detectives, Ben Mason. I'm working this case on behalf of the family of the victim and wanted to ask Taylor a few questions about what he may have noticed last night. Ben will keep you company, Ms. Nelson, and explain the situation to you while I visit with Taylor in my office. Make yourself comfortable." Coop motioned to the couch.

"Uh, okay. Are you going to be okay by yourself, Taylor?" she asked.

"Yeah, Mom. I'm fine," he rolled his eyes. "Funny shirt," he said as he followed Coop.

Coop showed Taylor to the chairs near the fireplace, the furthest seating area from the door. He offered him some M&M's from his bowl. "So, I have a few questions. You must not have heard yet that there was a man found dead this morning out at Silverwood."

"No, sir. I've been doing homework all day and haven't talked to anyone. I don't work again until next weekend. Mom told me right before we came here. Who was it?"

"A man named Grayson Taylor. He was an executive at Global Records, but based in Los Angeles." Coop showed him a picture Ben had provided, courtesy of Global Records. "Do you recognize him?"

Taylor concentrated on the picture. "Yeah, I saw him at the party. I saw him several times at the appetizer stations."

"Did you see him talking or arguing with anyone at the party?"

"No, sir."

"Did you talk to him?"

"No, sir. I may have said something like could I help him or did he have everything he needed, but I don't remember. We were busy."

"Yeah, I was at the party, too."

"Hmm. I don't remember you, sorry."

"Did you spend any time on the terrace while you were working last night?"

"Um," he looked at the wall above Coop's head. "Not really. We had to clean up so I went out there after the party to make sure there were no glasses or anything, but we didn't serve on the terrace."

"Did you find any glasses?"

"Yeah, a couple in the garden area by the terrace, but not on the terrace."

"Where in the garden area did you find the glasses?"

"On the stone ledge. I collected them and turned them in to be washed."

"Anything else unusual out there?"

Taylor's shoe tapped the floor and he shook his head. "No, not that I remember. It was pretty clean, didn't take long."

"Did you have to clean or inspect any other areas outside the mansion?"

"Only the garden area by the terrace and the lawn off the main dining room. There were some tables set up out there and lots of plates and glasses to collect.""Okay, Taylor. Is there anything unusual you noticed at the party or anyone who drew your attention?"

"Nope. I was stationed at the appetizer stations on the upper floors until we had to clean up. Then Uncle Andy picked me up and that was it. I didn't see much of anything weird."

"What time did you clock out?"

"It was close to midnight. It takes a few minutes to walk to the parking lot and when I got in Andy's truck it was midnight, so right before."

"Did you walk with other people to the parking lot or by yourself?"

"With other people. There were a few of us leaving at the same time."

"Were there any strange cars in the staff parking lot that didn't belong or cars you didn't recognize?"

"No, nothing out of the ordinary."

"Do you know how long Andy had been waiting for you?"

"He said he'd been there a while, because he commented on all the fancy limos he saw leaving. He said he got there early because he went to dinner and sat in his truck working on bids for some jobs while he waited."

"Okay, Taylor. You've been very helpful. If you happen to think of anything else, I'll give you my card or call Ben, the Chief of Detectives. He'll give you his card before you go." Coop stood. "How about a Coke and I'll check and see if they're ready for us?"

"Sure, I'll take one. Thanks."

Coop left his office and when he glanced at Ben and Abby he saw she was quietly crying and her parents and Andy had joined them. He wandered to the kitchen and retrieved a cold can from the refrigerator. He approached Ben and asked if they were ready.

Ben nodded. "Okay, folks. Coop is done talking with Taylor so we can have him join us and help explain the significance of Mr. Taylor's death."

Abby scowled at Andy. "I can't believe you went to see him."

Coop interrupted. "I could try to explain it to Taylor in my office first, if that's easier."

Andy nodded. His parents gave helpless shrugs, but their

eyes pleaded with him. Abby wiped her eyes. "That might be better right now. I don't want him to see me so upset." Andy offered her a tissue and she swiped it out of his hand.

"Okay, we'll be out in a few minutes." Coop took the drink and went back into his office.

"Here you go, Taylor. Your uncle tells me you've got college plans. Where are you heading?" He tossed a few M&M's in his mouth while he waited for Taylor to answer.

Taylor smiled. "Vanderbilt, sir. I want to be a lawyer. I'll graduate high school next year."

"I recommend it. That's where I went to school. I'm a lawyer as well as a detective. This was my uncle's firm and he died last year, so now I run it. He was a police detective and retired and opened this agency."

Taylor took a swig of his drink. "Cool. Did you like Vanderbilt?"

"I loved it. I always take on a couple of interns, so when you get further along and if you're interested, you let me know and maybe you could do some work here."

Taylor's eyes brightened. "Really?"

"Really. Now, I have some other information to share with you. This is something that won't be easy, so I'll do my best to explain it and then you can visit with your family. Your mom and grandparents are out in the reception area, along with Andy."

Taylor furrowed his brow. "What do you mean?"

"Well, the man who died is someone who was close to your family. He grew up here in Nashville and went to school with your mom. In fact, your mom and Mr. Taylor dated in high school."

"Oh, wow. That's weird. Mom didn't mention anything."

"She didn't know he was the victim. Ben just told her."

"Oh, she's probably upset if she knew him."

"Actually, there's a bit more to it. When she was dating

Grayson, she became pregnant. He thought she had an abortion, but she didn't. He didn't know about her child. You're their son, Taylor." Coop's eyes, the color of expensive cognac, softened.

The can in Taylor's hands began to shake. "What? He was my dad?"

Coop nodded. "I'm afraid so. I'm sorry you had to learn about it like this and I'm very sorry he died. That's a lot to take in."

Taylor set the can down on a table. Tears welled up in his eyes. "Why didn't she ever tell me I had a father? I used to ask about him and she told me he was dead."

"I can't answer that, but I'm sure she thought she was doing the best thing she could do for you. Moms like to protect us, that's their job. I can tell your mom's a good one, so don't be too hard on her. Your family loves you."

"Man, I could have known him. All this time..." he couldn't continue, as his voice cracked and silent tears leaked down his face.

Coop placed a firm hand on his shoulder. "I know this is hard, Taylor. Your uncle feels horrible about the situation. He went to see Gray Friday morning and told him about you—without telling your mom. He was trying to get Gray to contribute to your college costs and Gray told him he wanted to help you. He was shocked to know about you too. Andy told him you'd be working the event at Silverwood."

Taylor's eyes widened. "He spent a lot of time at my appetizer station, maybe that's why."

"Could be. I'm sure he wanted to know you, Taylor. I've only talked to you for a short time, but I can tell you're a bright and special young man. He'd have been proud of you."

Taylor nodded and wiped his face. "I wish I would have talked to him last night."

"You ready to face your family now? They asked me to break

the news to you, because your mom is pretty upset and worried."

"Yeah, I'll be okay." He stood and went to the door. Coop opened it and they joined the others in the reception area.

Abby rushed to him and hugged him. "I'm so sorry, Taylor. I thought I was protecting you."

He hugged her back. "I know, Mom. Mr. Harrington explained you were doing your best."

She looked at Coop and mouthed her thanks. "I was. I really was. Do you need us for anything else tonight?" she asked.

Ben shook his head. "No, ma'am. You're all free to go. If we have any more questions, we've got all your contact information and we'll be in touch. I've told everyone else we've interviewed, not to leave the area without letting me know. Do any of you have travel plans?"

They all shook their heads and Abby's father moved in to hug his grandson. "Let's go to our condo tonight, huh? Have some ice cream and talk things through."

Coop shook Taylor's hand. "Remember, if you need to talk, stop by anytime and come see me when you get into Vanderbilt or if you need help with your admission."

Taylor shook his hand. "I will, thanks, sir."

"It's Coop, okay?"

"Thanks, Coop. See you later," said Taylor, as he left the office with his family. Coop shut the front door and sunk into the couch, looking at Jimmy, Kate, and Ben. "So, what did you learn from the others?"

"Nothing new. The parents didn't add much. They were home together all night. We can confirm with the security at their building, but I don't think they had anything to do with it," said Jimmy.

"We validated Andy's arrival at Silverwood and his departure, which match the times he gave us. There's no footage to confirm he stayed in his truck, so technically, he was at the scene and could have done the deed," added Kate.

Coop reported on his conversation with Taylor which didn't add much to the investigation. "He confirms Andy's departure and the story about him going to dinner with friends and arriving early. The only noteworthy item lies in the fact he cleaned up outside and there were some glasses on the ledge in the garden area to the side of the terrace. So, it's obvious people were there, we just don't know who or when."

Ben yawned. "Let's meet again in the morning and start going through the guest list. You two do your best to confirm Andy's story with his friends and the restaurant and see if anyone saw him sitting in his truck."

"You got it, boss. We'll confirm Abby's whereabouts, but I don't think she was involved or even knew Grayson was in town. See you in the morning," said Jimmy, as he and Kate left.

"After our meeting in the morning, I'm going to drive over to Bowling Green and talk with Emily Taylor. I'll tell her what we know so far and see what else I can learn from her," said Coop.

"Good idea. Thanks for the help tonight. This worked out better for the family. See you around ten tomorrow. Should have the cause of death and Gray's phone records by then," said Ben, as he made his way to the back door.

"Sounds good, I'll be there. I like Taylor—he's a neat kid. I hope things work out for him."

7

When Coop got home, he found Gus and Aunt Camille both asleep on her flowery sofa. Her rhinestone encrusted reading glasses had slipped down her nose. He patted her hand. "Aunt Camille, time to get to bed. It's late."

Her eyes fluttered open and she smiled when she saw him. "Oh, I must have dozed off." Gus opened one lazy eye and sighed as he shut it again. Coop saw her notebook open on her lap.

"What are you up to?" He glanced at her entries. "Where did you get this list of people?"

"Oh, nothing. Eula Mae mentioned a few people who were at the party and I thought I'd make some notes about those I know. It may help you boys out."

He shook his head, but smiled. "Aunt Camille, come on, let's get you to bed." He gave her a hand up and she drifted to her bedroom. Gus moseyed to Coop's bedroom and climbed into the oversized chair he claimed as his own.

As Coop got ready for bed his thoughts turned to Taylor. He wished Gray had gotten the chance to meet him and do the right thing. The dread of telling Emily Taylor about Gray's son kept him awake and thinking too much. He inhaled the natural lavender oil he kept on his nightstand. His latest attempt at inviting sleep hadn't proved to be successful, but he kept trying. Thoughts of his father blended with theories about Gray's case as he closed his eyes. He finally slept, only to be wakened a few hours later by the alarm.

Mrs. Henderson had breakfast ready when Coop emerged from showering. He went for coffee first, hoping to stave off one of his signature headaches brought on by a constant lack of sleep. Anticipating a trip to see Emily Taylor, he opted for a button-down and jeans. "Good morning, Mr. Cooper," she said, presenting him with a plate of her famous eggs benedict over waffles.

"Morning, Mrs. Henderson. This looks delicious." He cleaned his plate and as was his habit, drank several more cups of coffee.

He kissed his aunt goodbye and told her he'd be late, but would take Gus to the office to spend the day with Annabelle.

"We'll keep supper warm in the oven, if y'all miss it. I'll have new information from the salon today, don't forget," she said, as he and Gus hopped in his Jeep.

Coop shook his head and chuckled as he drove away. Gus was smiling with his head out the passenger side, ears flapping in the breeze and lips ruffled by the wind. It was a short ride to the office and Coop spent the first part of the morning telling Annabelle about the new case.

"See, it's a good thing you went to Silverwood with Shelby," she winked, as she finished making a pitcher of sweet tea and stashed it in the fridge.

"It was definitely more interesting than I thought it would be." He signed a few checks she had ready and added, "I'm going to a meeting at Ben's office, then I'm driving to Bowling Green to talk to the wife."

"No wonder y'all look so professional today," she said with a smirk.

"I may be late. Depends what happens today. If I'm not here when you close up, leave Gus in the office and I'll pick him up before I go home."

"You have a meeting tomorrow on the Simpson divorce. I'll have the reports done this morning and they'll be on your desk, plus I'll email you copies." She cleared her throat. "Speaking of your desk, I was surprised to see it cleared off, until I looked on the floor and in your credenza. Coop, you've got to let me get in there and organize your mess."

"I know," he hung his head. "Go ahead and file everything, except anything I have on Grayson's case. I'll try to keep it clean this time."

She shook her head and rolled her eyes. "Yeah, yeah, I've heard that before."

"Thanks, AB. I'll catch you later or see you tomorrow," said Coop, as he gave Gus a rub. He filled his travel mug from the fresh pot on the burner and left through the back door.

He arrived at Ben's and was welcomed with a box of sinful pastries. "I stopped by the Donut Hole on my way," said Ben, choosing a salted chocolate caramel topped confection. Coop snagged a maple bacon donut, helped himself to a cup of coffee, and prepared to listen to the latest developments.

Jimmy and Kate joined them at the table. "Gray's phone records showed calls to a real estate company, some song-writers and a few performers, The Bluebird Café, his lawyer in Los Angeles, Andy Nelson, his parents, and his wife. There were no calls or texts to Pamela, Mel, Beau, Abby, or Taylor. There was an appointment reminder for Monday about a call with Beau. He texted his wife, as she indicated when she was inter-viewed, and also his lawyer about transferring a large sum of money for a scholarship for Taylor," said Jimmy, as he read from his notes.

"So, he was going to do the right thing. I hope his lawyer got that done for him," said Coop.

"I talked to him this morning," added Kate. "He has authority to handle Gray's finances and did in fact get the transfer of funds completed after hearing from Gray. Sounds like he's one of his VIP clients and he jumps for him. He also told me he knew Emily wouldn't be happy to learn about Taylor and she could be difficult and demanding. He didn't envy us the task of talking to her and hinted he hoped we would so he didn't have to." Kate's eyebrows rose as she bit off a hunk of cinnamon twist. "I thought she was a piece of work when we met her and he confirmed it."

Ben glanced at Coop. "You're in for a fun meeting with the missus. Good call on skipping one of your usual humorous shirts."

"Yeah," Coop shrugged. "Hopefully, the lawyer was good and she can't undo the money for Taylor."

Jimmy spoke up. "Speaking of money. Gray's so rich, he buys a new boat when he gets one wet. The guy is loaded, with millions in the bank. Everything is paid for—a huge house in Malibu, right on the ocean. Expensive cars, boats, you name it, he has it. I don't see any money problems; it all comes from his job at Global Records. He clears around three million a year, plus a bonus. Looks like his wife's family had a little money, but nothing like what they have now. Her family has always been in Bowling Green—horse people."

"We plan to talk to his parents this morning and we'll verify the calls to the artists and real estate office, but they make sense if he was planning his own label," said Kate, dusting her hands of cinnamon and sugar. "He took a cab to the Silverwood, so there wasn't a driver waiting to take him back to the hotel."

"I've got the autopsy results. Doc says she estimates time of death between ten-thirty and twelve-thirty in the morning. That fits with our eye witness account of seeing Gray around ten-thirty," Ben glanced at Coop. "She says preliminary cause of death is blunt force trauma to the head from a heavy object consistent with the stone sculpture on the terrace railing. Trace indicated small fragments matching the statuary. They're doing more tests, but found blood and tissue on it. No good prints, just smudges, due to the porous nature of the stone. Only a small amount of alcohol in his system, nothing to indicate he would fall on his own and no drugs. The full tox screen will take weeks, but she's certain it was the trauma to the head."

"I was hoping for better news," said Coop. He took another sip from his cup. "What did you guys get on Beau's alibi?"

"His limo left the party at ten-forty, with three adoring women and they went downtown to a bar. He hooked up with one of them and they spent the night together at his hotel. Gray's phone showed a reminder to call Beau set for Monday, which means he was planning to continue the conversation. We verified Beau's story and it checks out. He was spotted by limo drivers and surrounded by adoring fans, until he got in the car, so he's not our guy," said Jimmy.

Kate said, "I checked Twitter yesterday and Gray's death was tweeted, so Mel could have found out that way. We also saw a record of a one minute call from Pamela to Mel right after you two left her place, probably warning him."

"She's trying to keep her apartment. Wonder if she still has a job?" said Coop, glancing at his watch. "I better get moving and see the widow. I'll check in when I get back."

Coop stopped for gas and a cold drink before hitting I-65 for the hour drive. He wasn't looking forward to telling a privileged woman her husband had an illegitimate son to whom he had just given hundreds of thousands of dollars, or that he was having an illicit affair with a secretary and planning to leave his job.

He scanned the directions and followed a driveway lined with white fencing, enclosing several horses, to a large brick home. He rang the bell and was greeted by a stunning brunette, dressed in a simple black dress, set off by a large diamond necklace and matching earrings.

"Mr. Harrington, thank you for coming," said the woman. "I'm Emily Taylor."

Coop extended his hand, noticing her manicured and polished nails, "A pleasure, ma'am. I'm so sorry for your loss."

"Thank you. Do come in. We're here alone. I didn't want my daughter to hear our conversation, so my mother has taken her to the stables. Would you like something to drink?"

"Sure, I'll take sweet tea, if you have it."

She led him to a room decorated with framed pictures of young girls with horses. He chose a leather chair and studied the photos. He recognized Emily as a young girl smiling with her horse, surrounded by ribbons and trophies. Another girl he assumed was Emily's sister was also in several shots. His gaze rested on a family picture with Grayson, Emily, and their daughter, which looked to be a recent photo.

"Here we are," she said, handing him a glass. "So, what have you learned?"

"Several things, actually, but no firm suspects yet. I've got some information to share that will prove difficult for you." He looked at her over the rim of his glass, gauging her expression.

She was ramrod straight, nothing showed on her blank face, except a slight widening of her pupils. "Go on."

"First, Gray was planning to leave Global and move back here to Nashville to start his own label. He gave his notice to Mr. Lewis on Friday."

She shook her head in disgust. "That had been something he'd talked about before, but I always thought it was an overreaction to things at work. I told him we didn't need to start over and worry about owning a business when he had a fabulous job with Mel. It doesn't make sense. What else?"

"These next two are harder, ma'am. Your husband had been having an affair with a secretary from the company for the past year, when he visited Nashville. On Friday he told her he wanted to discontinue their relationship because it wasn't fair to you and his family. He wanted to end it."

"Name?" she said in a flat voice.

"Pamela Hargrove. Do you know her?"

"I've met her a few times at events, but no, I don't know her. And, what's next?"

"Gray learned on Friday he had a son. He's seventeen years old and from a high school relationship with a girl named Abby Nelson. The boy's name is Taylor."

"A son? So, did this woman kill him?" she asked, her eyes glossy with rage.

"No, ma'am. She didn't know he was in town. Her brother visited with Gray at his hotel and told him about Taylor. Abby never wanted Gray to know about the boy, but her brother was hoping Gray could help him with college."

"Of course he was," she said, in a loathing tone. "I'm sure he thought Gray could afford it and why not hit him up for some cash. *If* the boy is even Gray's son."

"From Gray's conversation with the uncle, your husband was shocked, but never doubted Taylor was his son. It seems Abby got pregnant in high school and he gave her money for an abortion, but she had the baby and never told him. Taylor works at Silverwood and was at the event Gray attended on Saturday night."

"So, maybe he killed Gray. Sounds like the whole family is in on it." Her voice could have cut stone. "Probably a bunch of trash looking for some easy cash."

Coop shook his head. "I don't think so, Mrs. Taylor. We interviewed them all at length and none of them appear to have any involvement. Your husband died from blunt force trauma to the head. Most likely from stone statuary in the garden. We don't have any strong suspects and will be going through the list of attendees, which number in the hundreds."

"You make sure and tell those bloodthirsty boondock people they won't get a penny for Gray's so-called son." Through clenched teeth and trembling lips, she added, "He's got a daughter and wife and we're his only family."

Coop took a slow drink of tea. "Do you know the Nelson family? Abby or her brother, Andy?"

She shook her head. "Of course not. I lived here in high school and didn't meet Grayson until I was in college. But I know their type," she said, her voice laden with petulance.

Dread worked its way into the muscles of Coop's neck. "Gray called his lawyer on Friday and sent him a text instructing him to set up a scholarship fund for Taylor Nelson and he did it immediately. From what I know, Steve, his lawyer, has authority to make such transactions and it was completed Friday."

"How much?" she seethed, anger oozing out of every pore of her perfect skin.

"Four hundred thousand."

Her dark eyes narrowed. "We'll see about that."

Coop finished his tea and began to ask his questions. "Do you know anyone who would want to harm your husband?"

She shook her head. "He had business dealings with people that didn't always work out, but he never received threats. Most people liked him."

"And you didn't know he planned to move back to Nashville within a month?"

She shook her head and frowned. "No. How ridiculous to think we could move so soon. Hannah has all her activities. My dad's terminally ill. I guess he wasn't thinking of anyone but himself." She brandished her cell phone. "He texted me Saturday from the party and said he wanted to make some changes." She showed him the text.

"I'm sorry to have to tell you these things, Mrs. Taylor. From all accounts, your husband was a good guy and was in the midst of trying to make changes he thought would be for the best."

She stared at him, silent, a storm brewing in her eyes and her lips a thin flat line.

"Once I get a copy of the guest list, I'll get in touch with you and see if you know any of the attendees or have information that would elevate any of them to a suspect status."

"I'll be here for the foreseeable future. Until I know more about my dad. If I go back to LA, I'll let you know." She stood, effectively dismissing Coop.

Coop followed her to the front door. "Thanks for your time. I'll be in touch."

She watched from the entryway and as soon as he turned to go down the steps, she flung the door shut, without a farewell.

Coop shuddered as he got behind the wheel of his Jeep. He hit the button for Ben and told him he was on his way back and would stop in and give him an account of his visit. He briefly considered calling poor Steve, knowing he'd be the next to face the wrath of the widow.

As he wound his way to the interstate, the mannerisms of Emily Taylor brought back memories of his Aunt Liz—technically, his ex-aunt. She was born into money and never let his dad's brother, Uncle Mike, forget it. He played professional baseball for a short time, but suffered an injury and his dream of a career in the major leagues vanished. He was a hard worker, but couldn't possibly keep up with her demands for material goods. They had one son, Phillip, who was much younger than Coop.

The Lizard, as she was referred to behind her back, avoided Mike's side of the family. It was clear none of them were good enough for her. She had the same thin mean lips as Emily. She was a cold-blooded reptile, hence the nickname.

Her thirst for fancy cars, new things, and better houses led Mike to work multiple jobs, trying to keep her happy. He dropped dead of a heart attack before he was forty years old. After Mike's death, The Lizard whisked Phillip away and settled close to her family in California, where she found a new rich prospect and remarried. Coop remembered his dad trying to keep in contact, but he finally gave up and none of them had talked to Phillip in twenty years.

Despite the heat, he shivered as he kept his foot on the gas. Emily and Liz, along with his mother, were three excellent incentives to stay single.

Coop ate a burger on the road and pulled into Ben's parking lot before three o'clock. As he opened the door to Ben's office, his phone chirped. He scanned the display and saw a text from Shelby asking for an update. He ignored it, and closed the screen. He found Ben at the table in front of the whiteboard with sheets of paper in front of him. "So, the wife's a real barracuda," said Coop, sliding into a chair next to Ben.

"Yeah, she was mad, huh?"

"More like cold, with a dash of nasty. Right away she wanted to blame Abby or Andy or even Taylor for the murder. Called them boondock people looking for a quick buck."

"Does she know them?"

"Not according to her. And our lawyer friend in L.A. is going to get an earful, I'm afraid. She was most displeased about the money for Taylor."

"We went through his laptop from the hotel today and all his files from his office computer. Nothing useful, except a letter he composed to Taylor on Saturday morning. I printed you a copy. Feel free to share it with his wife, maybe it'll help."

Coop took the printout Ben slid to him. "What did you learn from his parents?"

Ben shook his head. "Nothing, really. They knew about the pregnancy, but didn't know Abby gave birth. They seemed like regular people, completely devastated about Gray; he was their only child. He planned to meet them on Sunday but called and let them know he had to get back to Emily because of her dad. He told them he'd call them from Kentucky and set up another time. He wanted to meet and told them he was planning a move back to Nashville. They were happy and looking forward to having him near them. They said they always liked Abby and her folks and were pleased to know they have a grandson. They want to see Taylor."

"So, you had a pleasant visit and I suffered through a conversation with Cruella Deville?"

"That's why you get the big bucks," laughed Ben. "Also, all the calls check out as legit on Gray's phone. He was trying to find an office for his new label and told the realtor he would need it in a month. He contacted several artists and told them he would work with them next week to sign contracts. Nothing suspicious."

"Is that the guest list?" Coop asked, pointing to the sheets of paper on the table.

"Yeah. We're getting it entered into the computer, but I started grinding on it by hand. Figure we can eliminate anyone who left before ten-thirty and start working them one by one."

"I told Mrs. Taylor I'd share a copy in case she recognized anyone who may be linked to Gray."

"I'll have one of the clerks email it to you once it's entered, before we make any notes. It should be done before five today."

"I'll take the staff and interview all of them. I can get started tonight."

"Yeah, go ahead and start there. I'll work on the music folks and we can tackle the politicians together. If anything pops, let me know. Otherwise, we'll meet back here on Wednesday morning and compare notes."

"Gus is at the office. I'm going to stop by and check on a few things and I'll be home if you need anything," said Coop, taking Gray's letter. He waved goodbye to Jimmy and Kate, both on the phone at desks across from each other.

He called Aunt Camille on the drive to the office and promised to be home in time for supper at six. He parked in the back of the office, hugging the shadow of one of the oak trees that graced the yard. Gus greeted him at the back door and he stopped and poured himself a glass of sweet tea over ice.

"Hey, AB," he said, as he passed by her desk, Gus at his heels. "Anything happening?"

"Not much, just finishing up the invoices. The folks at Rochester referred another firm and they want us to do their background reports, so I sent them a contract and will work on those tomorrow. I spent most of the day cleaning up your paper disaster in your office. What did y'all learn on your road trip?"

Coop slumped onto the couch and let the cool air-conditioned breeze blow over him. "Not much except Mrs. Taylor could freeze hot lava with her stare and she probably drowns puppies. She's angry about the affair, Taylor, and especially the money Gray set up for him. I've got to work on the guest list. I'll need your help with that this week." He unfolded the letter, "Ben gave me this. It's a letter Gray wrote to Taylor on Saturday. Wanna hear it?"

"Sure, go ahead."

Coop scanned the sheet and read it aloud:

Dear Taylor, This is a difficult letter, but I want you to know I just learned about you yesterday. I'm your biological father. I went to high school with your mom and we were in love and careless and she ended up getting pregnant. I never knew she had a baby until now. I'm so sad and sorry I've missed the last seventeen years. I'm honored that she chose to name you Taylor.

I live in Los Angeles right now, but will be moving back to Nashville in the next month. My parents, your grandparents, still live in Nashville in the home I grew up in. They're going to be thrilled to know you—they always thought the world of your mom. Andy came to see me yesterday and told me about you. I know it isn't much, but I've set up a scholarship fund for you. He told me you want to go to college and I'd be honored if you let me help you. I want you to go and not worry about expenses.

If your mom will allow it and you want it, I'd like to meet you and get to know you. It would be great to spend some time with you. My life is a bit complicated right now. I'm married to a woman, Emily, and we have one daughter, Hannah. I haven't told them yet, but will be doing that tomorrow. It might be hard at first, but it will work out. I'll be back in town in a few weeks. Let me know if you want to get together for dinner. You pick the place and I'll meet you or I'll pick you up.

I know I haven't been there for you, but I want to be. I hope you'll give me a chance to prove I'm up to the task. I'm including my cell phone and e-mail, please get in touch. With all my love, Gray.

Coop looked up when he finished and saw Annabelle dabbing her blue-green eyes with a tissue. "How sad," she whispered.

"Yeah. This case sucks. I know Gray made some mistakes—big ones, but deep down he was a good person. He was going to do the right thing by Taylor. I want to find out who killed him."

Annabelle looked at her computer as it chimed. "Ben sent the guest list. I'll get it printed out for you so you have a working copy. He put a red line through everyone who left before ten-thirty, but sent a second complete list. He's also indicated each person's affiliation, whether it be politician, employee, musician, or guest."

"Send a complete copy to Mrs. Taylor under my name and

ask her to review it and get back to me if she recognizes anyone associated with her husband."

Annabelle's fingers danced over the keyboard and within minutes she sent off the message and sorted the list so Coop could concentrate on employees. "I'll call Silverwood and get contact info on all the staff."

"Great work, thanks, AB," said Coop, as he and Gus shuffled into his office. "Wow, this place looks terrific. You outdid yourself, as usual."

She mumbled something under her breath and went back to her work.

He reviewed his messages, noticing four from Shelby, and ran a background on Emily Taylor. He wanted to know more about her in case he needed it later. Her maiden name was Emily Dutton, the youngest child of Wheelock and Iris Dutton. Her sister, Isabelle, was two years older and married to one of the wealthiest developers in Nashville, Harold Palmer. Nothing jumped out, but he printed the reports and slipped them in a new file, beaming with pride as he filed it in his desk drawer, not wanting to taint the freshly cleaned desktop.

As Annabelle was leaving for the day, she dropped off the printed list for Coop. "We've got almost fifty employees on this list. I talked to the manager and she's going to be emailing you the time each of them clocked out on Saturday night. She's happy to help and said to call her if you need anything else."

She bent down to pet Gus and he rolled over for a belly rub. "I'll see you boys in the morning. I locked the front door," she said, as she left through the kitchen.

Coop preferred to interview in person rather than on the phone, so settled in to contact staff members and arrange meetings. The only full-time employees were the gardeners, security personnel, and the manager and her assistant. Everyone else who worked the event wouldn't be working until Friday afternoon. He set up appointments with the ten permanent

TAMMY L. GRACE

employees for the next morning at Silverwood and turned his attention to the remaining part-timers.

He made some decent progress by the time he left for supper. He thought about calling Shelby on the way home, but didn't have anything to report and didn't feel like answering her questions. He knew he and Shelby weren't cut out for each other and figured he needed to end it before she got even clingier. She was too young for him and too focused on the music world. He could see her morphing into Pamela as she yearned to be more.

He and Gus arrived home to find Eula Mae's car in the driveway and the aroma of Mrs. Henderson's meatloaf and fresh biscuits wafting through the house. Aunt Camille and her friend were in the sitting room sipping sweet tea.

"Hey, Eula Mae, how you doing?" asked Coop.

"Hotter than a billy goat's butt in a pepper patch," she replied, as she took a swig of tea.

Coop smiled. "I hear ya. I think it's a good night for a swim." Gus thumped his tail in agreement. "I'm glad you're here. I wanted to interview you about the night of the music event and the murder of Grayson Taylor."

"Let's eat while you interview Eula Mae and after I'll share what I learned at Bella's," said Camille, standing and ushering them into the dining room. "Supper's ready."

As they passed platters and ate, Coop asked Eula Mae about her schedule and duties the night of the murder. "I got out there early to help set things up and we always get treated to a free meal when there's an event. So, lots of the workers were there to eat around six. I went up to the ticket booth before seven with my guest list and checked off names as they arrived. I closed up the ticket booth a little after eleven and turned in my list and went home. The security guys watch the entrance and exit after I leave, as a deterrent to mischief."

"Did you have any problems with anyone that night or any

unexpected guests not on the list?" asked Coop, buttering another biscuit.

"Well, the thing is, I have a list of names of the invited guests and many of them brought along other guests, but I didn't have their names. It's not important; it wasn't an event that required me to collect money. All those limos with their dark windows, I couldn't see anything inside. The driver would give me the name of the guest and I'd check them off. Some of them told me they were bringin' more guests with them, so I made a note on my sheet. Those politicians all had a slew of people with them."

"But you didn't have names of anyone besides the invited guests, right?"

"Right. But, I'm meticulous about my notes, so anyone who said they brought extras I noted."

"Do you think someone could slip into or out of Silverwood without being seen, say if they were on foot?"

"Mmm. There's only the one road in or out and it goes right to the ticket booth, but if the murderer was walkin' he could probably get in or out and dodge the ticket booth. I know there's a camera at the booth, but I'm not sure what it picks up outside of the road."

He paused and hesitated before asking his next question, knowing he would be fueling the amateur sleuth inside his aunt. "Do either of you have any theories?"

Camille and Eula Mae looked at each other. "It was the topic of conversation at Bella's Salon," said Camille. "The consensus at the shop was he'd been having an affair. I'm still thinking his wife could have been involved and had him killed. We need to find a motive."

"Some of the staff saw Mr. Taylor talkin' to a young blond woman. They suspect they were involved...you know," said Eula Mae arching her brows, which Coop suspected she drew on her forehead each morning.

"Yeah, I've spoken to the blond. She's a secretary at Global

Records and they were having an affair. Which," he added in a stern voice, "is not for publication."

"And, do you think she killed him?" asked Camille.

Coop shook his head. "So far nobody who appeared to have any type of motive was involved. Gray argued with the secretary, Mel Lewis, and Beau Branson."

Mrs. Henderson brought out plates of strawberry shortcake for dessert.

"Eula Mae, do you recall Beau Branson leaving while you were still in the booth?" asked Coop.

"Not for sure. When cars leave there's nothin' we check and several limos left before I closed the booth. They don't stop and with the tinted windows, I couldn't tell you who was in any of them."

"Did you see Andy Nelson when he came in to pick up his nephew, Taylor?"

She smiled. "Yes, I spoke to Andy. He was early but said he had some work to do while he waited for Taylor. They're both always nice and polite."

Camille got up and retrieved Eula Mae's list from her notebook. "Here are the notes we made on anyone we knew on the list. Lots of money and power on that list, Coop."

"Yeah, I know. Like you said, we need to find the motive."

"Well, there's one more thing I learned at Bella's today," said Camille, her eyes sparkling. "Seems like there's some gossip about Mrs. Emily Taylor. She dated a young man in high school by the name of Seth Hill. His family is friends with Beulah's cousin so she knows about him. Anyhoo, when Emily moved to Los Angeles, she hired Seth to manage their stables in California. Claimed she didn't trust anyone but him to look after her prized horses. So, he's been living out there. There's some speculation she and Seth are still an item. Beulah said she talked to her cousin this morning and confirmed Seth had visited his parents in Bowling Green this past weekend, so he was in town."

Eula Mae clucked her tongue. "Well, that there's some motive."

Coop scribbled some notes and Camille supplied him with Beulah's phone number and her cousin's name and number. "I knew you'd be interested. Here's his parents' address too." She beamed as she handed him another piece of paper from her flowered notebook.

"Good work, Aunt Camille. You too, Eula Mae. I'll follow up on this tomorrow." He motioned to Gus and headed to the pool.

8

Usually an evening swim tired Coop out, but not last night. Gus, on the other hand, was zonked out and snoring as soon as he fell onto his bed. The case nagged at Coop, causing him to give up on sleep and go to the office early. He brewed a pot of coffee and studied the list again. He scanned the staff names and job titles and stopped when he noticed the photographer's name. He picked up his cell and tapped Ben's icon, noticing several texts from Shelby asking him to call.

"Hey, Ben. Aunt Camille did some nosing around at Bella's and came up with some information on Emily Taylor. Sounds like there's a rumor she's involved with her boyfriend from high school, who she happened to hire to work with her horses and he's been living in California. According to Camille's friend, Beulah, this guy, Seth Hill, was in Bowling Green this weekend. So, we need to take a look at him and the wife. I'll text you the info I have."

"First, you must not be sleeping at all, if you're calling me at five in the morning. You need to take care of yourself, Coop. As soon as I get going I'll dig into it and check him out. Seems odd for her to hire you to find the killer if she's involved, but I've seen crazier things," said Ben.

"Yeah, this case is bugging me, so I'm sleeping even less than usual. I'll be fine." Coop paused for a sip of coffee. "I'm working on the staff list and came across a photographer. It got me thinking about all the photos that would have been taken during the party. Is there any way to have your techs go through them and see if we can piece together whereabouts for people during the kill window? I bet the music folks were having photos taken for publicity and with everyone having a camera on their phone, I'm sure they'll be lots of photos posted."

"I'll get on it. Great idea, by the way. I've been trying to build a matrix myself of the location of each guest during those two hours and it's overwhelming."

"Also, I talked to Eula Mae last night and she said she has notes on her guest list from the ticket booth where she wrote down additional names not included on the original list. You'll need to ask the manager about getting Eula Mae's list, since some of the official guests brought people with them. I noticed my name was on the list, Shelby must have submitted it, but I don't think our list is complete."

"Got it, I'll call over there first thing."

"One more thing I was thinking about last night. Is there any chance of getting any epithelial cells off the stone?"

"I mentioned that to the lab. They aren't hopeful since there was a huge party on the terrace the night before. It's hard to get a quality sample and with it being in such a public place, chances are there will be several samples. They're collecting everything, but we'll need to have a suspect before we can justify the expense of running DNA on such a long shot. Talk to you tomorrow, unless we learn something significant today."

Coop hung up and made himself wait until seven o'clock to make any more calls. He needed to get a look at the photos. The photographer, not happy at being awakened early, grudgingly agreed to meet Coop at Silverwood and show him the video footage and photos from the event.

Gus shot off like a bullet for the back door, announcing the arrival of Annabelle. "You two are early today," she said, stashing her lunch in the fridge and depositing two oversized bags of peanut M&M's in the cupboard, before petting Gus. She poured a cup of coffee and wandered into Coop's office. "Wow, two days in a row of button down shirts. I'm impressed."

He rolled his eyes at her. "Yeah, this case is nagging at me. I've got appointments starting at nine out at Silverwood. I'll be there until noon and then I've got some of the staff scheduled to come here starting at one." He handed her the list. "Go ahead and work on the rest and try to get them scheduled today or tonight. The sooner the better."

Annabelle took the list and Gus padded after her, content to situate himself at her feet while she worked the telephone.

Coop made the short trip to Silverwood. The manager, Sarah, showed him to a small conference room overlooking the terrace garden. She gestured to a sideboard set up with coffee, tea, pastries, and icy silver water pitchers. "I hope y'all find this to your likin', Mr. Harrington. We're all just sickened about this murder business." Her accent flowed like warm syrup.

"Yes, thanks so much for your help. I appreciate the refreshments."

"I was able to get our docents who volunteered Saturday night to come in this mornin', so they're available whenever y'all can squeeze them in."

"Wonderful. Oh, did Chief Mason call you about the guest list?"

"Yes, sir. I hadn't even considered the box office notes. I've been a bit out of sorts with all this. I made a copy of Eula Mae's guest register with her notes. I'll get it for y'all. I emailed a copy to Chief Mason already."

She returned a few minutes later with the paperwork and

Coop's first appointment, one of the gardeners. "When y'all are ready for the next, just buzz me. The phone is on the sideboard and my extension is on a li'l pink sticky note on the phone." Coop watched her leave, taking in her proper lace covered sheath dress and high heels, which served to accent her shapely figure and fit legs.

He welcomed the first of the gardeners and began his interview process asking him to describe what he saw and where he was the day of the murder. Coop's appointments continued and he filled a pad with notes by the time he finished with all the security officers, gardeners, and docents.

Sarah's assistant was next and offered to escort Coop to the photographer's area as soon as they finished. She helped fill in some of the names of the missing additional guests.

Jake, the photographer, commanded several large monitors in his editing room and began clicking through the hundreds of images from the party. Coop learned there were a few other photographers at the event. Both the record companies and the politicians brought official photographers with them and Jake pointed out their names on the guest list. Coop asked if he could have copies of all the photos and video footage and Jake offered to organize the photos by timestamp to make it easier. With a few clicks of his mouse, he announced he was done. He loaded the photos and video files online and gave Coop a password to view and download anything he needed.

Jake also emailed Coop the link to the Facebook event where several photos from attendees were posted. "If I run across more sites with photos from the party, I'll email you," he offered.

While Jake worked, Coop asked him questions to see if he could shed any light on the murder. Jake's whereabouts were tracked through pictures and with his eye glued to his camera he'd only seen what the photos revealed.

"Thanks for the help. Sorry to call you so early, but this case is important. I'll share this information with Chief Mason and he'll have the techs get on this right away." Coop found his way to Sarah's office and was shown in immediately.

"How'd y'all do?" she asked.

"Jake went above and beyond to help with the photos. I only have one interview left—you," he said, taking a seat. "Was there anything unusual about the event on Saturday night?"

She smoothed her skirt with her hands. "Not that I can think of. It was a busy night, but nothing comes to mind." She took a sip of water. "I'm trying to think back, since after the body was discovered it's been so crazy around here. I'm on the verge of a panic attack with all this."

Coop nodded and spoke in a calm manner. "What time did you leave?"

"It was a bit after one in the mornin'. I was one of the last ones out. One of the security guys walked me to my car and he and I left at the same time."

"Walk me through your duties after the event that kept you here so late."

"Well, I have some paperwork to complete for an event report. This one wasn't too hard, since we're invoicin' for the bar charges and the food was preordered, so I tallied the bar receipts. We ring up the drinks so we can itemize the invoice."

"Do you check the mansion and lock up?"

"I do a walk through to look for damage or lost and found items that haven't been turned in by staff. We keep a log of all the lost and found items and put them in a plastic tub with the name and date of the event."

"Do you have a tub from Saturday night?"

"I sure do," she smiled. She picked up her phone and asked to have the items brought to her office.

"Did you see anything unusual on the terrace or in the garden area?"

"No, it was all cleaned up. Usually we find glasses and plates out there, but the staff had cleaned it up. I didn't see anything out of place anywhere."

Her door opened and her assistant deposited the tub on her conference table and left.

"May I?" Coop gestured with his head to the table.

"Sure. Help yourself."

He opened the lid and rifled through it, finding cell phones, sunglasses, reading glasses, perfume, lipsticks, a couple of evening bags filled with makeup, a necklace, a tie, two sets of keys, and two sweaters. He scrolled through the cell phones and found the numbers and wrote them down. "I'd like to take the cell phones and turn them in to the police, in case they contain any helpful information or photos. I'll sign a receipt for you."

"That's fine. I'll make a note of them and keep it in the box in case the owner calls."

"Do you get many people calling for their things?"

"We usually do. Some events, like this one, involve a lot of alcohol and people leave their stuff and forget about it until the next day or two, after the hangover wears off." She looked at a file in the box. "We've had three calls on this event. One for a set of keys, one for sunglasses, and one for an earring."

"I didn't see an earring in your box."

"No, we didn't find any that night." She held the sheet with the inventory of items and caller information. "I'll make y'all a copy of this."

She glided out of the room and was back in seconds with a warm copy of the list for Coop. "Thank you. Just a couple more questions. Did you have any problems with anyone at the event?"

"The only thing I heard about was Beau Branson and poor Mr. Taylor having a bit of a verbal scuffle out on the terrace. From what I know it didn't last long and Mr. Branson seemed to calm down after they talked for a few minutes. A lot of the guests were watchin' them when they were on the terrace, but saw them leave down the outside stairs."

"Do you have any theories or ideas about who killed Mr. Taylor?"

Her hand flew to her chest. "Me? Why, no, not at all."

"You haven't heard any staff talking about theories or ideas?"

She shook her head, her blond curls bouncing. "No, nothin'. We're all shocked by it, and a bit scared."

"Any employees you're uneasy about?"

She gasped, her cornflower blue eyes wide in surprise. "No, of course not. We have a wonderful staff. I can't imagine anyone at Silverwood's involved."

"I had to ask, it's not personal," said Coop.

She nodded. "I understand. Sorry, I'm on edge."

"Okay, Sarah. Thanks again for your help. I'll be talking to the other employees over the next few days." He closed his notebook and stood. "If you think of anything helpful, be sure to give me a call." He handed her his card. "And if anyone calls for their cell phones, let me know."

She took the card. "I will. I sure hope y'all catch the murderer soon. I want all of this to be over." She paused and added, "You're welcome to stay for lunch."

"Oh, how kind of you, but I've got another appointment and need to get going."

She plucked one of her own cards from a holder on her desk and scribbled on the back. "Here's my card. I've given you my cell and home number in case you need me outside of business hours." She fluttered her eyes when she handed it to him.

He flirted with the idea of asking her to dinner, but dismissed it as foolish. "Thanks, Sarah. I'll be in touch." She was easy on the eyes, no doubt, but a bit of a damsel in distress and he wasn't sure he needed more drama. He had to resolve the situation with Shelby before he could even think of going out with another woman. He hurried to the Jeep intent on finding lunch before his next appointment.

He drove to The Pickle Barrel and enjoyed a barbecue sandwich and coleslaw while perusing his notes. He sent Ben a text with the online photo information, so the techs could start their research. He climbed over the wooden bench at the picnic style table and settled in with his notebook and a glass of sweet tea. His phone rang and Shelby's name appeared. He poked the red button to ignore her call. "I don't have time for this," he muttered. He reread his interview notes while he finished his sandwich before heading back to the office.

Gus welcomed him as soon as he opened the back door of the office. He sniffed the air and took in the aroma of fresh baked cookies, Aunt Camille's pecan chocolate chunk, if he wasn't mistaken. "Hey, AB, I'm back," he hollered. As he passed through the kitchen he spied a plate of the cookies and nicked a handful.

Annabelle glanced up from her desk. "I see you found the cookies. You just missed your aunt. She offered to deliver food later when I told her it looked like it'd be a late night."

Coop licked a dab of melted chocolate from his hand. "These are my favorite. You gotta have one."

She smiled. "I know and I will, as soon as I finish this up. I left you a schedule on your desk. I'm waiting for two more calls, but have everyone else slotted in today. That means we'll be working until nine tonight."

He nodded, chewing on his second cookie. "Okay, sounds doable. You didn't have plans tonight, did you?"

"Nope. I'm all yours."

"Tell Aunt Camille we'll take her up on her delivery offer and if she asks tell her Ben's following up on her lead from Bella's. You pick the best time for us to squeeze in a bite." He scurried to his office to get ready for his first interview. A pitcher of sweet tea and iced water were already set up on the conference table. He smiled, "She really does think of everything, before I even know I need it." Gus wagged his tail in agreement, eyeing the last cookie.

Moments later he heard the front door open and Annabelle ushered in the first appointment. She gave Gus a look and motioned him out with her head and closed the office door. He followed her to her desk, where she promptly rewarded him with a bite of her cookie.

The afternoon went by in a flurry of activity with interviewees coming and going. Camille stopped by with a picnic basket full of deliciousness, fresh lemonade, more cookies, and leftover strawberry shortcakes. "Anything new on the murder?" she whispered, as she stashed items in the refrigerator.

"No, Coop's doing all the employee interviews tonight. I haven't had a chance to talk to him all afternoon. We've been booked solid, but he told me to tell you Ben's following up on your lead."

Camille proceeded to share the news about the connection between Seth Hill and Emily Taylor and the suspicions of the girls at Bella's. "I've got a book club meeting in Franklin, so I need to run, but call me if you two need anything. I'll see if I can learn anything new that might help tonight." Camille hugged Annabelle and bustled for the back door. Gus brushed up against Camille for a pet before she left.

Coop was ahead of schedule, leaving them a half hour gap for a quick meal. Annabelle unpacked cold chicken salad sandwiches on buttery croissants, fruit salad, and macaroni salad. She filled their glasses with the fresh lemonade and uncovered the strawberry shortcakes.

In between mouthfuls, he caught her up on his progress. "I haven't learned much of anything new from the staff. Nobody saw anything or anyone suspicious on the terrace. There was a lot of traffic in the garden area, which is only a few feet from the terrace, but nothing specific to tie anyone to the murder. Did you hear anything back from the widow on the guest list?"

Annabelle nodded. "She sent an email and said she recognized some names from Global, Beau, Senator Wagner, Speaker Evans and a few other political names, but none of them caused her any concern."

"I think this is going to be a long case. It's funny, Eula Mae and Aunt Camille both said we need to find the motive and that's what's nagging at me. All the motives surrounding his affair, money, and his illegitimate son are dead ends. There's some question on the timeline about Andy, but I don't think he has a motive. Maybe this new rumor of an affair between Mrs. Taylor and the horse guy will prove to be something."

They heard the front door. "You finish supper, Coop. I can eat while you're interviewing," offered Annabelle, as she rose and greeted the next appointment.

They finished a little after nine o'clock, even working in the two employees who called back after supper. Coop sunk into the couch and clutched his shoulder, twisting his neck from side to side. "Wow, that was a marathon day. Thanks for staying, AB." He studied Gus flaked out on the floor by Annabelle's desk, face resting near the vent.

"No problem. Did you get any new information?" She lifted the plate of cookies and placed them on the table by the couch, causing Gus to perk up and relocate.

"Not really. Nobody saw Gray talking with anyone other than Pamela, Mel, and Beau. I was reviewing my notes from the security guards and two of them assigned to patrols in the staff parking area confirm Andy was in his truck, but can't say he never left the parking lot. He could have slipped out and walked to the mansion unnoticed. There's a span of about twenty minutes between the patrols, so technically he could have hoofed it to the terrace, whacked Gray, and returned to his truck before anyone missed him. They both remember seeing him each time they passed and even chatted with him, but their testimony can't clear him."

Coop picked up a cookie and took a bite. "So, back to motive. There are a handful of basic motives for murder. Money, love, drugs or other crimes, hate, and revenge come to mind." He chewed another bite, licking a speck of sea salt from his thumb.

Annabelle added, "Don't forget killing to protect someone or to keep a secret."

Coop nodded. "If it's not love in the form of the wife having an affair, or hate from Andy, I think we might be dealing with a secret." He got up and retrieved his interview notes. "Could you type these up for me? I'll give it a fresh look tomorrow. I'm beat."

"Sure, I'll do it first thing in the morning. I can have them done by the time you meet with Ben."

"You're the best," he said, giving her a peck on the cheek and calling to Gus, who licked her knee on his way to the door.

9

E very few weeks, pure exhaustion forced Coop's body to
sleep. After his marathon day at work, he fell into a deep
sleep and awoke to a soft knock on his bedroom door.

"Coop, are you awake?" asked Camille.

"Yeah, I'm up," he mumbled, sliding the cocoon of
comforters from his head. He squinted to block out the slit of
light coming from the opening in the door, focusing on his aunt.

"Breakfast is ready. It's after eight, I didn't want you to wake
you any earlier." Gus squirmed through the door, opening it
wider.

"Okay, I'll be out in a minute." He dragged himself upright
and took a hot shower, hoping to loosen the tightness grabbing
his neck and shoulders.

He helped himself to breakfast and read the paper while Gus
lounged beside him. His eyes fixed on an article about the
murder. Ben was quoted as saying the department was pursuing
all leads and questioning hundreds of people who attended or
worked the event.

He knew Ben would be under pressure to make an arrest
soon. Murder wasn't good for politicians or tourism, especially

the murder of a millionaire music executive in an exclusive neighborhood.

Coop pocketed his cell phone, seeing another message from Shelby, plus more texts. He'd only gone out with her twice, but knew there wouldn't be a third date. He'd make some time to call her later and tell her he wasn't interested in a relationship. He liked his life like it was; he did what he wanted without answering to anyone.

~

He and Gus sauntered through the back door of the office at nine-thirty. "AB, we're here," he called out.

"I've got your notes ready. Let me know what else you need. I'm working with Madison and Ross to finalize a report today and then I'll be free."

He took the folder off his desk and deposited Gus in his chair. "I'll be at Ben's office the rest of the morning. Not sure after that. It depends on what we can put together from all these interviews."

"Oh, Shelby called this morning and sounded irritated. She said she needs to hear from you and it's personal," she said, handing him a message slip.

Coop rolled his eyes. "Yeah, I need to talk to her today sometime. I can't deal with her constant calling. We've only gone out a couple of times and she acts like we're permanently linked."

Annabelle said nothing and turned her attention back to her computer, leaving Coop to look at the back of her blond head. Coop scanned the typed summaries as he walked through the office. He lifted a bottle of tea out of the refrigerator, wiped the condensation on his "4 out of 3 People Struggle with Math" t-shirt, and hollered out his goodbye.

He found Ben, Kate, and Jimmy gathered around the table and the murder board. Ben asked a clerk to make copies of

Coop's materials and handed him a packet containing their notes. "So, did you catch a break?" asked Ben.

Coop shook his head. "No. I was hoping to clear Andy, but he's still in the running. There's twenty minutes in our kill window where he could have done the deed and hurried back to his truck. How about the photos?"

"Tech is still going through them, but they helped us eliminate some people and Jimmy and Kate have been whittling down the list of limos and attaching names with the car services." Ben paused and picked up another sheet of paper. "And, it looks like Aunt Camille was on the money with her tip. We confirmed Seth Hill and Emily were indeed an item in high school and he was hired to manage her horses. He lives near the stables and is paid quite well. We're working on financials and cell records and hoping to talk to Gray's lawyer to see if he can shed some light on any of this. Mr. Hill was in fact in Bowling Green this past weekend. He arrived on Friday and left on a flight back to California on Sunday. His return ticket was booked Sunday morning."

Coop's brows arched. "Interesting. We'll have to nail down his movements to see if he's a possible suspect and look a little closer at the missus." Coop grinned. "I should say *you'll* have to look a little closer at her. That should be an amusing conversation."

"Yeah, I'm looking forward to it," smiled Ben. "Kate and I will make a trip up to see her when we have more information."

Kate added, "We've been hitting the guests related to the music industry and have come up empty. No ongoing issues with anyone. Most of them liked Gray. Beau was our best candidate for revenge and his alibi is solid. Nobody we talked to saw anyone with Gray or anything suspicious." She reached for her notes. "We have a small list of half a dozen people from the music biz who were seen in the garden area. We questioned them more than once and they admit to being in the garden, most of them to get away from the noise or sneak a smoke. None of them saw Gray or anything out of the ordinary. They estimated the time they were in the area, and two of them were there in the two-hour window, so we'll keep looking at them."

"I didn't do any better with my interviews," said Coop. "I did get a list of lost and found items and brought in the cell phones they collected. Thought you guys may be able to find something on them." Coop slid two phones across the table. "The list is in with my interview notes."

"We checked the additional guests from this group and got nowhere. Most of them didn't have a clue who Gray was and were focused on Beau. He was the most significant draw of the night," said Jimmy.

"If we can't tie this to Emily, Seth or Andy, we'll be left with the politicians, right?" asked Coop.

Ben nodded. "Yeah. I think they're even more of a pain in the ass than the musicians."

"Both Senator Wagner and Speaker Evans were by far the heaviest hitters at the party. A few junior legislators tagged along, but none of them with the name recognition of those two. Plus they all had staff and interns with them, and the ever present lobbyists lurking in their wake," said Coop.

"I guess we'll need to visit the capitol and start talking to everyone we can find. I saw in the paper today meetings were still going on for the fiscal issues, which means both Evans and Wagner will be working. We'll have to see about the rest," said Ben, looking at the list. "Where do you suggest we start?"

Coop had interned at the Tennessee General Assembly and worked in the House of Representatives during law school. He understood the inner workings of the political process and still maintained some contacts in the building. "I'll call my buddy David. He's the Chief Clerk of the Senate now. He'll point us in the right direction. I'll use your office."

While he was gone, the three cross-referenced the list of cars that left the grounds by ten-thirty with the list of politicians. Kate used a red marker to delete anyone on the list they could ignore. "It looks like there were some extra guests with the politicos. We'll have to account for them," reminded Kate. She highlighted the extras for Ben.

It was close to lunch and Ben called for a pizza delivery. By the time the pizza arrived, Coop emerged from Ben's office. "Sorry that took so long. They're busy today trying to get the budget done. David said he didn't anticipate the legislators having much free time, but suspected Friday morning would be our best bet. There's a confidential leadership meeting scheduled and he knows our two bigwigs will be in attendance. The junior legislators on the list would have more availability and he suggested we call their office and make an appointment. He said it would be a waste of time to try to schedule an appointment with the other two, since he knows staff has been told to refuse all requests. He said we'd be better off to show up early Friday, with the help of Ben's badge, and insist on talking to them."

"Kate and I need to head up to Bowling Green and talk to the widow. Gray's lawyer in California, Steve, offered to have his investigator look into Seth and Emily and see if he can get confirmation of an affair. He's going to question Seth today. He offered his services at no charge because he liked Gray and is hoping to find anything he can to help find his killer."

"I can keep working on the list while you guys visit her. I don't want to be involved in that chat. You'll probably get me fired anyway," said Coop.

"I'll see if I can get in to see the junior legislators and we can meet up and compare notes tonight or tomorrow," offered Jimmy.

"Let's make it tomorrow morning and if we haven't been able to link Seth or Emily, we'll start in on the rest of the political animals," said Ben.

Kate and Ben decided to surprise Emily Taylor and from the scowl on her face when she answered the door of her parents' house, they succeeded. "Chief Mason, I didn't know we had an appointment," she said, like a teacher chastising her pupil.

"We didn't, ma'am. There are some recent developments and we need your help to clear up a few things."

She glanced across the property and said, "My mother took Hannah to visit the horses again. She'll be back soon, so you'll need to make it quick." She opened the door wider and motioned them inside. She led them to the trophy room.

Ben opened his notepad. "We need to ask you some questions about Seth Hill."

Emily's eyes widened for a moment and she licked her lips. "What about him?"

"What's the nature of your relationship with Mr. Hill?" asked Kate.

"He manages our horses in California."

"And he was here in Bowling Green this past weekend?"

She shrugged and said, "He had the weekend off and mentioned something about visiting his family here."

"So, you two didn't have any contact during his trip to Bowling Green this past weekend?" asked Ben.

She shook her head and glared at him. "No."

"We understand you and Mr. Hill were high school sweethearts. Is that true?" asked Kate.

"We dated in high school, but that was a long time ago. Seth's always been good with horses and when we moved, we wanted someone we could trust, so we hired him."

"And your husband knew about your history with Seth in high school?"

She sat taller in her chair and said, "I don't like what you're insinuating, Chief Mason."

"Ma'am, we're investigating the murder of your husband and need to look at anyone who may have had a motive in his death. If you and Seth were having an affair and he was in the area, it's our duty to investigate him fully. Please just answer the question," said Ben.

"This is utterly ridiculous. Y'all should be out lookin' for Gray's killer and instead y'all are here interrogatin' me, implyin' there's something going on between us." She rambled as her usual proper speech slipped into that of a native Kentuckian.

"That's what we need to know," said Kate. "Were you now, or at any time in your marriage, having an affair with Seth Hill?"

Emily's nostrils flared and her face turned red. "How dare you," she hissed.

"We need an answer, ma'am," said Ben. "Or we could transport you for more formal questioning." Ben thought a tad of bluffing never hurt during a hostile interrogation and delighted in playing worse cop to Kate's bad cop persona.

"You will do no such thing. I. Am. Not," she turned and gave Kate a defiant stare, "nor have I ever had an affair with Seth Hill."

"Do you know if Seth had any reason to harm Gray?" asked, Kate, watching Emily for a reaction.

"He most certainly did not. He and Gray got on just fine. They didn't see much of each other. Seth lives out by the stables and focuses on the horses. Hannah adores him." The polished Los Angeles socialite was back.

"Did your husband ever suspect you two were involved romantically?" asked Kate.

Emily's dark eyes narrowed to form slits. "No, he did not. He had no reason to suspect such a thing. He was the bastard who was sleeping around, as y'all learned."

"To confirm, you did not have any contact, in person, by email, text, or phone with Seth Hill while he was visiting his family in Bowling Green?" Kate continued her litany of questions.

She nodded, while twisting her diamond ring. "That's right. I've been a little busy tending to my ailing father, as y'all know." They heard a door slam and running feet. "That'll be Hannah. You can see yourselves out." She got up and left the room.

Kate raised her brows and Ben shrugged. They made their way to the door without encountering anyone in the house. When they got in the car Kate said, "It'll be interesting to see what Steve's investigator has to say and if they contact each other now." She tapped her phone and continued, "I've got tech set up to alert me if either of them calls the other."

They rode back to Nashville recounting the conversation and took a call from Steve in Los Angeles. His investigator interviewed Seth Hill, who confirmed he was in Bowling Green Friday through Sunday. Steve said Seth became squirmy when he was asked about any contact with Emily while he was in Kentucky, but denied any communication. Seth did go into Nashville Saturday night with some friends and provided names and numbers. "Seth was nervous when he was questioned about any romantic involvement now or ever. He said they weren't involved, but there's something there," said Steve, his calm voice filling the car. "We're going to keep looking into friends and neighbors who may know something, but what we do know is Emily spends a lot of time at the stables without Hannah."

Ben added, "She denies any relationship and became very indignant when we asked anything related to Seth."

Steve reported Seth wasn't rude or irritated, but came across tense and jumpy. "I think he's your weakest link, if there's anything there."

Kate and Ben thanked him and promised to be in touch once they reviewed phone records and followed up on Seth's trip to Nashville.

As soon as Coop hung up the phone, Annabelle buzzed in to let him know Emily Taylor was on the line. He cringed and took a deep breath before picking up the receiver and said, "Hello, Mrs. Taylor," in what he hoped was a cheerful voice.

"I've just withstood the most upsetting visit from your friend Chief Mason and that woman detective. They harassed me to no end about my relationship with my horse manager. You need to do your job and find the real killer, Mr. Harrington." Her voice hissed with annoyance, "This nonsense of thinking Seth had something to do with Gray's murder is ridiculous."

Coop paused, not wanting to interrupt her rant and suffer another reprimand. "I'm sorry they upset you. I know this whole situation has to be very troubling for you, especially with your father so ill. The police have to follow up on every possible lead and with Seth being in the area at the time of the murder, they'd be remiss if they didn't ask questions. When the real killer is caught, his or her defense attorney would make an issue out of them not looking at every possible suspect. It's really to your benefit to have them be thorough." He winced, waiting for her to pounce.

She harrumphed. "My point is I'm paying you to find Gray's murderer and I need you to have my interests in mind. Seth and I had nothing to do with Gray's death. Please make that clear to Chief Mason. And, I expect some results for my money."

"Mrs. Taylor, I understand your frustration and believe me I've been focused on this case and nothing else. I cannot and will not control what the police investigate—no private detective can do that. I know the police are looking at several leads, Seth being one of them. If he's innocent, there's nothing to worry about. Chief Mason will eliminate him when the evidence bears out that fact. If you're not happy with my services, you're free to terminate our relationship. I'm committed to finding Gray's killer, but real crimes don't always get solved like what you're used to seeing on television. It's still very early in the case. It takes time to sift through everything, especially with such a large guest list at the party."

"You're not fired...yet," she said, anger replaced by confidence, followed by a loud click.

He shook his head and instead of slamming down the phone, reached for a handful of M&M's to appease his temper. Annabelle peeked around the corner. "I couldn't help myself and listened to your side of the conversation. You've always been a diplomat and did a terrific job with her."

Coop's jaws worked to chomp the candy. "I don't care if she fires me. I'm still going to work this case. Gray deserves justice and I'm beginning to question her involvement. I resent being used, if that's what she's doing."

"It's too bad Gray wasn't able to change his will. I don't think the wicked witch will do anything kind for Taylor."

Coop nodded. "I like the kid and feel bad for him." He rifled through some papers. "I've been looking at the guests to come up with all the lobbyists we'll need to interview and can name three big hitters I saw at the party that aren't on this list, so they're probably guests of Wagner or Evans. They would be Craig Baker, Reed Simmons, and Anna Prosser. Plus we've got these other lobbyists for the recording industry and entertainment venues," he said, pointing to names and highlighting them.

"Tomorrow's going to be a long day," she said.

10

The foursome met early in the morning at Ben's office. Jimmy reported nothing gained from his visit with the junior legislators. Kate yawned and glanced at her notes. "I worked late last night and dug into financials and phone records on Seth and our favorite widow. No calls to Seth's home or cell from her numbers, but I found a couple of interesting things. She receives several calls each month from a burner phone and has placed a few calls to the same burner. Looking closer, the majority of those calls have been made when Gray was in Nashville. And, she made a call to the burner phone last night. Nothing in the financials jumps out, but they're paying Seth a whopping ten grand a month."

"I should've gone into horses instead of law enforcement," said Ben. "I think we need to put some pressure on our buddy Seth. Kate, you and Jimmy get a flight to L.A. today and contact the locals and give them a courtesy heads up. We need some truthful answers out of him. Coop and I will tackle the lobbyists today and be ready to canvass the halls of the capitol tomorrow and hang out as long as it takes."

"You got it, boss," said Jimmy.

"Give me a call when you're done with Seth and we'll plan to meet back together Friday night, unless one of us is lucky enough to get a confession out of somebody before then."

"I'll call another friend with the Capitol Police and see if he can help us on logistics tomorrow morning. They have cameras all over and will be able to tell us the best time and place to find Speaker Evans and Senator Wagner. They'll both have layers of gatekeepers and I'd rather try to find them without going through a staffer," offered Coop.

"Good idea. I'll get the list of lobbyists organized and we can spend the rest of the day interviewing some of Tennessee's richest bottom feeders." He smirked, "We'll need to shower when we're done."

"I know that's the general consensus about lobbyists, but when I was an intern I met a few good ones who are respected for their knowledge and ethics," said Coop, as he piled into the unmarked Crown Victoria.

"I'm sure there are. I'm tired and hate dealing with politicians and their ilk. I'm not sure any of them are capable of telling the truth and was hoping to solve this one without having to spend the day with them." Ben used his courthouse parking permit—one of the few perks of being Chief of Detectives. From there walking was the easiest way to reach most of the lobbying firms, which tended to have space in office buildings between the courthouse and the Tennessee State Capitol Building.

There was a total of eight lobbyists listed on the guest register, plus the three Coop remembered seeing at Silverwood. They started with Anna Prosser, a longtime lobbyist who, with her father, owned one of the most respected firms in Nashville. Ben flashed his credentials at the receptionist and he and Coop were escorted to a plush conference room and offered cold drinks.

Anna, dressed in a navy blue silk suit that hid her pudgy

figure, greeted them with a friendly smile. "What can I do for y'all today?" she asked. She took another look at Coop. "You're Camille's nephew, right?" The sweet twang in her voice revealed her Nashville roots.

"Yes, ma'am, that's right."

Ben explained they were investigating the death of Grayson Taylor at the Silverwood event. "I read about his murder. Horrible," she said.

Ben and Coop traded questions and learned Anna didn't know Gray personally, only through his work at Global. She asked her assistant to research her invitation to the event and discovered she was invited by both Senator Wagner and Speaker Evans and she met with both of them in the garden area, separately.

They learned Anna had been in the company of her intern, Jackson and both of them had shared a car with Peter Collins, another lobbyist. Coop looked at their list and saw Peter was noted on the register and Eula Mae had scribbled a notation of two additional guests next to his name. He glanced up and nodded at Ben.

"Any reason you can think of someone would want Mr. Taylor dead?" asked Ben.

"Not at all. I've never heard much about him, until now. I knew he ran the L.A. office for Mel, but other than that, I'm afraid I'm not in the know."

During the interview, Ms. Prosser revealed they left around eleven-thirty that night and she hadn't seen anything suspicious when she was in the garden. "It was a quiet place to chat and we were only there for maybe ten minutes. I don't remember seeing anyone else around."

"How'd you arrange to meet Speaker Evans and Senator Wagner?"

"I didn't arrange it. I walked up to them when they were outside and suggested we wander over to a quiet corner to talk."

"Do you know what time it was you spoke with them?"

"I met with Lois first. I would guess around ten o'clock. Her daughter was with her and was antsy to listen to the music, so it was a quick conversation and they left."

"How about the senator?"

"It was shortly after Speaker Evans left. He was chatting with some people outside and I interrupted him. He brought his Chief of Staff, Meredith Stevens, with him. It was a short conversation, just remindin' him of my clients' positions on the budget bills and I left them there in the garden. It must have been close to ten-fifteen or so."

Ben wrapped up his questions and asked to speak to Jackson. He was summoned and Anna left them in her office to finish their interview. Jackson looked like a kid playing dress up in his father's suit, a serious look on his flushed face. He chewed on his fingernails between answering questions, and gulped down three glasses of water during the ten minute interview. His lip was lined with beads of sweat and when it seemed Jackson could add nothing new, Coop and Ben pressed further.

"Is there anything you haven't told us, Jackson?" asked Ben. "Do you have some information that would be helpful to our murder investigation?"

"No, no, uh, no sir, not that I can think of," replied Jackson, gripping his water glass so tight Coop was afraid it would shatter.

"Say, Jackson, you seem awfully nervous. Are you okay?" asked Coop.

The young man nodded. "Yes, sir. Uh, I'm, not used to being questioned by the police. I'm only an intern. I do research and um, prepare reports, and uh, analyze statistics and bills."

"Are you attending Vanderbilt?" asked Ben, in an effort to put Jackson at ease.

"Yes, sir."

"Coop and I both went to Vanderbilt. It's a fine school. Do you have political aspirations?"

"I want to be a lawyer, but, um, I'm interested in politics." His grip relaxed. "I'll be done with the internship at the end of June."

"Good luck to you, Jackson. If we need anything else, we'll be in touch. I've got your contact information down," said Ben.

As they walked out of the building Coop shook his head and smiled, "I think they better keep that Jackson kid in the back room doing research. I don't see him holding up in a trial."

Ben said, "I thought maybe he was holding something back about the murder, but I think he's just a skittish kid, who should rethink his career."

They chuckled as they left the Prosser office and trekked to the next lobbyist on the list. Stopping to speak with Peter Collins proved to be a quick visit. He was friendly, dressed in workout gear on his way to the gym, but substantiated Anna's arrival and departure. They were nearing the end of the list and failed to learn anything of consequence, other than most of the lobbyists they interviewed were in the garden area the night of the murder and none of them saw or heard anything.

One of the lobbyists on the official list, Susan Bates, said she had asked Reed Simmons to join her. They were working together on an issue and were hoping to negotiate language in a bill that would be advantageous to both of their clients. "We lobbyists are actually quite a close-knit group and tend to work together often," she said. "Reed and I spent most of our time at one of the tables outdoors on the edge of the garden area, since that's where the legislators gathered after their glad handing inside."

"From your vantage point at the tables outside do you remember who went into the garden that night?" asked Ben.

"Boy, that's tough. I know most of the lobbyists used the space at one time or another, since it was relatively quiet with the trees and shrubs helping to muffle the music. Plus it afforded a bit of privacy. I can't remember exactly, but it would be safe to say all the legislators and close to all the lobbyists were in and out of that area often. I also saw some of the other guests and staff, but didn't pay much attention."

She couldn't pinpoint the times she spoke with the legislators in the garden, but knew she left the event around eleven. "I know Senator Wagner was the last one I spoke with. I caught him coming out of the garden area and we chatted at the tables. Had to be around a quarter to eleven, I would guess."

They caught Reed as he was returning from a late afternoon workout. He confirmed Susan's account and admitted to being in the area during the time of death, but didn't remember seeing anything strange. Like Susan, he didn't know Grayson Taylor personally, only by reputation. His story matched up with Susan's with regard to timelines. Ben and Coop thanked him for his time and set off for the last stop.

Craig Baker's office was the closest to the capitol building and the most impressive. He was one of the partners in Whitehead, Baker, and McCord, the oldest lobbying firm in Nashville and well known for their prowess. Coop and Ben waited almost thirty minutes, but were eventually ushered back to a conference room overlooking the grounds and the massive limestone building atop a hill. They were led to a supple leather couch and offered a variety of beverages and snacks, but declined.

Craig Baker entered as soon as they were seated. "My apologies, gentlemen, this time of year is busy with our friends hard at work across the street," he said, glancing at the view from the window and offering each of them a firm grip.

Coop took in Craig's expensive suit, matching suspenders, tie and handkerchief, and monogrammed cufflinks, noting the jacket stretched to accommodate his muscular form. The man looked and smelled like money. Ben thanked him for seeing them and explained they were following up with all the guests of Saturday's event. "We noticed your name was not on the official guest register, but Coop remembers seeing you at the event," said Ben.

Craig nodded. "Yes, I actually went as a guest of Senator Wagner. We had some bills to discuss and he suggested I attend as his guest so we could chat, plus we represent Global and I always enjoy the music. I took my own car and met the Senator there."

"I'll need to get your license plate and car make and model," said Ben. Ben made a note of a BMW sedan and continued asking him questions. Craig confirmed he spoke with both Senator Wagner and Speaker Evans, along with the other legislators throughout the night. Eula Mae's list showed a BMW as a guest of Senator Wagner's.

Craig confirmed he spent time in the garden area, along with the other lobbyists. "The garden offered a semblance of privacy for those meetings we all wanted to have, especially with the legislative leaders. There are important budget bills in the works."

Craig didn't know the exact time he was in the garden, but said he spent most of the evening outside at the tables near the garden. He said he got back to the office at eleven-thirty, putting his departure time from Silverwood somewhere in the neighborhood of eleven o'clock.

He didn't spend any time on the terrace and entered the garden from the other side near the tables. He knew Mr. Taylor only in passing from his visits to Global and he didn't know anyone who would want to harm him. They discussed his separate meetings with Speaker Evans and Senator Wagner. He remembered Speaker Evans was alone and added, "Senator Wagner was with Meredith, of course."

"I take it Meredith goes with the Senator often?" asked Coop.

"Yes, she's his right hand woman. It's best to stay on good

terms with Meredith if you want to get access to Senator Wagner. It's a busy office and she rules it with an iron fist."

Ben left his card with Craig and asked him to call if he thought of anything else. They were led down the hall, their tired feet relished the thick cushioned carpeting. They left the reception lobby and began their journey to the car. It was after six o'clock and Ben suggested they stop at a Starbucks on the way to the parking garage. They splurged on frozen blended drinks topped with whipped cream and sank into chairs at a table in the back.

"So, what do you think?" asked Ben, letting out a sigh.

"I think the odds are tipped in the direction of our killer being on the political list, since we've confirmed several of them spent time in the area. It will be interesting to see what we learn from the actual politicians."

"Yeah, nobody stood out today as being our guy...or gal," said Ben, taking a gulp of his icy drink. "We haven't found anyone even remotely connected to Gray."

"Don't you think that stone piece weighs at least thirty pounds?"

Ben nodded. "Thirty-three to be exact."

"That leads me to think it must be a man. None of the women on our list look like they could heft that and swing it hard enough to bash Gray in the head. All the male lobbyists look muscular and fit and appear to be gym rats."

"Not to mention all the women are on the short side and all the men are tall. I tend to agree," said Ben, spooning the rest of his drink into his mouth.

They finished their drinks. Coop retrieved his Jeep and stopped by the office to pick up Gus. On the way home his phone beeped and he saw another text from Shelby. "I've got to call her tonight. That should be fun," grumbled Coop. Gus whined and put his head out the window, preferring not to get involved.

As soon as he reached the door of his aunt's house his phone chirped. Gus bounded in and headed for his bowl. Coop checked his phone and saw a message from his old friend at the Capitol Police. He suggested Coop and Ben show up around seven-thirty tomorrow morning, since that's when the two leaders were expected to arrive. He said they could catch them as they came into the building.

He texted back his thanks and followed up with a text to Ben. They decided to skip Peg's and have breakfast downtown, so they'd be close to the capitol. Ben offered to pick Coop up at his office at six in the morning.

11

After dinner Coop excused himself, poured a large glass of sweet tea, and shuffled to his home office. He needed to call Shelby. He'd been putting it off, dreading how unpleasant it would be. He knew it was bad when he opted to update Mrs. Taylor first.

He hammered out an email, preferring not to have another conversation with her in the midst of Ben's investigation into Seth. He reported the dozens of interviews with staff and attendees and the lack of a solid suspect, but promised his commitment to continue the investigation. He scanned and attached the letter they discovered on Gray's computer, hoping it would soften her heart.

He straightened his desk, filed the stack of papers that had lingered on it for months, and organized the guest list, placing a set of colored markers and several highlighters next to the documents. He retrieved a cold beer from his stash in the mini fridge. Gus stared at him from his resting place on a leather chair. "Don't look at me like that," muttered Coop. "I'm going to call her."

He scrolled to Shelby's name, took a long swallow from the

bottle of Yazoo Pale Ale and hit the button. She answered on the first ring. "Hey, Shelby. It's Coop."

Gus picked his head up off the arm of the chair and his ears stiffened as he heard the high pitched voice on the other end of the phone. Coop rolled his eyes and looked at Gus.

"I know, I'm sorry, Shelby. I've been working day and night on this case. No, I don't have any solid leads."

Her voice went down an octave as Coop bobbed his head while he listened to her. "Say, Shelby. I don't think this thing with us is going to work out anyway. You're in a different place in your life and my work makes me unreliable at times. I think you'd be happier seeing someone else. Uh, someone who shares your same interests."

Shelby shrieked, causing Gus to leave the chair and stand next to Coop. He let go of his grip on the cool bottle and petted the dog's head. After listening to her unyielding rant, she finally took a breath and he said, "I'm truly sorry, Shelby, but I think it's best if we end this now. You're beautiful and deserve someone who can dedicate more time to you. You take care now."

He was met with silence. She'd hung up without a goodbye. He shook his head and hit the button to disconnect the call and with a stroke of his finger deleted her from his contacts. "Ok, Gus. That's over. I should have known it wouldn't work."

Gus sighed and jumped back in the recliner opening his mouth to yawn and his giant tongue lolled out. Coop took a long draw from his beer. He and the dog stared at each other. "Don't judge me," said Coop.

After a couple of hours of highlighting the list, his eyes grew tired. He turned off the desk lamp and the noise caused Gus to tilt his head in inquiry. "Come on, Gus, let's go to bed."

He tossed and turned, feeling guilty about the call to Shelby. He'd been on dozens of first and second dates, but nobody made the cut to even a semi-permanent status in his life. He wasn't getting any younger and knew he needed to get serious if he didn't want to end up alone. Then again, even if he found someone, there was no guarantee he wouldn't end up alone.

∼

At breakfast Ben reported he heard from Kate and Jimmy late last night. Their flight was delayed, which meant they arrived late. They would be interviewing Seth and promised to call when they had more information, but wouldn't be back for a meeting tonight.

As Coop put jam on his last piece of toast he grinned. "Guess what I'm wearing under my politically correct suit today?"

Ben laughed and said, "Do I want to know?"

Coop unbuttoned the top of his dress shirt to reveal a white t-shirt with a picture of the U.S. Capitol and "Never Underestimate the Power of Stupid People in Large Groups" stenciled below.

Ben laughed out loud. "It's perfect, but you better hope you don't have an accident that requires removal of your shirt today. They might not have a sense of humor."

"It satisfies my rebellious urge." Coop picked up the tab. "This one's on Mrs. Taylor."

Since Coop's aunt knew Speaker Evans, he'd volunteered to talk to her. Ben agreed to tackle Senator Wagner. They downed the last of their coffee and stationed themselves at the end of the tunnel, ready to intercept them as they made their way from their offices and secure parking in the Legislative Plaza. Coop spotted Speaker Evans walking toward them. She was on her cell phone, but her eyes flickered with recognition when she glanced at Coop.

She disconnected and extended her hand. "Coop Harrington, right?"

"Yes, ma'am. Sorry to catch you like this, but I'm working

with the police in the investigation of Grayson Taylor's murder at Silverwood."

"Oh, yes, that was unbelievable. It upset my daughter when we heard about it the next day. Silverwood isn't a place I expect to encounter a homicide. Y'all are sure it was murder, huh?"

"Yes, unfortunately. Do you have a few minutes to answer some questions?"

She glanced at her watch. "Sure, let's scoot into one of the small conference rooms."

Coop verified her arrival and departure times with the video log from the gate. She outlined her evening, which consisted of a bit of campaigning and legislative business with lobbyists. "My priority that night was my daughter. She was excited to see Beau Branson and some of the other musicians, so I tried to keep my political antics to a minimum," she chuckled. "I've been busy with session and wanted to give her some of my time."

Coop smiled and took out his notebook. "I understand. Do you recall spending time in the garden off the back lawn and what time you may have been in that area?"

She furrowed her brow and rattled off the lobbyists she remembered speaking with outside. "As far as time, I'm not sure. I know it wasn't during any of Beau's performances. I missed one artist right before the short intermission and left my daughter to listen while I tried to get my commitments out of the way. I also spoke with my colleagues from the legislature while I was in the garden. Just for a few moments here and there. I went back in the mansion and listened to the bands until we left around eleven."

She also entered the garden from the lawn side and didn't spend any time on the terrace. As with the others they had interviewed, she didn't remember seeing anything suspicious or out of the ordinary. She knew who Grayson was, him being a hometown boy, but didn't have a personal relationship with him. She confirmed she was accompanied by her daughter and no staff members.

"Do you know of any reason someone would want to kill Mr. Taylor?"

She shook her head. "No, I'm stunned. It seemed like such a civilized affair. How was he killed?"

"All the evidence hasn't been analyzed, but from what we know, he was hit on the head with a decorative stone piece from the terrace and fell to the stone wall below."

"Oh my, that's horrible. I honestly don't think he was involved in any political dealings. Perhaps his death was related to his work."

Coop handed her Ben's card along with his. "Please call either of us if you remember anything that may help."

"I will. I understand he left a wife and young daughter behind. Please extend my sympathies."

Coop nodded. "I appreciate your time, Speaker Evans. I know how busy you are."

She gathered her satchel and slipped the business cards into her purse. "I think we could be done soon. I hope so. Give my best to Camille."

Coop followed her out and sent Ben a text telling him he'd wait for him in the cafeteria. He got a cup of coffee and reviewed his notes from the interview with Speaker Evans, watching the bustle of power moguls press through the halls.

Ben was seated in a conference room waiting for Senator Wagner, who stepped out for a moment to take a call. Ben intercepted him, along with his Chief of Staff, as they made their way to the building via the tunnel connecting the Tennessee State Capitol with the Legislative Plaza. A seasoned politician, Senator Wagner masked his annoyance, but Meredith Stevens did little to hide her irritation. She huffed as she left the room, when Ben asked to speak with the senator in private. She reminded Ben more than once they were on a tight schedule today and he was interrupting budget negotiations.

The door opened and Senator Wagner said, "Ah'm sorry, Chief Mason. We're in the last stages of getting this budget ironed out. How may ah help y'all?"

"I'm sure you know about Grayson Taylor's murder at Silverwood Saturday night. We're in the midst of the investigation, questioning everyone who attended the event." Senator Wagner nodded. "Sir, did you interact with Mr. Taylor during the event?"

"Ah may have greeted him, along with a room full of others, but ah didn't know him. Ah knew of him, with his position at Global, but had no dealin's with him."

"I understand you met with several lobbyists in the garden area that night. Did you spend any of your time on the terrace?"

He shook his head explaining he was in the garden area and entered from the tables area on the lawn. He recounted his conversations with the lobbyists and said Meredith would have a list in the diary of those with whom he spoke.

Senator Wagner said they left the event at eleven-thirty and estimated he spent about two hours mingling with lobbyists and other legislators outdoors.

"Was anyone with you in addition to Ms. Stevens?"

"There were a couple of interns who needed to talk to me about some campaign issues. They left around nine. Meredith has their contact information if you need to talk to them."

"Did you see anything out of the ordinary or anyone acting suspicious in the area or on the terrace?"

"No, nothin' comes to mind. The terrace isn't visible due to the trees and foliage in the garden, but the only people ah saw were my fellow legislators, staff, and lobbyists." He paused and looked at his phone. "You know ah did hear a bit of a ruckus that I thought was comin' from the terrace. From what people were sayin' it was Beau Branson and Mr. Taylor."

Ben nodded. "Yes, they were involved in a verbal disagreement on the terrace around ten-thirty."

"How was Mr. Taylor murdered?"

"Blunt force trauma to the head. He was killed with one of the decorative stone pieces on top of the balustrade."

"Oh, that's awful. Perhaps you'll get some fingerprints."

Ben smiled. "We're hopeful and waiting on further results from all the evidence. If you think of anything that may be helpful, please give me a call." Ben handed him his card. "Please send Ms. Stevens in."

"Keep up the excellent work, Chief." Senator Wagner palmed his phone and opened the door.

"Meredith, he's ready for you," he bellowed. "Ah have that meetin'. Text me if you need anything."

Meredith came through the door. "I don't have much time, Chief Mason. I really must get back to the office."

"I understand. I need to ask you a few questions about Saturday night at Silverwood."

She stared at Ben. "Get on with it," she said, tapping the toe of her shoe on the carpet.

"Tell me about your evening Saturday at Silverwood. Where did you go and what did you do?"

"I assisted Senator Wagner and made sure he met with some of the lobbyists we asked to be there. I also made sure he got in some greeting time with his constituents."

"Were you always with him or did you leave him alone during the evening?"

She gave him an icy stare. "I believe I used the ladies room during the evening, but outside of that, I was with Senator Wagner."

"Did you know Grayson Taylor or have any interactions with him at the event?"

"Only by reputation and his position at Global. He may have come through the greeting line, I don't know." She didn't remember any irregularities except the loud voices on the terrace that she later found out belonged to Beau and Mr. Taylor.

"Did you go out on the terrace that night?"

"No, I spent most of my time in the garden area or by the tables on the lawn, except for a bit of campaigning in the art gallery and fetching food." She glanced at her watch and twisted the brooch on her jacket. "Is this going to take much longer? I need to get back."

"Almost finished. Do you know who may have wanted to kill Grayson Taylor?"

She frowned and said, "Of course not. I had no relationship with him at all."

She flipped the pages in a worn leather bound diary and ticked off the names of the lobbyists Senator Wagner met in the garden. She said they left the party at eleven-thirty and she estimated they arrived outside around ten o'clock.

"And you heard nothing on the terrace except for the loud argument?"

"That's right."

Ben handed her a business card. "Please call me if you remember anything else."

She slipped the card into her diary.

"Oh, will you and the senator be available if we have further questions in the coming days?"

"Once session ends we'll pack up. I'll be in the office for the better part of two weeks cleaning things up, but the legislators all go home upon adjournment."

"Thanks, Ms. Stevens. You've been very helpful."

She picked up her diary and phone and opened the door, her heels clicking on the floor as she hurried to the tunnel.

Ben removed his phone from his pocket and saw Coop's

text. He made his way through the now crowded halls and slipped into a chair at Coop's table. "Have you been waiting long?"

Coop looked at the clock on the wall. "Only about thirty minutes. Speaker Evans didn't have much to add." Coop and Ben recapped their interviews.

"Do you think we could catch your friend David? I'd like to get some insight into these people."

"Sure, I'll text him and see if he could meet up with us." Ben got a cup of coffee while Coop typed a message on his phone.

As Ben sipped his coffee, Coop watched the parade of people rushing past the cafeteria. His phone beeped and he scrolled through the text. "David says he'll meet us in Victory Park in half an hour. He'd rather not be seen chatting with us in the building."

Ben took a swig of coffee. "I think Gray was killed by one of these political types. Most of them were in the garden area and could have slipped through to the terrace. Nobody remembers seeing Gray after you saw him, but Beau says when he left, Gray was headed back up the stairs to the terrace. I think he was killed soon after he got to the terrace. Somebody in this group of lobbyists and politicians is lying."

Coop nodded. "I feel the same way, but can't figure out what links Gray with any of them. The timeline sure points to one of them."

They tossed their cups and made for the exit. Outside they crossed to Victory Park and found a bench in the shade, which offered a modicum of relief from the oppressive heat. Coop focused on the walkway, keeping an eye out for David.

Coop raised a hand in greeting as he saw his old friend. "Hey, David. Thanks for meeting."

"Sure, sorry for making you come out here, but I wouldn't want any of the members to think I'm talking out of turn."

Ben extended his hand. "I'm Chief Ben Mason. Thanks for

coming. I wanted to get a feel for a few of the people we've been speaking to from someone like you. An insider, so to speak."

David nodded. "Sure, I'll tell you what I know."

"Tell me about Meredith Stevens and Senator Wagner."

David whistled. "You guys know how to start with the major players." He took a breath and began, "Well, Senator Wagner has been in the General Assembly for decades. He's powerful and connected. Has a reputation for getting things done that seem impossible. He's polite and always a gentleman, but not someone I want to cross. He has years of chits to collect from other members and is the main broker for deals. He'll be the one to get us out of session with some type of budget compromise bill. He's responsible for the bulk of the economic development boom over the past several years and has banked a lot of good-will for it."

"And Ms. Stevens runs his office? Has she been with him a long time?"

"Yeah, Meredith's his golden girl. She's bright and talented, but can be, uh, dismissive, rude, condescending, and plain difficult. Working with her over the years, I've found if we question what she wants or suggest an alternative, she gets downright offensive. She pretty much gets what she wants around here, because it's easier to comply than to get a call from Senator Wagner, who backs her on every little thing. To stay in his good graces you have to make Meredith happy."

Coop asked, "How about Lois Evans. I know she's in the House, but do you know much about her?"

"I've had some dealings with her. She's one of the favorites around here. Polite to staff and reasonable in her requests. She's not a slacker though. If she wants something she'll stay in the fight and get it done. She's quieter about it and being a home-town girl from a wealthy family, she's got a lot of support. She also has a rather aggressive Chief of Staff, Susannah Tyler. She and Meredith could be evil twin sisters."

Ben looked at his notebook and showed David the list of lobbyists they had interviewed. "What about these lobbyists? I'm curious to know their relationships with either of the legislators. Which of them has the closest relationships with the two legislators?"

David scanned the list. "You've got a lot of heavy hitters on the list. They're the most prominent with regard to the budget and money bills. Lots of formidable clients." He studied the names. "I'd say Anna, Craig, and Peter are the top three, as far as influential with leadership. Anna is closer to Lois, both being from old families. Senator Wagner does a lot with Craig. He's a constant fixture on the couch in Senator Wagner's office during session. Peter is also someone you'd find in both of their offices."

"Do you know of any connection these people may have had with Gray Taylor?"

David shook his head. "None that I know of. I didn't know Gray. I could do a search through our databases and see if he's ever testified or lobbied, but nothing rings a bell."

"How long have you been working at the General Assembly?" asked Ben.

"Oh, since I got out of college, almost twenty years. I interned here and decided to try for a job and worked in the House of Representatives first and took this job in the Senate about twelve years ago."

"Do you know anything about the personal lives of either the lobbyists or the legislators?"

"I've been to a few staff parties at Senator Wagner's place. He's got a huge estate in Brentwood. His first wife died and he married a younger woman. Probably younger than his own kids. Speaker Evans is married to a professor at Vanderbilt and has a teenaged daughter. She's got a massive estate in Green Hills. Meredith Stevens lives in a townhouse in Forest Hills. I don't think she's ever married. I've been to a few parties hosted by Anna Prosser and Craig Baker. Craig has a place in Hidden River in Franklin. He's got quite the spread with a few horses. Anna lives in Belle Meade near her parents' estate. Peter's in Green Hills. That's the extent of my personal knowledge."

Ben scribbled in his notebook. "Okay, thanks for the information."

Coop asked, "Do you think they'll wrap it up today or this weekend?"

David nodded. "If I had to predict, I'd say tomorrow or Sunday at the latest. They're all tired of being here so long and in the mood to settle things."

"Meredith told us staff would be around for a couple of weeks, but legislators would vacate as soon as the gavel goes down. Is that how you see it?"

"For the most part. They're generally in a hurry to get back to their home districts and get out of here. Most of the staff will be gone within two days or so. Meredith likes to, uh, exaggerate her importance and will stay. She and Susannah tend to compete with each other and both like the power. I think they hesitate to leave, because when they vacate their session offices here, they won't have a building full of people to command," David said with a grin.

Coop laughed. "I remember the gigantic staff party we used to throw when all the legislators and their high maintenance staff finally vacated the building. It was such a relief to see them leave."

David gripped his phone and scanned the screen. "I need to get back." He stood and scanned the crowd. "Let me know if you need anything else."

Ben shook his hand. "Thanks for the help. We appreciate the time and Coop owes you a beer," he said with a grin.

David smiled and jogged off with a wave.

12

Ben dropped Coop back at his office and they promised to keep in touch with developments. Coop removed his jacket and shirt and added a pair of shorts to his politically incorrect t-shirt and plopped into his chair, palming a handful of M&M's.

He settled in and spent the rest of the day trying to connect dots between Gray and the remaining names on the guest list. Gray wasn't involved in the lobbying efforts at Global, so he didn't have any direct links to the politicians or the lobbyists. Mel and another executive in Nashville handled the lobbying. Gray had relationships with lobbyists in California, but Coop couldn't connect any of them to Nashville.

He looked up from his computer and files when Annabelle came in with his lunch. "You need to take a break and eat something. I fixed you a plate of leftovers from your aunt's picnic supper."

He glanced at his watch and saw it was already mid-afternoon. "Looks good, thanks." She took the couch and brought him up to date on their other cases while he ate. He offered her a cookie and she took it and smiled as Gus camped out at her feet. "He knows you're a soft touch."

"Yeah, I know. I can't resist. I don't give him much and avoid the chocolate chunks." She bent over to reward Gus with a nibble and got a quick lick on the nose as a thank you.

"I've gone over and over this list and can't tie Grey to anyone who could be a suspect. It's driving me nuts."

The phone rang and Annabelle hurried to chew her bite of cookie before reaching for the phone on Coop's desk. She put the call on hold. "Taylor Nelson's on the phone for you."

Coop stuffed the remaining chunk of his cookie in his mouth and nodded. Gus followed Annabelle out as she shut the door.

Coop answered the line and Taylor asked if he could stop by and talk. He had the use of his mom's car for a few hours and was hoping Coop was available. Coop agreed to meet within the hour.

Coop hung up and cleaned up his lunch mess. "Hey, AB, do we still have some cookies left?"

"They're in the kitchen. Don't tell me you're still hungry?"

"No, I'm fine. Taylor's on his way over and I figured he might want a few."

"I'll get a plate ready and put it in your office. I wonder what he wants."

"He didn't say." Coop picked up his notes and lists and cleared off the table. He refilled his iced tea and sat on the couch in reception, waiting for Taylor.

Annabelle busied herself with some filing. "Any big plans for the weekend with Shelby?" she asked.

"No, no plans, big or otherwise, and Shelby's history."

"Oh, I'm sorry."

"Don't be. She was just a date, nothing serious. I keep finding myself with the wrong type of woman. I need to find someone more my speed, with my interests, and not so needy and clingy."

He shook his head. "What about you? Are you doing anything fun this weekend?"

She continued filing folders. "Nah, hoping to stay cool. I might go to a movie, but nothing too exciting. There's a new comedy at the theatre."

He laughed. "Sounds fun. And, it will be nice and cool in there."

She nodded and began to say something when the front door opened and Taylor stepped across the threshold.

Coop stood and Gus extricated himself from the slick floor and hurried to Taylor, offering a wet-nosed greeting. Taylor reached down to pet the dog. "Hi, Mr. Harrington."

"Remember, it's Coop. And, this is Gus. I don't think you've met AB," he said, gesturing to her. "She runs the place."

Taylor stopped petting Gus and moved to offer his hand to Annabelle. "Nice to meet you, ma'am."

Annabelle shook his hand. "Hi, Taylor. Call me AB or Annabelle, but not ma'am—that makes me feel even older," she smiled. "How about a Coke or iced tea?"

"Iced tea sounds terrific, thanks."

Coop led Taylor into his office and Annabelle delivered the tea, made sure Taylor took a cookie, and ushered Gus out of the office. "So, what brings you by?" asked Coop.

"Well, I was hoping you could help me with something. You mentioned you went to Vanderbilt and it would help me to have a letter of recommendation from an alumnus. Would you be willing to write one?"

"Sure. I'll need some information from you about your studies and activities, but I'd be happy to write one."

Taylor's smile widened to fill his face. "Cool, thanks. The other thing is my grandparents." Taylor looked down and took a drink of his tea. "I mean Grayson's parents. I overheard Mom talking to the lady from the police and she said they would like to meet me. My mom isn't sure about it, but I thought maybe if we could meet here, like we did the other night and you could help, she'd let me meet them."

"I could do that, but I don't want to get in the middle of a problem with you and your mom. If she's open to it, I'm fine with hosting a meeting here. I know from talking to Chief Mason your grandparents want to meet you."

Taylor nodded and finished his cookie. "Yeah, I think she's overwhelmed and feeling bad about not telling me about my dad. She's worried and upset, but I'll talk to her. I want to have a plan, if I can get her to agree. It will have to be on a weekend."

"I can work it out anytime that works for all of you. If you get the okay from your mom, I'll call the Taylors for you."

"That would be great. Mom and I are going to Grayson's funeral tomorrow. She agreed to go and changed her schedule at the pizza place. I was hoping we could do it Sunday. She's off all day and so am I."

"I'm open all day Sunday. I'm glad you're going to the funeral." Coop took a sip of his tea. "I talked to Grayson's wife, Emily. She's obviously upset about his death and was more than a bit surprised to learn about you. She may not give you a warm reception at the funeral. It's been an enormous shock."

Taylor looked down at his lap. "I figured she probably won't be happy to see me or Mom, but I want to go."

Coop nodded. "I think you're doing the right thing. Just wanted you to be warned about her. She's my client and I'm doing my best to help figure out who killed Grayson, but so far we aren't having much luck."

"I understand. Grayson's lawyer from California called and said he'd like to meet with us when he's here for the funeral. He said he wanted to tell us about the provisions Grayson made when he found out about me."

"I think your dad was a good man and I know he wanted to get to know you and help you." Coop was reluctant to share

Grayson's letter with Taylor without his mom's approval, but the urge to give it to him was overwhelming.

Taylor's eyes misted and he nodded his head in silence.

Coop made sure Taylor had his cell phone number and told him once he talked to his mom to give him a call and he'd contact his grandparents about Sunday. He made him take a few cookies for the road and put his arm around Taylor's shoulder. "It's gonna be okay, Taylor. You send me your information and I'll get a letter done and we'll talk again, okay?"

"Okay, Mr. Harrington— I mean Coop," he smiled. He said goodbye to Annabelle as he left.

Madison and Ross came through the door moments after Taylor departed. "Hey, y'all," said Annabelle. "You two ready for another night of espionage?"

Madison rolled her eyes. "I can't believe the number of cases we have with cheating spouses."

Coop interrupted. "Are you two available to go to a funeral tomorrow morning?"

They both nodded. "Why?" asked Ross.

"I'll be recognized and I need somebody to scope it out. Keep an eye on the widow and her family along with folks from Global and see if any of the politicians show. It's at Memorial Hills with a reception to follow. Funeral's at ten. I'll be there too, but it'll be a huge event and I'll need some help covering it."

"Okie dokie," said Madison. "Hopefully, nobody will ask us how we knew him. We'll wing it and say we knew him in school."

"You'll figure it out. Don't acknowledge me; just see if you notice anything. I'll get you a copy of the names we haven't been able to clear and AB can get photos for you."

"You got it, boss," said Ross.

He and Annabelle worked on the list, whittling it down to the names of people yet to be cleared through alibis, photos, or other means. She searched databases and made a photo layout of the remaining pool of suspects. Most of the lobbyists and politicians, plus a few music industry guests, and the late addition of Seth Hill, stared up at them from the pages she printed.

Coop and Ben texted all day and neither had anything solid to report, until Ben called as they were closing up the office. "Kate and Jimmy broke Seth. He admitted to using a burner phone to contact Emily and said they've been involved with each other for several years. She told him to keep his mouth shut about it, because she's worried about losing out on Gray's millions and his insurance money. He said he didn't murder Gray and he wasn't at Silverwood, but there's a time gap in his alibi between leaving Music Row and getting home where he could have done it."

"Do they think he's telling the truth?" asked Coop.

"Kate said he's nervous. He's concerned he's going to be blamed for Gray's murder and says he had nothing to do with it, but admitted to lying about the affair. He also confirmed he met Emily at the stables in Bowling Green while he was there."

"Sounds like you're in for another talk with dear sweet Emily," joked Coop.

"With the funeral being tomorrow, I'll take a run at her on Monday. It'll be fun to catch her in a lie. I think Kate and Jimmy scared Seth enough he won't dare contact her now. According to Kate he's the picture of cooperation. Kate thinks he's nervous about Emily's wrath and thinks he's telling the truth, but we're going to have to dissect his alibi and movements."

"I'll catch up with you Monday, unless we get lucky this weekend," said Coop, as he hung up.

"We need to get somewhere. I can't believe we haven't been able to solve this one yet," said Coop, as he slid his copy of the photos into a folder. "Thanks for staying late again, AB. How about we grab some dinner, on me?"

She glanced at her watch. "I could eat."

He loaded Gus into the backseat and offered to drive to the

Gas Lamp, a neighborhood grill a few blocks away. They were shown to a table on the patio.

"This place brings back memories. We ate here all the time during law school," she said.

"Yeah, I haven't been here in ages, but it sounded good tonight."

They decided on a signature pizza loaded with chicken, bacon, pineapple, red onions, barbeque sauce, and cheese. They spent the evening talking about the past and their time at Vanderbilt and split a piece of chocolate mousse cake for dessert.

Annabelle asked about Coop's dad. "I'm due for a visit soon. I wish I could talk him into flying out here, but he's a homebody."

"Camille would love it if you could get him to Nashville. Maybe if you start on him now you could convince him to spend the holidays with you."

Coop smiled as he surrendered his dessert fork. "Yeah, I miss him. Our client in this case reminds me so much of my uncle Mike's wife. She was an ice queen like Emily. Drove my poor uncle to an early grave and took off with their son and never let our family see him again. Her family was loaded and none of us, including Mike, was good enough for her. I think the only reason she latched onto Mike was his promising baseball career. Once that was over, she was done with him."

"I remember you mentioning them when we were in school. She made quite the impression on you."

"Yeah, plus my mom walked out on my dad…and me. Not the best of memories." He paused and took a swallow of his tea. "Luckily, I have you and Aunt Camille, the only two women I've been able to count on."

She smiled and slid the last bite of cake into her mouth. "You can always rely on us, Coop."

He carried the box of leftover pizza to the Jeep and kicked

Gus out of the driver's seat. He dropped Annabelle at the office to get her car and ran in to stash the pizza in the fridge.

"Thanks for the company tonight, AB. It was fun," he said, as she opened her car door. "You've always been a true friend to me."

"I enjoyed it. I haven't been out in a long time. Give me a holler if you need anything this weekend," she said, waving as she pulled out on the street.

Coop drove home with Gus in his appointed position in the passenger seat. "Too bad I can't find somebody like AB, huh?" he asked Gus. Gus turned his head and stared at him with his soulful brown eyes for several seconds before turning his attention back to the open window.

13

The funeral surveillance on Saturday was a bust. The politicians and lobbyists were no shows. With the legislative session still going strong they were busy at work. The funeral was packed with people from the music industry. All the people who had been at Silverwood, plus hundreds more attended the service, even Beau Branson.

Coop paid his respects to Grayson's parents, who thanked him for contacting them about Taylor and moved to greet Emily and her family. When he shook her hand, she gave him a cold look and said, "I expect to see some progress from you this week, Mr. Harrington." She added in a robotic tone, "Thank you for coming," before moving to the next person in line.

He walked away from the receiving line, feeling sorry for the little girl, Hannah, who was sobbing, but made to stand alongside her mother, shaking hands. He noticed Abby and her family didn't linger and didn't go through the receiving line. He caught up with them as they were trudging to their cars.

"Hey, Coop," said Taylor.

"How y'all doing today?" asked Coop.

Abby was leaning her head on her dad's shoulder, her face red and her eyes puffy. "Not so good," she mumbled.

Taylor shook Coop's hand and said, "Thanks for arranging the meeting with Grayson's parents." He paused, "I mean my grandparents. I didn't want to bother them today, but I saw them."

"They're excited to meet you. We'll see you tomorrow afternoon at my office." Coop looked at the somber group. "I'm so very sorry for your loss and the circumstances of Gray's death."

He shook hands with Andy and gave Abby a squeeze on the shoulder before heading to his Jeep. He knew Madison and Ross were going to stay until the bitter end, observing, but didn't feel there was anything more to learn from hanging out at the reception.

Coop stopped by the office to get caught up on some other work and found Annabelle at her desk. "What are you doing here?" he asked.

"I stopped by for a few minutes to finish up a report before I catch a movie."

"How about I join you and treat you to lunch?"

She grinned. "Sure, sounds good." She glanced at her watch. "We've got about an hour."

Coop hurried to his office and looked through his basket, signing off on a number of reports and reviewing files. He thumbed through his notes from the interviews with the lobbyists and politicians and changed into a pair of jeans and his "I did it…I Let the Dogs Out" t-shirt from the armoire in his office.

"You ready, Coop?" hollered Annabelle, as she shut down her computer and gathered her purse.

He offered to drive and return her to the office when they were done. They enjoyed the coolness of the theater and the distraction of a goofy comedy. They stopped at a cheeseburger place near the mall after the movie.

They both indulged in extra thick chocolate shakes served in the metal containers. "So, did you get any leads at the funeral?" she asked, spooning a dollop of ice cream into her mouth.

He shook his head. "Nothing at all. I talked to Taylor and Abby. He's excited about meeting his new grandparents tomorrow. Cruella gave me the evil eye and stern orders to make some progress."

She rolled her eyes. "Her tune might change tomorrow after Ben visits with her."

"I hope so. I hate this case. There's still no clear motive, unless it turns out to be Seth, but I trust Kate's instincts. I'm beginning to think you were right when you suggested a secret."

"It could be something Gray didn't even know he knew. Seems like a crime of opportunity, using the stone from the terrace. Makes me think it wasn't planned. Andy or Seth would have made a plan to kill him if they went there with intent."

"So, what would cause someone to pick up a thirty-three pound piece of carved stone and whack a guy?"

They were interrupted by the buzzer vibrating on the table announcing their order. They retrieved their burgers and fries and doctored them up with toppings at the long condiment bar.

"Beau seemed like the best candidate since he was arguing with Gray on the terrace, but he's clear and so are the others who had an axe to grind. Ben and I are convinced the killer is in the political pile."

"So why would someone in the political circle kill Gray?" she asked, taking a bite of her giant burger.

"There's no direct line between any of them and Gray."

"So it has to be something that happened at the party, right?" she asked.

"That's the theory that makes the most sense."

"Political types are notorious for shady deals and protecting their interests. We've got to figure out how Gray could be connected to something like that." She dipped a fry into ketchup.

"With him being from out of town and no apparent links, whatever the motive, it must have been spontaneous."

"Except the person didn't leave any fingerprints, DNA, foot-prints, nothing. That sounds like someone with experience."

"I know, it has the markings of a crime of passion, but zero evidence and zero motives." He finished his shake and wiped his hands. "What would be worth risking murder to protect? I miss Uncle John. He could unscramble this one."

"He was the best, but he taught you well. You'll figure it out —you always do," she said, pushing her plate away. "I'm stuffed. Thanks for lunch."

"It was a good day. We should do it more often. We're always working and don't hang out like we used to," he said.

"Yeah, well my boss is a slave driver," she grinned.

On the way back to the office, she offered to come in on Sunday for the meeting with Taylor and his grandparents. "I could make some snacks and try to lighten the mood."

"That would be fantastic, but you don't have to, if you're busy."

"I'm happy to do it. I like Taylor and want this to work out for him."

"That's kind of you," he said, pulling into the parking lot of his office. "I'll see you tomorrow afternoon."

"I'll make some of your aunt's cookies," she said with a wink, as she climbed from the Jeep.

Sunday morning Coop slept late, having been awake most of the night. Gus was lounging with Aunt Camille when Coop finally made his way to breakfast. He found a fresh pan of cinnamon rolls and an egg casserole waiting for him in the oven.

He lingered over coffee and read the paper until it was time to go to the office. He put on another button-down shirt, noticing only one left in the closet and made a mental note to make sure Mrs. Henderson laundered his others. He opted to take Gus, since greeting people was one of the dog's favorite activities. Aunt Camille was engrossed in a movie, so he gave her a peck on the cheek and motioned Gus to the Jeep.

The aroma of fresh coffee and warm cookies greeted them when he opened the door of the office. He saw a vase of flowers on the reception table and heard noises from the kitchen. Gus trotted ahead of him and accosted Annabelle. She was fixing a tray with cookies, banana bread, and some sort of cinnamon swirl concoction.

"Wow, everything looks wonderful, AB," said Coop.

"Help me carry out the tea and lemonade and we'll be ready."

The reception area was always welcoming, but today it had been transformed into a cozy living room. "I figured if they were comfortable with each other and we needed to give them some privacy we could scoot back to the kitchen," she said, arranging the napkins and plates. "I even stashed some extra cookies in the kitchen in case we're stranded."

Coop laughed. "You're always prepared, AB. That's what I admire about you."

The rapid wagging of Gus's tail announced visitors. Abby and Taylor arrived first. Coop shook hands and said, "Abby, I don't think you've met my associate. This is Annabelle Davenport. She's really in charge here."

"Nice to meet you and feel free to call me AB," she said, shaking Abby's hand. "Great to see you again, Taylor."

"You too, Miss Annabelle, I mean AB," said Taylor, his voice cracking.

"AB made some treats and we've got lemonade and iced tea. How about a glass, Taylor?" asked Coop.

"That'd be good. My throat gets dry when I'm nervous."

"Your grandparents are so excited to meet you. They appreciate you agreeing to the meeting, Abby," said Coop, handing her a glass of lemonade.

"They've always been kind to me and my parents." Abby smiled at her son. "I want Taylor to have the opportunity to have a relationship with them. I should have done this a long time ago."

"Here they are," said Coop, gesturing to the window overlooking the porch. "Mr. Taylor, Mrs. Taylor, nice to see you again," he said, opening the door.

"Please, call me Chase and my beautiful wife is Lila Rose," said the white haired man with gentle eyes.

"Chase and Lila Rose it is. Please come in and make yourselves at home. My associate Annabelle has made some delicious snacks for all of us."

Abby and Taylor both stood to greet the couple. "Oh, Abby, dear how are you?" asked Lila Rose, moving to engulf her in a hug.

Her head shook as silent tears trickled down her face. "I'm so sorry about Gray," she whispered.

Lila Rose sighed, "I know, dear, I am heartbroken."

Chase extended his hand to Taylor. "Taylor, we are so happy to meet you."

"Yes, sir. Me too," he said, shaking hands with his grandfather as he noticed some of the sadness leave his eyes.

"You are the spittin' image of your daddy," said Lila Rose, her eyes full of tears.

"That he is. That he is," smiled Chase, as he took in the scene of Taylor hugging his grandmother for the first time.

"Please sit down and help yourselves," said Coop. Abby took a chair and Taylor took the couch, sandwiched between his grandparents.

Annabelle helped serve up slabs of her homemade breads and cookies and she and Coop sat on the loveseat with Gus at their feet. He used his eyes to give Coop his dejected look, until he succumbed and shared his banana bread.

The conversation turned to Taylor's school and his aspiration to attend Vanderbilt and become a lawyer. "Mr. Harrington is writing me a letter of recommendation and told me Gray, uh, I mean my dad left me money to attend school."

"How wonderful," said Lila Rose. "He would be very proud of you."

Taylor continued answering questions and explained he didn't play sports because they were expensive and he was focused on getting an academic scholarship.

At a lull in the conversation, Coop walked to his office and returned with a sheet of paper. "During our investigation we discovered a letter Gray composed to Taylor on Saturday morning. I thought it best for Taylor to read it here, in the company of his family." He passed the letter to Taylor and added, "AB and I have some work to do in the back. If you need us, give a shout."

Gus followed the two of them to the kitchen and they sat in silence, trying not to eavesdrop, but listening for sounds of any distress. They heard Abby ask Taylor to read it out loud and took note as he struggled to get through the entire letter without breaking down. Soft sniffles and murmurs emanated as the group continued to talk after Taylor finished reading.

Coop let out the breath he had been holding. "Well, we made it through the worst part. I think they'll do fine together."

She nodded. "Yeah, they seem like very loving grandparents. It'll be good for them to have each other."

"I was thinking about what we talked about yesterday. I think we should focus on the politicians and lobbyists and see if we can figure out if any of them have something to hide that would lead to murdering Grayson."

Annabelle opened the laptop and her fingers flew over the keyboard. "Where do you want to start?"

"Let's focus on all the male lobbyists, Wagner, Evans, and Meredith. Ben and I don't think a woman would have the strength to heft that stone piece into Gray's head, but they're both tall and in good shape. Let's look at financials, partnerships, key legislation or causes, and anything else that pops up." He paused in thought and added. "I'm going to call Ben and see if he'll pull some records on our short list."

"Okay, I'll start checking them out," she said, taking a cookie from the plate, while she perused the screen.

Gus wandered between the reception area and the kitchen, pleading for nibbles as he visited each room. They worked for hours, smiling as they heard Taylor laughing and happy chatter coming from the front of the office. Gus surrendered to boredom and slept in the corner.

Coop's phone pinged and he read the text from David aloud. "Session has finally adjourned sine die and I checked our records for Grayson Taylor. He provided testimony about eight years ago on some legislation pertaining to digital music recordings. Nothing controversial, just going on the record for Global. Sorry, nothing more to add. Taking a couple of days off, but I'll be home if you need more."

"I don't see how that would lead to murder," said Annabelle.

The printer was spewing forth reams of paper from her research. Coop removed a sheaf and began sorting through the papers. He established piles for each of the suspects in the pool.

Taylor came into the kitchen. "Hey, Coop, we're going to take off and grab some food."

"We'll come out and say goodbye to your mom and grand-parents," said Coop.

They thanked Coop for hosting the gathering and Annabelle for the treats. "I hate the circumstance, but I'm grateful for the chance to have Chase and Lila Rose in our lives," said Abby, embracing Coop.

They said their goodbyes with hugs and handshakes and

Coop reminded Taylor to stop by next week to pick up his letter. Coop locked the front door and looked at the time. "It's Sunday and Aunt Camille would love it if you came to supper," said Coop, as Annabelle picked up the leftovers from the coffee table.

"Sure, I'm in," she smiled. "Let me get these files organized."

He locked up and followed the gecko green Beetle down the street. He called Aunt Camille on the way to warn her he was bringing a guest. They pulled into the driveway minutes later and Gus bounded for the door.

"AB!" gushed Camille. "I'm so glad Coop convinced you to join us for supper."

"It smells delicious," said Annabelle, returning Camille's hug.

"It's ready y'all, so sit right down. Coop, you can help me carry out a few things."

They devoured pork roast, green beans with bacon and pecans, applesauce, and buttered new potatoes with fresh biscuits as they shared their progress on the case. While they enjoyed the meal, Coop made his aunt's day by letting her know her tip had proven to be very important and shared the latest about Seth and Emily. The size of Aunt Camille's grin matched the giant scoops of cobbler she dished up for dessert.

Coop had stashed the new files on their suspects in his satchel and after dessert they gathered in the sitting room to peruse the information.

Aunt Camille scanned the documents in the file on Lois Evans. "I can't believe Lois would have anything to do with murder. I've known her since she was a baby and she comes from one of the most upstanding families in Nashville."

"My instincts say she wasn't involved, but right now we're looking for any anomaly to connect one of these people to something involving Gray."

"We're working a theory Gray may have learned something

134

that didn't even register and was silenced to keep the secret," added Annabelle.

Camille nodded. "I understand and agree most political types have questionable scruples, but Lois is the exception."

They worked late into the night, toiling to analyze each of the clients of the lobbyists for potential underhanded activities that would spark one of them to murder anyone who discovered the corruption.

Annabelle ran the companies through a search engine and printed out newsworthy items. Most of them had to do with ribbon cuttings at new facilities, charity events, or social affairs. As she combed through the stack, she fingered two articles touting headlines of car crash victims.

She read the reports, the oldest from five years ago telling the story of the assistant to the CEO of a manufacturing company, who was involved in a fatal accident. There were no witnesses to the one car collision where her car left the roadway and went off a steep embankment. She was pronounced dead at the scene. The other article gave the account of another fatal car crash from two years ago involving the Chief Financial Officer of one of the semiconductor firms on the client list. He suffered a similar tragic end when his car went off the road and struck a tree. They both left behind spouses and children. Taglines from colleagues littered both articles describing them as hardworking and kind people who would be missed not only as coworkers, but as friends. Both companies had established funds to support the families involved.

"Hmm," she said, handing the articles to Coop. "I've still got a ways to go in analyzing this pile I pulled from the web, but these two are interesting."

Coop rubbed his eyes and said, "I've got to call it a night. My eyes are killing me and my brain is numb." He placed the two articles on the table. "I'll take a look at these tomorrow."

"You never kept that eye appointment I made you, did you?" asked Annabelle. "I think you need reading glasses."

He flicked a harsh eye in her direction. "My eyes are just tired. " He worked to pile the papers in a stack. "This is difficult, since all we can do is speculate about underhanded deals, unless they've been publicized."

"We just got started, so let's give it this week and see if we can connect anything. Maybe something in the records Ben's getting will lead us in the right direction," said Annabelle, straightening her file.

"If nothing else it was delightful to visit with you, AB. I hope you'll come to supper again very soon," said Camille.

"It was wonderful, thanks so much for the lovely meal," she said, hugging Camille. "I'll see you in the morning, Coop."

He walked her outside. "Thanks for all the extra work today, AB. I'd be lost without you."

"Probably," she said, smiling as the engine came to life. She gave a wave as she looped through the driveway.

14

Ben called early Monday and told Coop he and Kate were headed back to Bowling Green. They planned to follow up on Seth's alibi in person and confront Emily about her lies. He also said Jimmy would be stopping by Coop's with the records they obtained. "I'll give you a call when we're on our way back and we'll compare notes," he said before disconnecting.

Coop just finished arranging the files on the conference table when Jimmy arrived bearing a pink box of pastries, followed by Annabelle. The three clustered around the conference table and in between bites of donuts and turnovers, looked through the financials and cell phone records Ben had obtained.

There were hundreds of pages to analyze and Ben's technicians turned up nothing in their search for calls made to Gray. They decided to concentrate on the days surrounding the murder. Armed with colored highlighters they each took a stack and began marking repetitive numbers and calls between the parties.

Only a handful of direct calls existed from the lobbyists to Speaker Evans and Senator Wagner. There were hundreds of calls between Meredith and Senator Wagner, as there were between Speaker Evans and her Chief of Staff. Anna, Peter, and Craig also racked up dozens of calls to each Chief of Staff, which could be attributed to the looming budget bills and the end of session.

With a few crumbs remaining in the pink box and two pots of coffee gone, the lone anomaly they found was a string of several calls from Meredith to Craig in the hours following the party at Silverwood. She placed seven calls to him starting at one in the morning. They ranged in duration from two minutes to ten minutes.

Annabelle pulled up the website for the Tennessee General Assembly. "They weren't in session late Saturday night or early Sunday morning. They had the weekend off."

"We'll need to pay a visit to both of them and see if we get the same story about why they were talking at such odd hours. I see some late night and early morning calls from other lobbyists on a few days, but none in the middle of the night like these," said Coop.

Coop's phone chirped and he put Ben on speaker. "We're on our way home," he said. "I think our visit put an end to Seth's romance with Emily and I wouldn't be surprised if he lost his job."

"She was madder than a nest of hornets, but finally caved when we told her we'd flown to L.A. to interview Seth," chimed in Kate, with a happy lilt to her voice.

"She said she only lied about the affair to spare them embarrassment and reluctantly admitted she was afraid to jeopardize any insurance money or have issues with the terms of Grayson's will."

Kate went on to say they were able to confirm Seth's alibi with regard to the times he was in Bowling Green. They still had some work to do from the time he left his friends on Music Row and returned to Bowling Green. "There are a couple of hours missing. He said he wandered around downtown and spent some time by the river. We're going to have to resort to surveillance footage to corroborate it."

"Sounds like you guys have been busy," said Coop. "We found some strange calls we need to follow up on when you get back." He explained the calls between Meredith and Craig.

"Maybe they're more than colleagues," said Annabelle, wiggling her eyebrows.

"Anything's possible. Coop, I think I'll have you go with Kate to talk to Meredith and I'll take Jimmy and see what Craig has to say. I want to see them at the same time, so neither is able to call the other with a warning," said Ben, suggesting they meet at two o'clock.

As Jimmy was leaving, Aunt Camille bustled in with a basket. "Yoo-hoo!" she called out. Gus bounded from Coop's office to greet her. "There y'all are," she said, plopping the basket on the edge of the table. "I brought yummy leftovers from last night."

Coop and Annabelle slid the files to the other end of the table and made room for the sandwiches, salads, and cobbler Camille arranged. "I figured you two wouldn't eat a proper meal unless I provided one," she winked.

Coop hugged her and murmured his thanks. As they dined, Camille asked, "So, did you learn anything from Ben's records?"

"Not much. We're going to dig into some calls Meredith Stevens made to Craig Baker in the hours following the murder. It seems odd for her to call him seven times during the middle of the night."

"Oh, my, that sounds a bit peculiar."

"AB thinks there might be some hanky-panky involved," he said, sliding a forkful of peach cobbler in his mouth.

"I'm going to my herb club meeting this afternoon. I'll poke around and see if anyone has heard rumors of an affair between the two of them. Several of the members have family who are connected to the legislature and the political world," offered

Camille with a sly smile. "My friend, Twyla Fay, lives near Craig Baker. I've never heard her mention anything about marital problems. And, believe me if she heard a whisper, she'd yap about it. She's the biggest gossip I know."

Coop almost choked on his cobbler. "Now, don't be meddling. It's only a theory and needs to stay confidential."

She flapped her hand at him a couple of times. "I know what I'm doing. I used to help your uncle all the time and know how to gather information without anyone getting the least bit suspicious."

Coop sighed and shook his head while Annabelle suppressed a giggle and stuffed her mouth with the sweet dessert. Realizing she only had ten minutes to get to her meeting, Camille hurried out the door.

Guessing Meredith Stevens wouldn't see the humor in his "Give Peas a Chance" shirt decorated with a line of the vibrant green vegetables, he traded it for another Harrington and Associates polo shirt. This case was wreaking havoc on his wardrobe.

Later in the afternoon, Coop gathered with Ben and his team around the table. "Jimmy and I talked to Craig Baker and asked about the calls from Meredith. He hemmed and hawed, but eventually told us Meredith was three sheets to the wind and called him suggesting they get together. Seems she wouldn't take no for an answer and he was reluctant to be too rude, since she's his main access to Senator Wagner. He said her last call was an apology."

"Didn't his wife think it strange he was talking to her in the middle of the night?" asked Kate.

Ben smirked. "We asked him the same thing and he said his wife was out of town, so he was home alone. He urged us to keep it quiet as he didn't want his wife to find out or Senator Wagner, for Meredith's sake."

Coop asked, "What's your take? Do you think he was telling the truth?"

"He didn't give any indication he was lying, but he's a lobbyist, so it's hard to tell," said Ben with an impish grin. "He was a bit squirrely, but I got the feeling he didn't want to mess things up with his wife or get shut out of the senator's office," said Ben. He nodded to Kate, "What about you two?"

"We found Meredith and she kept us waiting for twenty minutes, for what I don't know."

"Because she's a pretentious tyrant and wants us to know she's in charge of her miniature kingdom," added Coop, rolling his eyes.

Kate smiled, "Yeah, there's that." She paused and continued, "She was indignant, reminding us her phone was a personal phone, not paid for by the State of Tennessee, and we had no right to access her calls. Once we showed her the warrant she tried lying and said they were discussing a bill. After we pressed her, she admitted to being tipsy. She said she and Craig have flirted for years and she was lonely and fueled with liquid courage she exercised poor judgment and called him to invite him over to her place."

Coop added, "She said she was extremely embarrassed and the last call she made to Craig was an apology after she'd slept for a few hours and woke up realizing she'd been out of line. She didn't' remember how many times she called him, but acknowledged several."

"And she was less than pleased and almost humbled at having to admit to such shameful actions. She hoped we would keep our inquiry confidential so as not to cause undue embarrassment to Craig, Senator Wagner, the legislature, and, of course, herself," Kate read from her notes. "I'm surprised she didn't mention the president," she mumbled under her breath.

"She's hard to read, because she's always in command and condescending. The only thing I noticed was she kept fiddling with her fancy pin on her jacket while we talked. That could be nerves and embarrassment from having to admit to being out of control," said Coop.

"Craig made it sound like she was a lot more sloshed than she did, but that's understandable. The stories link up, so I guess we've explained it. Now we're back to square one," said Ben with a sigh. "You guys go ahead and get back on the other case," he said, nodding to Jimmy and Kate. "I'm supposed to get an update on the surveillance footage from downtown soon."

Coop pulled the articles about the fatal car crashes from his notepad. "AB has been pulling articles off the web featuring the major clients on Baker's lobbying list. She thought these two were interesting. Could you guys pull the files on these accidents and check them out? AB and I will keep going through the records and see if we can find anything else," offered Coop. "We're missing something."

Ben's phone buzzed and he looked at the screen. "Gotta run. I'll catch up with you on Friday at breakfast, unless you get somewhere before then. Kate, go ahead and look into these accidents," he said, handing her the papers.

Coop dedicated the remaining hour of the day to Taylor's letter for Vanderbilt and some other casework. He spent the evening watching television, hoping the focus on something mindless would help his brain uncover the missing link in the case.

Tuesday morning Coop dug back into the research files and made another call to his friend David in the Senate. He wanted to know if there had been any rumors over the years about Meredith being involved with Craig Baker. David was reluctant to discuss such gossip, but relayed he had never heard anything about a romance between Meredith and anyone, except old speculation about her and Senator Wagner after his wife died. "I'm not sure there's any truth to it," he added. "Because of what appears to be his total support for her, that's led to conjecture, and she's an easy target, especially with her acidic personality."

Coop chuckled at his apt description of Meredith and thanked him again, apologizing for disturbing him on his day off. He sent Ben a quick text and relayed his conversation with David.

As much as he dreaded talking with her, he placed a call to Emily Taylor. He knew calling her was better than getting a lecture from her when he wasn't ready. As he expected, she was displeased with the lack of progress and reiterated her demand for the arrest of the murderer. She also launched a new diatribe against Taylor and Abby, labeling them despicable trash. She was equally angry with Gray's attorney, Steve, and had secured her own attorney to try and nullify the $400,000 Gray set up in a scholarship for Taylor.

Although Coop did his best to change her mind and emphasize the positive attributes of Taylor, reminding her of Gray's own letter to his son, his words fell into an abyss of silence. He gave up and ended the call with, "I'm still hopeful. I'll get in touch as soon as we have something definitive."

He hung up the phone, shaking his head. "Brrr, she's one cold woman, Gus." Gus raised his head off the seat of the leather chair, plonked it back down and shut his eyes, content to go back to his peaceful snooze. Coop was thankful she chose not to mention the latest encounter with Ben and Kate or Seth. He wasn't going to introduce the topic.

The days dragged into one another, with them no closer to a solid suspect. Over pancakes on Friday morning, Ben told him he had to pull back on resources related to Gray's murder, since he'd been hit with some other cases with promising leads that demanded his attention. "The techs found Seth on some camera footage, but still have a ways to go. They've been pulled for another case," said Ben, shaking his head.

"I'd like to clear Andy, too. Twenty minutes is really pushing the realm of possibility anyway. I honestly don't think he did it." Coop moved his cup as Myrtle came by to top off his coffee. "I've gone back and talked to other employees and a few guests to see if any of them saw Andy near the terrace or even the mansion. Nobody did."

"Kate checked on those accidents and said there was nothing suspicious about either event. She talked to the investigating officers and they both wrote it off to driver distractions and speed. No foul play was suspected."

Coop shook his head. "This case is like looking for one needle in a whole stack of needles."

Ben nodded. "We don't have any evidence linking Andy or Seth to the crime, only holes in their alibis." Ben shoved his empty plate away. "Oh, the only good news is Steve called last night and said there's a fidelity clause in Grayson's will, so our favorite widow isn't going to end up with the windfall she thought she was. He said Taylor's scholarship is safe."

Coop's eyes twinkled. "Sometimes there's a glimmer of justice in the world. Now if Seth is found murdered, I think we'll have a prime suspect," he laughed and took a swallow from his cup. "I wonder if I'll get fired now."

"I wouldn't be surprised. She'll have to conserve some of her money and according to her you're not doing anything anyway," Ben winked and picked up the ticket. "My treat, since you'll probably be unemployed soon."

Coop carried the take-out box and followed Ben outside. The hot blanket of summer hadn't subsided and even this early in the morning, Gus was panting when Coop got in the Jeep. Once they arrived at the office, Gus barreled through the door to his personal water fountain.

Over the loud slurps, he heard Annabelle yell out a greeting and delivered her breakfast. She popped open the lid, "Mmm, strawberry waffles, thanks." Gus licked his lips and plopped onto the floor next to Annabelle's vent.

Coop adhered giant sticky notes to his wall outlining suspects, timelines, and his observations. Every morning he looked it over, hoping for inspiration.

Annabelle had left Mrs. Taylor's file on his desk with the spreadsheet showing the hours spent had more than exhausted the retainer. They would need to bill her for the remaining hours. He composed a standard email and attached the spreadsheet, along with a bill for the remaining hours, indicating he would need another deposit if she wished to continue to retain the firm. He anticipated the termination of their relationship once she received the bill.

On Thursday afternoon he received a terse reply to his email letting him know his services were no longer needed. She was, albeit reluctantly, sending a check for the remaining balance and would be sure to let her circle of friends know how dissatisfied she was with his performance. Coop was relieved when he read the email, knowing he wouldn't have to endure her patronizing criticisms any longer, but was still dedicated to finding Gray's killer, for Taylor's sake.

The singular bright spot of the week was when Andy and Taylor dropped by the office on Friday afternoon. Taylor was on his way to Silverwood and wanted to pick up his letter. Annabelle suggested they meet in reception, since everyone but Coop and Gus were gone for the day. She didn't want Taylor to have to look at the murder notes all over Coop's office walls.

Coop shook hands with Andy and presented the letter to Taylor. He scanned the page and as he read it, his grin widened.

"Wow, Mr. Harrington, it's perfect. You said so many nice things about me. How'd you know about the stuff at school and my volunteer work?"

"I'm a private detective, remember," chuckled Coop.

Andy's cell phone rang and he excused himself to the porch to take the call. "I keep hoping I can save enough to get my own car, so I can quit bugging Uncle Andy to take me to work," said Taylor. "I'm working more now that school's out and hate being a burden to him or Mom."

"What kind of car are you looking for?"

"Anything, just something reliable."

"I've got a friend who owns a garage and comes across some good deals at times. I'll have him keep an eye out for something," offered Coop.

"That would be great," he said, as Andy returned from the porch.

"Sorry, I have a work issue I need to take care of. I have to get moving."

"Go ahead, Andy. I can drop him at Silverwood," said Coop.

Andy glanced at his nephew, who was nodding and smiling. "Okay, if you're sure you don't mind. Thanks, Mr. Harrington."

Taylor followed Andy to the truck and removed his backpack, waving as Andy drove away. He plopped the pack on the couch and nuzzled Gus. "I meant to tell you we talked to Gray's lawyer and he said my scholarship is for real and it's all set up. He said he's the administrator of it and will pay my college bills. I need to send him the statements and he'll handle it."

"Now, we have to get you into Vanderbilt," Coop said with a grin.

"The application is due November first and I've got it done. Your letter will be a big help. I'm applying for the early decision, so I'll know by the middle of December."

"I'm sure they'll accept you. Your grades are excellent and you've done plenty of volunteer work in the community. With all that and Coop's glowing letter, how could they refuse?" joked Annabelle.

The phone rang and she returned to her desk. Taylor's grin faded, replaced by a solemn expression. "Have you found out who killed him?"

"No, I'm sorry, we haven't yet. We're still working on it and have followed up on several leads, but nothing has come of them." Coop paused and slid his hand over Gus's head. "How's your mom?"

Taylor shrugged and said, "She's sad. She tries to hide it, but I've caught her crying a few times."

"How about your new grandparents?"

The boy's smile returned. "They're great. They've been having us over for dinner each week."

Annabelle hung up the phone and swiveled around in her chair. "That was Justin. He said he's not going to be able to take care of the lawn any longer. I'd been calling all week and he finally called back."

"I knew it was risky to make a deal with him. I was hoping he'd stay on the right path."

"I'm looking for more work, I could do your lawn," offered Taylor. "I work every weekend at Silverwood this summer. I could do it then, if you can give me a ride to work on those days?"

Coop thought for a moment and nodded. "Let's give it a try and see how it works out for you."

"I work tomorrow at ten. How about I come by here early, before it gets too hot?"

"Works for me. I'll meet you here around seven," said Coop.

"Cool, that will be a good time for Uncle Andy to drop me. We better get going. I like to be early."

They said goodbye to Annabelle and Gus was relegated to the backseat for the short ride to Silverwood. As boys tend to do, Taylor opened up on the drive and talked about how concerned he was Andy was still a suspect in the murder. "He would never hurt anyone and I know he's worried, but you gotta believe him."

"I don't think your uncle harmed Gray and Chief Mason doesn't either. He's still considered a possibility only because of those twenty minutes where we can't corroborate his whereabouts." He looked over at Taylor as they pulled into the staff parking lot. "By the way, I'm no longer employed by Mrs. Taylor, but I'm going to keep looking into this case. I want to find out who killed your dad and why."

"What happened?"

"I got fired. She wasn't happy with the time it was taking to close the case."

"Don't take it personally, Coop. I don't think she's a very happy person and is taking out her grief on you."

"You're a wise man, my friend," said Coop, with a slow smile.

15

Coop showed Taylor the yard equipment and tools he kept in the shed on the edge of the parking lot. After a short tutorial on the sprinkler system, he left him to work for a couple of hours and tried to get something done in the office.

Taylor finished the yard and borrowed the office bathroom to shower and change for his shift at Silverwood. Coop got up from his desk and clutched his stomach, feeling a sharp twinge of pain in his right side. He'd felt off all morning and chalked it up to eating too much last night. He walked around the office, thinking it was a cramp he needed to work out.

He dropped Taylor off and drove back to the office. Attempting to take his mind off the pain he concentrated on paperwork. He jolted as a stabbing sensation bore into his side, delivering a heightened level of pain. He pressed low on his right side and gritted his teeth. He made his way to the sofa and Gus whined as he placed his head next to his master. He struggled to reach for his cell phone. He groaned as the pain mounted. He didn't want to bother his aunt, who was at a garden club luncheon and show, so he poked the icon for Annabelle.

She answered after a few rings. "Hey, AB, sorry to bug you, but—" he shrieked as another wave of pain hit. "Something's wrong, I'm in a lot of pain and need a ride to the hospital. I'm at the office."

After she said she was on her way, he dropped the phone to the floor as he gripped his side. When she rushed in a few minutes later, she found him slick with sweat, writhing in pain. "Coop, can you make it to the car?" she asked, with a hint of panic in her usually calm voice.

His eyes were glassy, but he nodded and grimaced as she helped him sit up. "I should call an ambulance," she said.

He shook his head. "No," he whispered. "I can make it." He put his arm around her neck and shoulders and she hoisted him up and out of the office. He clenched his jaw as they made their way down the steps and was out of breath when they arrived at the parking lot. He motioned to his Jeep, unsure if he could fold his body into the seat of her Beetle. She slipped her hand in the pocket of his shorts and pulled out his keys.

She held the door and helped him slide into the passenger seat. She saw Gus at the window, watching. "It's okay, Gus. We'll be right back," she tried to sound confident.

She maneuvered the streets like a Nascar driver as she made her way to the emergency room at Vanderbilt. The Jeep squealed to a stop in front of the glass door entrance and she hopped out to get help. Moments later, attendants ran out with a wheelchair and lifted Coop out of his seat. She followed and took his wallet and whispered, "I hope they don't have to cut off your shirt," before he was bustled through the door to the treatment area. She wasn't sure if the panic on his face was from the pain or the fear his vintage "World's Tallest Leprechaun" shirt was in danger.

She asked them to contact Dr. Alex Weston, a classmate of theirs from Vanderbilt and went about filling out the admitting forms. She completed all the forms except for his signature and approached the desk. She was buzzed through the door and directed to one of the dozens of treatment rooms. She found him curled on the bed in his room, shrouded in a flimsy hospital gown, hooked up to intravenous fluids and resting. "Coop," she whispered.

His eyes fluttered open. "Hey, AB, sorry I ruined your Saturday."

She smiled. "I've got your forms filled out and need you to sign. How are you?"

"They gave me something for the pain. They're trying to rule out appendicitis, but Alex thinks it's most likely kidney stones."

Her brow furrowed. "Oh, both of those sound bad. Sorry, Coop." She brushed his forehead. He scrawled his name on the paperwork and she went in search of the clerk at the admission desk.

On the way back, she passed Alex in the hall. "Hey, AB. I'm on my way to talk to Coop," she said.

"He said you were doing some tests."

"Yeah, I've got the results," she said, holding up the clipboard.

"Good news, Coop," said Alex. She waited for him to open his eyes and Annabelle slid into the chair by his head.

"I reviewed the scan and you've got kidney stones. You're also dehydrated and need to see your doctor on a regular basis." She eyed him over the top of her glasses. "We'll do our best to manage your pain, but until you flush them out, you'll be dealing with the discomfort. They're small enough to pass, but they'll hurt like the devil."

"How long do I have to stay in this place?"

"A few more hours. We need to make sure someone stays with you when you're discharged though. And, you need to follow up with the urologist.

"Aunt Camille's at a garden party—"

Annabelle cut him off. "I can watch him today."

"That works. So, you'll need to drink a ton of water and we'll send you home with some filters you'll use to collect the stones. You'll need to bring them to your appointment for analysis. Chances are they're calcium based, which means you need to lay off caffeine, chocolate, nuts, greens, and drink a lot more water."

Coop scowled at the doctor. "You've eliminated his basic food groups," said Annabelle. "Coffee, tea, peanut M&M's."

Alex shook her head. "Those will be on the list of foods to avoid. And you need to get in to see me once a year, like I've told you before."

"I know," murmured Coop as his eyes closed.

"He'll be tired due to the pain meds. I'll check on him again in a few hours and can give you a call when he's ready to go," offered Alex.

"That'd be great and will give me a chance to run some errands." She made sure Alex had her cell number and gripped Coop's hand before she left.

She stopped by the market before picking up Gus and driving to Camille's. Knowing the Henderson's were off and the house was empty, she used her emergency spare key.

She unloaded the groceries and prepared a pot of chicken soup. Gus moped around the house, but finally settled down on his chair in Coop's office. She poured herself a glass of iced tea and plopped to the couch as her cell rang. It was Alex reporting Coop was being released.

She checked the soup and turned it down to simmer and told Gus to stay. Coop was already dressed and in a wheelchair when she arrived. After more discharge paperwork, she got him loaded in the Jeep. "I see your shirt survived," she said, snapping his seatbelt.

He gave her a feeble grin. He was peaked and drowsy, but wasn't complaining about the pain. She stopped by the pharmacy on the way home and picked up his prescriptions.

By the time she got him settled in bed, it was seven o'clock and Gus barreling to the door, announced the arrival of

Camille. Annabelle followed Gus and met up with Camille in the kitchen.

"Hi there. I didn't want to startle you."

"Oh, dear, it's delightful to see you. Are you two working on the case?"

"Not right now. Coop wasn't feeling well and I ended up taking him to the hospital. He's fine, but in bed."

Camille's hand flew to her chest. "Oh, no, what's happened?"

"He has kidney stones. So they gave him some pain meds and want him to drink a lot of water. He's supposed to stop eating chocolate, nuts, caffeine, and greens."

Camille wrinkled her nose. "Oh, that won't be good." She paused and added, "Especially for us."

"I know. He starts the day with twelve cups of coffee and eats handfuls of peanut M&M's. He's not going to like the new diet."

"Something smells good in here. You must have been cooking," she said, taking the lid off the pot. "Looks delicious."

"I made some soup and stopped and got some juices and stuck them in the fridge. He has to drink plenty of fluids, mostly water, but I know he hates water."

"Sit down, dear, and I'll go check in on him and see if we can get him to eat some of your wonderful soup." She shuffled off in her dress adorned with giant peonies, the material swishing with her movement. Her oversized pink hat bobbed as she made her way to Coop's wing, Gus at her heels.

While she was gone, Annabelle readied a tray for Coop. She left him a large glass of water on his nightstand, but put a fresh glass along with some juice on the tray. She made her way through the house and found his door ajar. She tapped with her finger and opened it wider.

Coop was sitting up, Gus was in the chair, and Camille was on the edge of the bed. "Here's some food for the patient," she announced, placing the tray across his lap. "How're you feeling?"

His eyes, normally full of spark, were dull and tired, matching his drawn and pale face. "Like I got hit by a truck."

"I brought you some soup. You need to take in liquids like Alex said, so I thought this might taste good."

He moved his eyes to the empty water pitcher on his night table. "I drank all of it."

"Good job, Coop. Now drink more," she said, thrusting the glass into his hand.

"You need your rest. You've been working too hard and not eating properly," said Camille. "I'll get changed and be back to check on you, so AB can get home."

Annabelle perched in the other chair and nodded to the tray of food. "Eat."

He glared at her. "Yes, ma'am. You're a mean nurse." He spooned some soup into his mouth. "Mmm, tastes good though."

"You need to stay home until you pass those stones, so plan to take the week."

"It better not take a damned week," he said, gulping the water.

"I can take care of the office. You rest and relax. I'll come by every night with anything you need to know or sign."

"I know you can handle it, AB. I hate sitting around and I really hate being sick." The grumbling continued as he ate the soup. By the time Camille returned, he had finished his soup and downed both the water and the juice.

"I'm going to hit the road. I'll call a friend to pick me up, since I have your Jeep and left my car at the office. Give me a call if you need anything, otherwise, I'll stop by Monday."

"Thanks, AB. Sorry, I'm so cranky. I appreciate all the help and you taking care of me all day," he said, with a sheepish grin.

She squeezed his hand and gave him a peck on the forehead. "Feel better, Coop."

Over the next few days, Camille and Annabelle kept a thumb on Coop, insisting he rest and drink gallons of water each day. His follow-up appointment was scheduled for Thursday and he was resolute in his desire to drive himself. Late in the afternoon he showed up at the office sporting a t-shirt that said "In Dog Years, I'd be Dead" with Gus trailing behind him.

"Shouldn't you be home resting?" asked Annabelle.

"I just saw the doc and he said I could go back to work. I turned in my collection of stones. He did another scan and said they're all gone, so I'm good to go."

"And what did he say about your eating habits?"

He scowled as he turned for his office. "Exactly what Alex said."

She shook her head and turned back to her computer screen, hoping she'd be gone before he realized she had disposed of his M&M's and replaced his normal robust coffee with several bags of decaffeinated beans she had ordered via express delivery.

16

The days evaporated into weeks, as did the newspaper coverage of the unsolved murder of Grayson Taylor. The oppressive heat had abated for a couple of weeks in July, but now in early August it was back with a vengeance. Coop's frame of mind matched the weather. He was irritated with the lack of progress on Grayson's case and aggravated by his new diet restrictions. He never realized how much coffee he drank or how many times he reached for the candies on his desk. Aunt Camille stopped making his favorite cookies, auditioning new flavors. So far, snickerdoodles were the sanctioned replacement.

Coop moved on with other cases and other work, but made a point of reviewing the evidence each week. He scoured his research, seeking the elusive string that, if tugged, might unravel the whole mystery.

Ben's workload forced him to prioritize resources and he chalked up Gray's murder to one that might not ever be solved without new evidence. The topic came up at their weekly breakfast.

"I can't let it go," said Coop, stirring the one cup of real coffee he allowed himself every morning. "I've gotten to know

Taylor more this summer and for his sake I want to figure this
one out."

"I feel bad for the kid and I'm angry that we couldn't solve it,
but I don't have the time to dedicate any more manpower. You
have more freedom to pursue it and if you find a lead, I'm all in,
but I can't keep going over and over the same stuff. Even after
the hours we spent on surveillance video, we couldn't clear
Seth, or for that matter, Andy. Nobody thinks they did it, but
there's nothing to link any of the others to the crime."

"This is the first case I've taken that I haven't solved. It makes
me feel incompetent."

"Oh, our favorite widow does that for me. She still calls each
week like clockwork to remind me how inept I am," said Ben.

A grimace contorted Coop's face. "I was really hoping she
was involved."

Ben smirked. "I'd enjoy making that arrest. I'd probably let
Kate, though. That woman burrowed under her skin."

"Steve contacted me yesterday and said Grayson's will has
been settled. Grayson's parents received millions, Emily got a
lump sum based on the number of years they were married, and
the rest is in a trust for Hannah. Steve's the trustee, so Emily
can't get her hands on it. He said Seth did get fired and moved
back to Bowling Green. He thinks Emily's planning to stay in
Los Angeles, because if she sells the house, the proceeds go into
the trust."

Ben sniffed the air. "Ah, the sweet smell of justice with a
hint of maple bacon pancakes." He smothered his stack in
syrup. "That reminds me about the insurance money. They
paid Global on the executive coverage they carried on Gray,
but are dragging their feet on the policy naming Emily as the
beneficiary. Seems they don't want to pay until they're sure
she's cleared of any part in his murder." He took a sip of
coffee. "Of course I told them I couldn't sign off on something
like that until the case was solved, since there's a small chance

she was involved via Seth." He grinned like a pig in a mud hole.

"Well, you wouldn't want the missus to think you were incompetent. Best to cover all the bases before you attest to something as important as that," said Coop, a devious smile hiding behind his sincere lawyer voice.

"This week's call from her should be interesting."

They mopped up their pancakes and made plans to get together for a weekend barbeque.

Coop was busy reading the paper the day after the Tennessee Primary Election. His phone buzzed as he finished the article showcasing Senator Wagner and his successful victory last night, pummeling his opponent with eighty percent of the vote. As the pundits had speculated for months, he'd be advancing to the November election in his bid for governor.

"Yeah, AB, what's up?"

"Chase and Lila Rose are here. Are you ready for them?"

"I'll be right out." He gathered the newspaper sections and piled them on the credenza behind his desk and put a fresh tablet and pen on the conference table. He stepped into the reception area and before he could suggest it, Annabelle appeared with a tray of coffee and iced tea, both decaffeinated.

He welcomed them into his office and after pleasantries were exchanged and refreshments poured, he said, "So, what can I do for you two today?"

Chase got a nod from Lila Rose and spoke. "Gray left us several million dollars and we've been talking for a few weeks and have decided we'd like to use some of the money to buy a house for Abby and Taylor."

"We've visited them at their apartment and it's..." Lila Rose glanced at Chase before she continued, "well, it's just they deserve better."

"We found a place not too far from us and close to Vanderbilt. That way Taylor could continue to live there while he attends school."

"I think Abby would be lost without him. It's been the two of them against the world for so long," added Lila Rose.

"He may decide to live on campus eventually, but regardless, we like the idea of having them closer and in a better part of town. A few weeks ago at dinner, she said she put in for a transfer to a better position at one of the schools out here. She mentioned she'd want to find a place near the school so she wouldn't have to commute far and thought it would be good for Taylor to be closer to us. She finds out if the job is hers tomorrow."

Lila Rose's eyes twinkled with excitement. "So, we took a drive around the area and looked at a few places. We found the cutest little neighborhood, only about two miles from us and not even five miles from the University, plus it's close to Abby's parents' condo. It's about ten years old, but like new. It's part of a housing community so they do all the yard work and upkeep outside. It's lovely."

"We can't think of anything that would make our Gray happier than knowing his son and Abby would be taken care of and have a safe place to live," said Chase, tears looming in his eyes.

Coop's throat constricted with emotion. "Well, I'd be honored to help you make this a reality. I know your son would be pleased."

"They're coming for dinner tonight and we thought we'd make the announcement if you think it's something we can get done without any problems," said Lila Rose.

Coop took the paperwork they provided and perused it. "I can't think of any issues. I'll get in touch with the realtor and put in an offer. We can do some research and make sure we get you the best price."

"That would be wonderful and we'd like to get our wills amended, now that Gray's gone and we know about Taylor. We don't want to leave Hannah out, but assume Gray provided for her in his will, so we'd like to make sure Taylor is taken care of in ours," said Chase, slipping another folder across the table to Coop.

"Not a problem. I'll take a look at these and draft the new wills. We'll meet next week and go over them and hopefully finalize the sale of the house. I think Taylor and Abby will be thrilled." He closed the folders. "Taylor will be here tomorrow to do the lawn. I have a surprise for him. He's been looking for a car and I found an affordable one through a friend who's willing to let him make payments."

Both of their smiles radiated happiness. "He'll be so excited. He's been harping about a car all summer. That would take a burden off Abby and Andy," said Lila Rose.

He walked them out and asked Annabelle to schedule another appointment. When they left, she remarked he looked more cheerful than he had in months. He smiled, his dark caramel eyes dancing with excitement. "I know, let's go to lunch and I'll tell you all about it."

The weeks following Chase and Lila Rose's visit were filled with happy events. Taylor secured a used silver Honda Accord and Abby was successful in her transfer request. Coop shaved a little off the asking price of the house and they finalized the transaction, with a closing date at the end of August.

With summer's end looming, Taylor's hours were cut back, so he found a second job at a popular restaurant near the university. He worked there after school and on the weekends he wasn't scheduled at Silverwood. He still found time for Coop's yard work and the place had never looked better. Taylor was meticulous about weeding and trimming and the grounds looked pristine.

Annabelle made sure there were fresh cookies, minus chocolate and nuts, on the days Taylor did the gardening and he always visited with her and Coop, if he was in the office. Taylor and Abby extended an invitation for both of them, along with Aunt Camille, to attend a small housewarming party scheduled for Labor Day.

As part of his newfound focus to improve his health, Coop took Annabelle up on her offer to accompany her to the gym. She went to a place close to the office with twenty-four hour access. She took him as her guest a few times after work and he discovered he enjoyed it. Most of the members they met were like Coop, middle-aged and trying to get in better shape. He signed up for a month of personal training sessions and began a new habit of visiting the gym three times a week.

Coop and Annabelle dedicated their spare time to Gray's case and if they were all caught up on Friday afternoons, they pulled the files and spread them out on Coop's conference table. Coop had been sticking with his new diet plan, but reserved Fridays for splurging on a few peanut M&M's. Every week he bought one regular sized bag and made it last all day. No more giant bags from the warehouse stores, just the measly little bag he kept in his top drawer. He hadn't yet opened the yellow bag of temptation, but with the task ahead, thought it was time and even offered to share. Annabelle smiled but declined.

Neither of them were experts in financial analysis or accounting, but on a gorgeous Friday afternoon in early October they spread out copies of the fiscal reports and records from Ben, along with pages gathered from online sources. They decided to tackle income tax filings first, since they seemed less daunting than some of the other pages with numbers and categories they didn't understand.

Meredith's were the easiest, since she showed straightforward income from her job, plus some modest interest earnings. All of the lobbyists required complex returns, with multiple corporations and partnership documents and they all made a substantial amount of money. Senator Wagner's was by far the most challenging. He disclosed several sources of income, including earnings from his position as special counsel and 'of counsel' at a handful of law firms. He had long ago retired from practicing law, but was still collecting some hefty fees. Coop highlighted the information. "The largest payment came from Whitehead, Baker, and McCord."

Annabelle pulled up the firm's website and scanned it for information about Wagner's position. She tapped on the keys and read from the screen. "He's listed as 'of counsel' and his bio talks about all his past work as a partner at another firm that merged with Whitehead, Baker, and McCord. Sounds like he works on special projects and provides consultations, specializing in government affairs and business development. Probably why he's so close to Craig Baker, too."

"He also has compensation from Peter Collins' firm," said Coop, as the highlighter squeaked across the paper.

She keyed in the search terms. "They list him on the website as special counsel undertaking complex projects that require his expertise in government affairs."

"I wonder if Speaker Evans does any special consulting. She was a lawyer and her husband's a law professor," said Coop, as he flipped through more paperwork. He scanned her income tax return and saw she didn't show any income from law firms, but her husband did. "Her husband shows income from Anna Prosser's firm. Same title of special counsel."

Annabelle scanned the website and found him listed. "His bio shows he was a partner at the firm before he became a professor. He's still on staff and takes on special projects as his schedule permits."

"Lots of things intertwined on this case," mumbled Coop. "It's mind blowing to see all of the corporations and partnerships on these tax returns. Who even knows what they are?"

"I'll start looking into them, if you think it might lead to something," she offered.

"Start with the principals or officers for each of them and I'm going to try to put together a chart that shows the relationships. Maybe it will help us make some sense of this mess. It could be nothing. I know politicians, especially those who are lawyers, have cozy relationships with their past firms. I can't get over the amount of money. How do you earn over a million bucks in consulting fees in a year?"

"I want to research the special counsel and 'of counsel' designations. I don't remember much about it from law school. I always associated it with old retired lawyers who were still on the letterhead," said Annabelle.

"Monday I'm going to circle back with Craig Baker and Peter Collins and quiz them on the relationship with Senator Wagner and their firms."

"We could always have an accountant take a look at this stuff if we can't figure it out."

"Let's see what we learn Monday and if we think there's something there, I'm willing to spend a few bucks to have an expert decipher some of this," he pointed to the array of papers on the table. "I don't think Ben has the time or budget to do any more, but I'll keep him in the loop."

Prompted by the need to turn on a lamp, Annabelle checked her watch and said, "I need to get going. I've got dinner plans tonight and didn't realize how late it is."

"Sorry, you go ahead and we'll regroup on Monday and

come up with a game plan. Enjoy dinner and your weekend." He busied himself gathering the papers and stacking them in piles, finding himself reaching for his candy bowl.

"You too, Coop. See ya Monday."

He established a semblance of order, breaking Annabelle's rule and leaving some stacks on the conference table. He retrieved a pack of giant sticky notes from the hall closet and put them on the wall. He attached the paper photos of Meredith, Senator Wagner, Craig Baker, Peter Collins, and Lois Evans to the sheets and began writing bullet points under each photo, making a note of the corporations and partnerships listed on the tax returns of each.

Gus vacated his leather chair and nudged Coop's hand with his nose, reminding him it was past supper time. "Okay, buddy. Let's go home."

He locked up the office and they loaded into the Jeep and arrived to find dinner in the oven and a note from Aunt Camille saying she went to a movie with friends. He made sure the dog's bowl was filled with kibble and retrieved his own plate. Gus attacked his supper with gusto and Coop carried his tray to the granite topped breakfast bar. He flicked the remote and forked the food to his mouth as he looked for something more interesting than an infomercial. He took in his reflection in the glass doors and despite the humorous "What if the Hokey Pokey IS what it's all about?" t-shirt he wore, a drained and forlorn man stared back. Albeit one with excellent hair.

The dog plopped on the floor with a heavy sigh and looked up at Coop. "I hear ya, Gus. I need to get a life."

17

After an uneventful— make that boring— evening, Coop was up early and stopped at the gym before heading to the office. On the way he detoured to the Donut Hole and picked up a small box. He set the box on the floor of the Jeep and sensed Gus staring at him. "I work out so I can be bad, okay?"

He gave Gus a few nibbles off his donut and dug into his project. He wanted to get all his thoughts down on paper about each of the suspects in the political pool before he and Annabelle met on Monday.

While he was busy scrawling more bullet points on each person's sticky note, he heard the whir of the lawnmower and saw Taylor outside. He stepped back to admire his work, impressed with his use of colored markers to connect points related to the suspects. Gus leapt off the chair and ran to the backdoor as Coop heard it open.

Taylor called out a greeting and Coop said, "I'm in my office, come on back."

"Hey, Coop, do you have a minute?" He laughed as he read

the shirt of the day—"I'm Not Anti-social, Just Anti-stupid" and added, "You must have like a hundred of those goofy shirts."

"At least," he said with a laugh. "Come on in—" he stopped as he remembered all the notes on the wall, but Taylor was already heading for the couch. "I've got a mess going on in here; maybe we should sit in reception."

Taylor's eyes travelled to the wall. "You're still working on my dad's case?"

Coop nodded. "Yeah, in my spare time. I want to figure out who killed him." Taylor moved to study the wall. "We should move to the other room, I don't want this stuff to upset you."

Taylor shook his head. "No, I'm fine. He stopped in front of Meredith's photo and moved closer, examining it with the intensity of a dermatologist evaluating a mole. "Who's this woman?"

"She's the Chief of Staff to Senator Wagner. She was at the party at Silverwood the night Gray was killed."

Taylor turned to face Coop, his eyes betraying despair. His voice wobbled as he spoke. "I...I lied to you." He hung his head and slumped into a chair.

Coop frowned. "What do you mean?"

"I've been worrying about this for months and wanted to tell you, but couldn't figure out how."

"We'll tackle it together— just tell me what you're talking about."

"Remember when you guys first talked to me and asked me about what I did that night cleaning up?" Coop nodded. "Well, I, um, I did something wrong." He looked down at his hands. "I found an earring on the terrace when I was cleaning up and I kept it. It looked like it might be worth something and I was worried about money and Mom working so hard, I thought maybe I could sell it."

"Do you still have it?"

Taylor nodded. "I think it belongs to that woman, Meredith.

It matches the earrings she's wearing in that picture. I think it does anyway." He shook his head. "I'm sorry, Coop."

"We need to get the earring and I'll call Ben." Coop grinned. "This could be the break we need in the case."

"What will they do to me?"

"I'm not sure, but the important thing is to get it and you'll need to write a statement for the police, since it's a piece of evidence."

"It's in the console of my car. I didn't want my mom to find it, so I put in a plastic bag and kept it in my car. Each time I was here, I kept trying to work up the nerve to tell you. It just got harder the longer it went on."

Coop squeezed his shoulders. "It's going to be okay, Taylor. You made a mistake and you'll have to face the consequences, but the bigger picture is what the earring means to the case." Coop initiated a frenzied search through his notes, while he pressed the icon for Ben on his phone.

While Taylor went to retrieve the earring, Coop explained the situation to Ben, who agreed to meet at Coop's office within the hour. Coop examined the earring and held the bag up to the photo of Meredith. "Looks like a match to me, plus it's got the Tennessee General Assembly flag on it."

Coop returned to his stacks of folders and unearthed a copy of the lost and found items from Silverwood. He scanned the information and ran his finger across the line noting a call on a missing earring. The caller's name was listed as "Steven" with a cell number and a local number containing the 741 prefix he recognized as that of the Tennessee Legislature. He remembered getting the inventory sheet from Silverwood, but with the name listed, he assumed it was the first name of a man, Steven. He never connected it to the possibility of Meredith Stevens. Coop thumbed through all the folders again and found the telephone records they had examined and highlighted. "It's hers," he looked up, grinning at Taylor.

Ben arrived and after he collected a statement from Taylor, he gave him a stern lecture about the importance of telling the truth and the crucial evidence and clues that had been overlooked because of his failure to be honest. "Taylor, I know you're a good kid and made a poor choice. I'm glad you told Coop the truth today, but this cost us a lot of time and wasted effort." He used a portable kit and took Taylor's fingerprints. He explained they would need to eliminate them in case they were able to retrieve any good prints from the earring.

Taylor nodded, his whole body shaking. He was on the verge of tears, but said, "I know, Chief Mason. I'm really sorry I let it go on so long. I panicked and didn't know what to do. I knew Coop would be so disappointed in me and after everything you've both done to help. I'm such an idiot."

"I think for right now the best thing you can do is keep quiet about this new evidence. Once we know more, you'll need to tell your family and your boss, but for now, let's keep it between us," suggested Coop.

Ben nodded. "Yes, I'm going to get this to the lab and we'll talk next week. But, do what Coop says. Stay quiet and go about your normal business. Do you work at Silverwood this weekend?"

Taylor shook his head. "No, sir. I'm not scheduled this week and won't know about next week until Thursday."

"Okay, good. We'll be in touch." Ben put a hand on Taylor's shoulder. "It's going to be okay." Coop followed him outside.

"I've got an idea or two about our next move," said Coop. "But, I need to make sure he's okay. I'm going to suggest he go to his grandparents' house for the rest of the day. Once he's gone I'll swing by your office.

Ben stuck the bag in his pocket and said, "This is getting interesting. I'll see you in an hour or so."

Coop, feeling a caffeine celebration was in order, grabbed

two cold Cokes out of the fridge and set one in front of Taylor. "Look, you made a mistake. It's not good, but it's fixable. I know you're worried about what will happen. I think you need to come up with what you think should be the consequence. You're going to have to face the fact you may lose your job at Silverwood."

Taylor took a sip of the drink and swallowed. "That's why I feel so stupid. I hope I can convince Miss Sarah to give me another chance. I know I screwed up. What about Vanderbilt?"

"I don't think it'll impact school, unless of course, the police decide to press the issue. If they do, you're a juvenile so it would only amount to community service."

"I'm so ashamed," said Taylor, his shoulders sagging. "I knew it was wrong."

"You need to pull yourself together. I think you ought to spend some time with your grandparents today while your mom's working. Try to relax and I'll get in touch with you as soon as it's safe for you to discuss it. We need to use it to our advantage while nobody knows about it."

Taylor nodded and drank down the rest of his Coke. "Thanks, Coop. I'm sorry I disappointed you."

Coop gave him a manly pat on the back and walked him to his car. He and Gus watched as the boy drove away with the weight of the world hanging on his shoulders.

He and Gus flew across town in the Jeep and made their way through the almost empty precinct. They found Ben in his office on the phone. Gus curled onto his bed while they waited for Ben to finish his conversation with the lab, calling in a favor for a rush on the earring.

As soon as he hung up, they both commenced talking at once. "Sorry, you first," said Coop.

"I was thinking about having the lady at Silverwood call Meredith and say they found her earring."

Coop grinned and said, "Great minds. I think I could

persuade the manager, Sarah, to call Meredith. We could surprise her when she arrives to claim her earring."

"And let's make sure she identifies it as hers before we surprise her. Regardless of what the lab's able to prove, she will have claimed it as hers," said Ben.

"I'll set it up with Sarah for Monday morning. I think she runs a bit on the nervous side, but all she has to do is treat her like any other patron who lost something. We'll do the dirty work."

"What happens after that will be determined by what she tells us. If she confesses, it'll be easy. If not, we'll have to put a tail on her and monitor her calls and see where she leads us." Ben scribbled in his notebook.

"I'll talk to Sarah and get it set up." He motioned for Gus and asked, "What are you going to do about Taylor?"

"Let him sweat for a couple of days. I don't want to be too hard on him. I think he learned his lesson and he's basically a responsible kid. Let's see how this shakes out Monday."

"I told him to come up with his own punishment recommendation. He'll be harder on himself than we could anyway."

Coop stopped for pizza on his way home, knowing Aunt Camille was attending a Victorian Society shindig at the Belle Meade Plantation. She was obsessed with preparing for the event and getting her elaborate dress fitted and sewn.

He rummaged through his notes and found Sarah's card and called her cell, thinking a girl with her looks wouldn't be home on a Saturday night. When she answered, he said, "Hello, Sarah. This is Coop Harrington. I met you at Silverwood when I interviewed your staff about the Grayson Taylor murder."

"I haven't forgotten you, Mr. Harrington," she said, her voice purring.

"There are some new developments and we need your help. I was hoping I could meet you for brunch tomorrow and explain things."

She agreed to meet at Granite Point at eleven o'clock on Sunday morning. He hung up with a twinge of guilt, regretting the fact he didn't correct her assumption that their brunch date was more of a social encounter than a business call.

He made one more call to the bartender who worked the event the night Grayson Taylor was murdered, before nodding off in front of the television.

Granite Point was upmarket, pressuring him to wear jeans and a button down shirt. He'd called and made reservations, since Sundays were busy. He disappointed Mrs. Henderson when he drank a solitary cup of coffee and resisted one of her cinnamon rolls, but asked her to save him one for later.

He arrived at the restaurant early and since it was a mild day, requested seating on the patio. As soon as the waiter poured their complimentary mimosas, Sarah was led to the table.

He stood as she settled in, taking in her memorable figure in a pair of tight jeans. "Thanks so much for taking time out of your weekend to meet me."

"Of course. I was surprised to hear from you...in a good way," she smiled as she brought the glass to her glossed lips. She wore a filmy blouse with something lacy underneath and flicked her blond curls off her shoulder as she sipped her drink.

"I usually have the brunch buffet. Would you like that or something off the menu?"

"Buffet sounds perfect to me."

Coop signaled for the waiter and placed their order. Sarah requested coffee and Coop asked for water. They made their way to the buffet inside and came back loaded down with delectable eggs benedict, waffles and bacon, fruit, and pastries. "So, you said you needed my help," she said, arranging her plates.

"Yes, it's a long story and I can't stress enough the importance of it remaining confidential." Her eyes widened and she nodded her understanding. "We found an earring related to the crime scene and it's the same earring you received a call about on your lost and found sheet."

He continued to explain the plan he and Ben had formulated and answered her questions. By the time they finished dessert, her open-mouthed expressions had diminished and he helped her rehearse the part she would portray by role playing. She followed him to his office for a few more practice sessions to buoy her confidence.

By the middle of the afternoon, Coop deemed her prepared and said, "You sound natural and I've tried to rattle you and you stuck to your part. You'll do a terrific job."

"I don't want to get flustered and blow it," she said, biting her lip.

He patted her hand. "You'll do fine. We'll be out early in the morning and be there when you make the call. If things go as planned she should be arriving before lunch to retrieve her lost jewelry."

He stood, signaling the meeting was over. "I need to get going, but we appreciate your willingness to help. Chief Mason and I will see you in the morning."

"I've had a lovely day. After this is all over, I hope we can do it again," she said, adding a giggle. "I mean, not all this cloak and dagger stuff, but enjoy a meal together."

"Brunch was delicious," he said, not wanting to commit to further engagements. "Until this case is solved, I'm afraid I won't have any spare time."

"I can wait," she said, batting her eyelashes as she'd done when he met her at her office.

He gripped his cell phone, feigning a call. "I need to take this Sarah, but we'll see you in the morning. Y'all have a good night." He guided her to the door while he answered his bogus call.

She waved as she sashayed to her car and he returned the gesture. When she drove away he locked the door and flopped on the couch. "Whew, that was close," he mumbled, as he tapped Ben's icon to send him a text.

He punched in *Good to go. Sarah's ready and will meet us at her office at 8:00 tomorrow.*

18

Monday morning, Coop and Ben, along with some techies who specialized in video and audio recording, arrived at Silverwood. After unloading, they parked their cars out of view in the staff parking lot. Ben shook his head and smiled when he saw Coop's shirt stenciled with "Sarcasm, just one more service I offer." Coop didn't feel Meredith was worth a button down this morning.

Sarah got through to Meredith Stevens and explained she was going through the lost and found items as she did each quarter and discovered an earring that had been found the night of the June event. "I do apologize Ms. Stevens, but it seems it was mislabeled and put in the wrong box, so we didn't see it when you telephoned about it back in June."

Coop and Ben nodded their assurance to her and gestured for her to continue. "Could you describe it and if it sounds like a match, we'll set up a time for you to pick it up?"

They saw Sarah nod as she listened and the tech at the recording station gave Ben the thumbs up.

"I believe you're in luck and this is definitely your earrin'. Your description matches perfectly. Could you come out before eleven today? I've got a luncheon party starting and will be tied up all afternoon." She bobbed her head and said, "Perfect, I'll see you at ten o'clock."

She was shaking as he hung up the receiver and fanned her hand in front of her face. "I was *so* nervous."

"You did great, thanks again," said Ben. "You have to get through one more step and we'll take it from there."

Coop suggested Sarah take a break and have a cold drink. He joined her in the staff break room and made them each an Arnold Palmer. He handed it to her and took a chair. "Let's go over the next step, so you're comfortable."

While they practiced the next phase again, Ben and the techs tested the equipment they installed in the conference room and at nine-thirty Coop returned with a tray of lemonade and iced tea for everyone.

Sarah instructed the front desk to direct Ms. Stevens to her conference room and her phone buzzed just after ten o'clock announcing her guest's arrival. She smoothed her skirt and rather than using the adjoining door, exited her office and stepped next door to the conference room.

"Oh, Ms. Stevens, thanks so much for making the trip out this mornin'. I'm Sarah Holley," she said, offering her hand. "Would you care for a beverage?"

Meredith shook her head. "No, I'm fine. Do you have the earring?"

"Of course, right here," said Sarah, removing the plastic pouch from a file folder. I need you to verify it's your missin' jewelry. And if it is, sign this form."

Meredith eyed the bag and nodded her head. "Yes, that's my earring. I brought the other one with me in case," she said, popping open a compartment in her purse and retrieving the matching earring. She scribbled her signature on the form and the phone on the side table buzzed. Sarah held onto the plastic bag as she answered it.

"Excuse me a moment, Ms. Stevens," she said, as she hung up the phone and opened the adjoining door. She passed through the door without waiting for a response and handed the bag to Ben.

Coop smiled at her. "All done. Now it's our turn."

They opened the door and when Meredith saw them she gasped. "What are you doing here?"

"We need to ask you a few questions about your earring, ma'am," said Ben, taking a seat across from her as Coop slid in next to him.

"I don't understand," she said. "Where's Ms. Holley?"

"She had to take a call. We interviewed you after the murder of Grayson Taylor and you denied being on the terrace that night. We'd like you to explain how your earring ending up on the terrace without you," asked Ben, his severe face devoid of any hint of kindness.

Splotches of red appeared on her neck. "I have no idea. It must have fallen off and someone must have found it and left it there. How do you know it was on the terrace anyway?"

"We have a sworn statement from the employee who collected it the night of Grayson's murder. It was found on the terrace at the base of the column below the stone that was used to bash Grayson's head in."

Her fingers twisted the ring on her finger before rotating the pin on her jacket. Her face hardened. "I do not appreciate what you are insinuating, Chief Mason."

"So, you're still sticking with the story you weren't on the terrace that night?" asked Coop, with a dark chuckle.

"Because I was not on the terrace that night," she said, her voice full of indignation. "I was in the garden and it must have fallen off and gotten kicked over to the terrace somehow. Or someone picked it up and dropped it there."

"Would it surprise you to learn the only fingerprints on it

are yours and the employee who found the earring?" asked Ben, bluffing.

"Maybe the person who handled it wore gloves. I don't know." She stood. "This is ridiculous. I just want my earring back."

"They're unique and from what we know available only to members of the legislature."

"Yes, they were a gift from Senator Wagner years ago," she snapped.

"Perhaps you hitting Grayson Taylor was an accident or self-defense?" asked Ben.

She harrumphed and said, "I didn't hit him." Her eyes bore into Ben's as she rotated the ring on her finger.

Coop added, "After you and Mr. Baker told us how sloshed you were the night of the murder, I talked to the bartender at Silverwood. He says you were quite memorable and drank only soda with a lime twist. When he tried to entice you with a glass of wine, you made of point of telling him you didn't drink at political functions."

"How could he possibly remember what I drank? I'm sure he serves hundreds of people." The redness continued to creep up face.

"That he does, but your condescending manner left quite the impression on him. He deemed you unforgettable...and not in a good way." Coop's gentle eyes hardened as they bore into hers.

Her hand moved to the pin on her jacket. "The lobbyists all brought us drinks and I didn't want to insult them, so I drank several glasses that the bartender wouldn't know about."

"Which lobbyist in particular brought you drinks?" asked Ben, poising his pen over the page in his notebook.

"All of them, I don't remember exactly." Her voice snapped as her cheeks turned pink.

"Do you know who killed Mr. Taylor?" asked Ben. "It would

be a shame for you to take the rap for his murder if you weren't the only one involved."

She spun the ring on her finger faster. The splotches on her neck deepened to a vibrant crimson. "I most certainly do not know who did it. I am done talking to both of you. If you have anything else to discuss, you may call my lawyer." She stood and made strides for the door.

"Who would that be, ma'am?" asked Ben.

"Lester Whitehead of Whitehead, Baker, and McCord," she hissed, as she turned the handle of the door.

"We'll be in touch, ma'am," said Ben.

As soon as the door slammed behind her, Ben picked up his cell phone and put a call in to Kate. She was coordinating the surveillance of Meredith and was standing by in the back of a plumbing van on Page Road. "No confession, Kate. Go ahead and run with her and keep me in the loop."

Coop smirked as he tapped his cell phone and brought up a grid map. "Tell Kate not to worry, I put a transmitter on her car when she got here. I'll be able to track her every move without risking her spotting a tail."

"I don't want to know about it," said Ben. "You private guys don't have to play by the same rules. I've got to do it the old fashioned way."

The techs cleaned up the room and packed their equipment while Ben packed the earring in an evidence bag and he and Coop thanked Sarah. She wished them luck and reminded Coop to give her a call.

Coop called Annabelle and told her to head downtown to Whitehead, Baker, and McCord and then Peter Collins' office. They still wanted to dig into the relationship between Wagner and the firms from which he was collecting substantial fees. She locked the office, dressed in a business suit and glasses, and pulled back her hair.

Coop promised to contact Ben with any developments and

hurried downtown in his Jeep, planning to rendezvous with Annabelle when she completed her inquiries. Madison and Ross were already in position at coffee shops along 5th and Union, near the lobbying firms. All four of them were outfitted with earbuds and would be listening to Annabelle's interactions and could track Meredith's car on their phones.

Annabelle parked her Beetle in a public parking lot and made her way through the heavy glass doors of the most prestigious law firm in Nashville. She waited at the reception desk and overheard the woman advising the caller Mr. Whitehead was out of the office for the week, but she would be happy to connect her with his assistant.

The young receptionist acknowledged Annabelle and asked, "How may I help you?"

Annabelle displayed her phony press badge in the name of Lauren McDonald, a freelance journalist, and said she was doing an article on Senator Wagner and exploring his 'of counsel' relationship with the firm. She was hoping to get some information now to meet her afternoon deadline. The receptionist asked Annabelle to have a seat and told her someone would be with her momentarily.

Annabelle feigned interest in a display on the wall next to a mirror, watching behind her to see who would be tasked with her inquiry. After a few minutes, another woman approached and said she could follow her to Mr. Baker's office.

Annabelle trailed her down the plush hallway and through a door bearing a brass plaque denoting the title of managing partner. The woman offered Annabelle a beverage, but she declined. As soon as the assistant shut the door, an interior door opened and Craig Baker strutted across the room and introduced himself. He was decked out in another impressive suit and gave Annabelle a warm smile.

"Thank you for seeing me, Mr. Baker. I'm doing a piece on

Senator Wagner and his law career and wanted to discuss his position as 'of counsel' here at your firm."

"Senator Wagner is and always will be a valuable member of our team. He was a partner in another firm that merged with ours many years ago. He, of course, was already a shining political star and we gave him a lot of leeway to pursue his political interests. Well over ten years ago we transitioned him to 'of counsel,' since his main concentration was in the Tennessee Senate, but he still provides us with valuable services. It's very common in law firms these days."

"I was surprised to learn from my research it's now acceptable for lawyers to serve in 'of counsel' or special counsel capacities for a number of firms. With his position in the legislature or by serving as 'of counsel' in other firms, does that ever create a conflict of interest?"

He shook his head. "Oh, I'm sure over the years, the senator has had to decline cases or consultations based on a conflict with another firm, but his expertise far outweighs the occasional missed opportunity. It's of no significance to a firm of our caliber and size." He grinned, his index fingers making a steeple as they rested on the desk.

"It must at least give the perception of impropriety with him being the Chairman of the Finance Committee. I would think his legislative work could make him privy to confidential information not available to the general public. Couldn't that create a conflict of interest?"

"Lauren, may I call you Lauren?" He continued without waiting for her to respond. "You must understand, he's bound by strict ethics as a senator and an attorney and would never violate either one."

"How many cases does Senator Wagner handle for your firm each year?"

"I wouldn't know off the top of my head, but his value is not so much in the number of cases he handles as the breadth and depth of the knowledge he is able to impart."

"His specialties are, of course, government affairs and business development?"

"Yes, with his judicial experience and his career in the legislature, he's the top expert in the State of Tennessee."

"I'm sure he's well connected with many of the so-called movers and shakers. Does he refer some of those clients to your firm?"

"We don't ever speak about our clients to the press, unless they've directed us to do so, but I know Senator Wagner holds this firm, along with several others, in high esteem. If he were asked for a recommendation he would provide a fair and honest opinion to assist a potential client in finding the right firm."

"How are 'of counsel' lawyers compensated in your firm?"

Baker continued his polished spin and like a gifted attorney, spewed forth a jumble of words, but never answered a question. He told Annabelle compensation packages varied by attorney, and droned on to explain they were generally made up of a salary, commission, and bonuses, or a combination of the three.

"With his million dollars a year from Whitehead, Baker, and McCord, would it surprise you to learn he's the highest paid 'of counsel' lawyer in Tennessee?"

He grinned and folded his hands. "No, ma'am, it would not. His talents are worth every penny and we're fortunate to have him on our staff."

"I'm trying to figure out how he's able to generate that much work and business for you when he basically works full time as a legislator and now all his spare time is taken up running for governor. Do you see him continuing in his capacity if he's successful in the election in November?"

"What newspaper did you say you were with?"

She smiled and said, "I didn't."

His pupils widened for a moment. "We don't count his value

in billable hours, like some lower level attorney. His counsel and advice are well worth what he's paid." He rambled on to describe what a wonderful person the senator is and how lucky the good people of Tennessee would be to have him as their governor. He left it up to Senator Wagner to answer the question about his plans after he's elected.

After his campaign speech ended, Annabelle heard the buzzing of a cell phone. Craig's eyes darted to the smart phone on his desk, the screen of which Annabelle could see was dark. His hand flashed to his breast pocket, but then he rested it back on the desk. "I apologize, but I do need to get going. That was a reminder of an appointment."

Annabelle slipped her pen into the crack between the cushion and the back of the chair and closed her notebook. "I appreciate your time. You've been very helpful."

"Good luck with the article," he said, shaking her hand and leading her to the door.

The hallway was empty and once the door closed, she dropped her bag to the ground, pretending to look for something, in case Craig's assistant appeared. She stalled for a minute or two before twisting the knob and opening the door. She heard him say, "They don't know anything. You need to keep your mouth shut and calm down, Meredith. Now's not the time to vacillate."

Annabelle mimicked writing with a pen in the air and pointed at the chair. She mouthed "sorry" and searched the cushion, holding up the pen and smiling in victory. She waved and hurried from the room.

She plucked her bag from outside the door and hustled down the hallway and through reception, not letting out her breath until she passed through the outer glass doors.

She checked her phone as she walked along the street. A text from Coop asked her to report to Starbucks. She hiked the few blocks and slid into a chair next to Coop, who was grinning and handed her a grande sweet tea.

She took a long sip and sighed. "That buzzing was a second phone, probably a burner he and Meredith use since they were questioned about the other calls."

He glanced at the map on his phone. "She drove to her house after our meeting at Silverwood and hasn't left. Sounds like we rattled her though."

She nodded as she took another drink. "I'll head over to Collins' office and see if we get a reaction. I know you heard my conversation with Baker, but I could tell I was getting to him."

"I wish Ben had enough for a court order to listen to their phones, but all this doesn't hold squat with a judge."

She finished her tea and promised to meet at another coffee shop down the street when she finished with Peter. Coop transmitted the plan to Madison and Ross and asked them to shadow Craig Baker.

Annabelle was greeted and shown to a conference room off Peter's office. She asked him the same questions she had asked of Craig Baker. They paid Senator Wagner less than a hundred thousand dollars, so she altered some of her inquiries, but kept with the same theme.

Peter said they'd put Senator Wagner on staff several years ago and used him as a consultant and specialist when it came to business development. "Senator Wagner's well versed in the laws related to incentives offered for businesses to locate or expand and saves us a lot of research in that arena."

When she asked about conflicts of interest, he mentioned ethics and careful attention to the interests of all parties to ensure no conflicts or improprieties exist in bringing the senator in on a consult. "At times we don't even tell him the client, just use his knowledge to obtain answers and advice to formulate the best approach for our clients involved in complex development projects."

Like Craig, he professed his allegiance and trust in Senator

Wagner, but without the air of superiority Craig displayed. Annabelle thanked him for his time and met up with Coop at a small coffee shop down the street.

As soon as she plopped in her seat, he received a text from Ross reporting they were on the move, having spotted Craig in his BMW leaving the parking garage at his office.

19

Coop followed Annabelle back to the office, where she changed her clothes and they monitored his cell phone for progress updates. Madison had followed Craig to I-65, where he was southbound. Ross picked up the trail after Madison exited and doubled back, both doing their best to keep from drawing his attention.

Craig took the Franklin exit for his home and they both eased off, since traffic was light and they didn't want to take a chance on being made. Now it was a waiting game to see if he was in for the evening or would emerge and lead them to another destination. Practiced in all things surveillance, Madison parked in a church parking lot near the turn for his house in case he took side streets, and Ross stationed himself in a shopping center close to the freeway.

Coop and Annabelle dissected her conversations with the lobbyists and unearthed the files on Senator Wagner, Meredith, and Craig Baker. "So, Meredith is either calling Craig for legal advice because of the interview at Silverwood, or she's up to her eyeballs in something sinister with him," said Annabelle.

Coop bobbed his head. "Since she's calling him on a secondary phone, I'm going with door number two."

"Combine the call I overheard today with the middle of the night calls after Gray's murder and I say those two are in cahoots. Now we need to figure out how to prove it," she said.

"And what it's about." Coop checked his phone again and saw the blinking light signifying Meredith's car was still at her house.

While they watched the transmitter, Coop put in a call to Taylor and told him they had made use of the earring and he was free to talk to his family and explain the situation to Sarah at Silverwood. Coop filled him in on her involvement in the trap they had set for Meredith.

"I've thought a lot about what I've done and have tried to come up with an appropriate reprimand. You mentioned community service, and I think something like that would be best. I thought about taking my car away, but all that does is inconvenience my mom, so I think I'm going to suggest I do chores for the elderly and work at the soup kitchen."

"Sounds like a good plan. If you explain it like that to your mom, I think she'll go for it. I'll tell Ben your idea and have him get in contact with you."

"Poor kid," Annabelle said when he disconnected. "I hope he doesn't get in any real trouble."

"I don't think he will. He's willing to work at the soup kitchen and donate his time to help senior citizens with chores. I think he's learned his lesson."

Not wanting to leave, they called for a pizza delivery and made a plan for Annabelle to go downtown in the morning and request all lobbying reports for Craig Baker's firm and Senator Wagner. Recent reports were available online, but older data had to be requested through the Ethics Division.

Coop pulled up a map of Craig Baker's neighborhood and after studying it, concluded there was no way to do a casual drive by the house to see if he was still there, without being seen. He lived in a gated equestrian neighborhood and short of posing as a delivery person or repairman, there was no way in… unless he asked Aunt Camille to pay a visit to Twyla Fay.

It was too late for an impromptu visit, so he called off the surveillance and told Madison and Ross to get an early start in the morning and focus on getting a tracker hidden on Craig's car tomorrow. The four established shifts to monitor Meredith's blinking light throughout the night.

When Coop got home, Aunt Camille was awake so he filled her in on the busy day they'd had. Her eyes twinkled with delight when he mentioned using her for cover to visit Craig's neighborhood.

Tuesday, Annabelle spent the morning retrieving copies of old lobbying records at the Ethics Division downtown. She had to fill out individual request forms and it took hours to have the staff locate the files and then copy them. She paid with her company credit card and made it back around noon. When she returned, Coop filled her in on the morning's progress.

"Ross was able to slip a tracking device on Craig's BMW when he parked at the office this morning. So, now we'll be able to watch him, along with Meredith. She left her house this morning and went to the grocery store, drug store, and a gas station. Nothing too exciting. By the way, she's the red dot and Craig is the blue dot on your phone app. She's at bistro in Green Hills now, apparently for lunch. Craig's car hasn't moved from the parking garage."

"I'll get started with these records. I'll highlight any of the lobbying activities or clients that are linked to Senator Wagner." She eyed the pile of papers. "This is going to take some time and it's a long shot."

Coop nodded. "I dug into Senator Wagner's campaign site and put all of the events for the next few weeks on the calendar. He's booked each day with campaign stops and fundraisers. I thought Craig or Meredith might attend some of them."

Madison arrived with sandwiches from the Pot Belly and Ben called to confirm he was able to get a pen register approved for Meredith's landline and cell phone. This would allow them to have real time data of all the incoming and outgoing phone numbers. "I suspect with the burner phone AB saw in Craig's office, it won't do much good. Chances are they won't use their own phones for any communications. I have to pull Kate from surveillance, since Meredith hasn't done anything overtly suspicious. I'll rely on you to alert me to anything you notice."

After lunch Coop dug into the stack of papers with Annabelle. They worked together for a few hours gathering clients involved in economic development projects in Tennessee. They also noted any events or expenses reported by Craig's firm for the benefit of Senator Wagner. Coop had to get to a meeting concerning another case and left Annabelle to comb the records. Madison and Ross were on standby should they be needed to tail anyone.

Coop called the office just before closing time. "I'm going to head on home, AB. I'll catch up with you at the gym in the morning." He urged her to call it a night and disconnected. Annabelle stretched her neck and shoulders and took Coop's advice and locked up at five. She even broke her own rule and left the records scattered across the conference table.

Annabelle's shift to monitor the transmitters began at four in the morning. So far both Craig and Meredith had done nothing out of the ordinary. During the day Meredith was at Senator Wagner's campaign office and her evenings were either spent at home or at campaign events. Craig's car was at the office or at home. It was proving to be a lackluster electronic stakeout.

After going to bed early, she was refreshed and ready to dig into the records again. Rather than watch the blinking dots from home, she decided to get an early start and work at the office for a couple of hours before meeting Coop at the gym.

It was still dark when she parked in front of the office. She fumbled with her keys in the lock and finally got it open. She didn't hear the normal beeping from the alarm and saw the screen on the wall behind the door indicating the system wasn't activated. She shook her head and swore under her breath. She thought back to leaving last night and was sure she had set the alarm. She flicked on the reception lights and poked her computer.

She heard a shuffle coming from Coop's office. That explained the alarm. "Hey, Coop, what are you doing here so early?" She hollered out as she made her way to his doorway. She stopped short, noticing a lack of light coming from the doorway. She turned to hurry back to her desk, but was struck from behind and collapsed to the floor. She registered shoes moving past her face and heard the front door shut before the blackness engulfed her.

∽

When Coop arrived at the gym he warmed up on the treadmill, watching the door for Annabelle as he kept pace with the program. He did his twenty minutes and she still hadn't arrived. She usually was no more than fifteen minutes late, but neither of them was religious about it. He moved on to the weights and finished his routine.

On his way out of the gym, he pulled his cell phone from his pocket and tapped her icon. It rang and rang and went to voicemail. He tried her home phone and didn't get an answer. Then he tried the office with the same result.

He frowned as he opened the door of the Jeep. Gus had been taking an early morning nap, but sat at attention when Coop slid into his seat. "We need to find AB, Gus," he said, nuzzling the dog's neck.

He drove to her house and rang the bell. No answer. He didn't have his spare key on him so he and Gus dashed to the side of the garage and Coop struggled through some bushes to see if he could peek through the window. It was higher than eye level, so he jumped up several times to get a look. No green Beetle.

They rushed back to the Jeep and headed to the office. "Maybe she was in the shower when I called and went to work early," he muttered to Gus.

As soon as he reached the office, he saw her car parked in front, and relief washed over him. He parked in back and followed Gus to the door. He tried the handle and it was locked. His brow puckered as he dug his key out of his shorts. Gus bounded through the door as soon as he opened it, busting through the kitchen on his way to Annabelle's desk.

"Hey, AB, whaddya doing parked out front?" he hollered.

Coop was still in the kitchen when he heard Gus barking, followed by the thundering sound of the dog running back to the kitchen and barking with urgency. Gus never barked. "What's wrong, buddy?" asked Coop, leaning down. Gus took off again for the front of the house.

Coop followed and found him licking Annabelle's cheek as she lay on the floor. "AB," he yelled, as he knelt to reach her. He saw blood on the back of her head, but looking around saw nothing that could have caused her injury. He fumbled in his pocket for his cell phone and called 911. Gus kept licking her and whining as Coop tried to rouse her. He put his fingers to the side of her neck and some of his fear eased when he detected a faint pulse.

The ambulance arrived and the paramedics checked her vitals, examined her head wound, and hooked up an intravenous drip. Her eyes fluttered open as they moved her to a gurney. Coop was holding her hand and squeezed it, "AB, you're going to the hospital. I'll be right here."

She looked at him and shut her eyes. He kept squeezing her hand as they loaded her into the ambulance. He finally let go and hurried back to lock the office and retrieve Gus. He rushed to the hospital and called Ben while he was driving. He explained what had happened and asked Ben to check out the office. He didn't think she had fallen and hit her head on anything; someone had knocked her out.

He paced around the emergency room in his shorts and "Trust me, I'm a lawyer" t-shirt, and gave the nurse Annabelle's personal information. While he was waiting he called Aunt Camille and told her what had happened.

"Oh, my heavens. You tell AB she can stay here with us when she gets out of the hospital. I'm happy to keep an eye on her," she said, concern unmistakable in her offer.

He assured his aunt he would make sure Annabelle was taken care of and sent a text to Madison and Ross so they would know what was going on and asked them to pick up the slack on the vehicle monitoring mission. Madison texted back and said she would handle covering the office and to let them know the prognosis.

Coop's phone vibrated and he stepped outside again to take Ben's call. "How's AB doing?"

"No word yet, I'm still waiting."

"We're treating your office like a crime scene until we know more. I talked to your alarm company and they said it was activated last night around five and then deactivated at three fifty-two this morning. We need to know if AB deactivated it that early or what she remembers as soon as we can talk to her. Your office is a mess, papers all over the table, on the floor, everywhere. I don't see that anything's missing, but it would be hard to tell."

"Was her computer on?"

"It was on, but she hadn't logged in yet."

"Then she hadn't been there long. She always turns it on first thing."

"We're dusting for prints. I'll keep you posted. Let me know when you can get back and take a look and see if anything is missing."

Coop rang off and when he walked into the waiting area, he saw Dr. Weston looking for him. "Hey, Coop. Come on back and you can see her. I'll go over everything with you." As they walked she said it was a shame they kept meeting each other in the emergency room.

He followed her through the maze to the cubicle where Annabelle was resting, on her side with an oversized bandage on the back of her head. He moved to the chair beside her. "Hey, AB, how are you?"

She squeezed his hand and said, "Okay."

"Annabelle has a severe concussion from whatever caused the wound on the back of her head. We're going to keep her here to monitor things at least overnight. She's got a bad headache."

"When you get out, Aunt Camille wants you to stay at the house," Coop said, still gripping her hand. "Do you want me to call your parents?"

She squinted and moved her head a bit to indicate a negative response.

"I don't see anything that worries me on her scan, so I suspect she'll be fine in a few days. We need to watch for headaches or changes in vision," said Dr. Weston. "You can stay as long as you like. They're getting a room ready for her. Give me a call with any concerns."

Coop nodded and thanked her as she left.

He rubbed his thumb across the top of her hand. "I know you want to rest, but I need to ask you a couple of questions. Do you remember what time you got to the office this morning?"

She moved her hand and held up four fingers.

"Not before four, right? The alarm was deactivated at three fifty-two."

Her eyes narrowed and she whispered, "No, it was off when I got there a little after four. I thought you were there."

"Did you see anyone in the office?"

She shook her head and winced.

"Do you know what hit you on the head?"

She swallowed hard and he reached for a cup of water and let her have a sip. "I heard a noise in your office and thought it was you and then realized it was dark. I turned around and something hit me. All I saw were shoes go by me when I was on the floor." Her eyes flickered and then closed.

He put her hand under the blanket and whispered, "I'll be back, AB." He made sure they had his cell phone number and drove back to the office. He found Madison sitting at Annabelle's desk.

"How is she?"

"Doc says a severe concussion. She's got a bandage on the back of her head and will have to stay overnight." Gus's nose was working overtime as he sniffed his way to Coop's office.

"Ben's crew left about an hour ago. Nothing new on Meredith or Craig, they're both at work."

Coop nodded and went to pour himself a cup of coffee. He carried the cup into his office and surveyed the jumble of paper scattered over every surface. All of the summary sticky notes were still on the wall and he couldn't be sure about the records, but found the outlines they had made of clients and lobbying events. He dialed Ben's number as he shuffled through the papers.

"Hey, I don't think anything's missing. I reason somebody was here to see what we did know and AB surprised them." He told her what Annabelle had related about the timing and the shoes and updated him on her condition.

"We didn't find anything that was used as a weapon, but we had a uniform at the hospital collect some trace from her wound. I'm having the lab try to determine what was used to strike her."

"Keep me in the loop if you come up with anything," said Coop, as he hung up.

He spent the day sorting through the documents littering his office and organizing them. He also talked with his alarm company and changed the code, plus ordered an updated system that would be less vulnerable to hackers. After speaking with Madison and Ross they decided to spend their monitoring shifts at the office, so as to keep an eye on the place and the blinking dots of Meredith and Craig at the same time. Since Coop didn't sleep much, he volunteered to take Annabelle's shifts. He removed his gun from the safe in his office and strapped on his holster. "I know we don't carry all the time, but I'm insisting we all do until this case is resolved," he reminded them. "We've poked the beehive and need to be careful not to get stung."

After he made sure things were handled at the office, he and Gus made a stop for some flowers on the way to the hospital. Being relegated to the Jeep didn't sit well with Gus and he grumbled as he watched Coop walk across the parking lot. He checked in with hospital security, and after showing his license and weapons permit, proceeded to Annabelle's floor.

Dr. Weston had pulled some strings and Coop found Annabelle resting in a large private room. Her eyes were closed and the television displayed gorgeous scenery and soft music.

He placed the large bouquet of colorful snapdragons on the shelf and slipped into the chair next to her bed. He studied the monitors showing Annabelle's heart rate and relaxed, content to watch the scenery and listen to the soothing melody on her television. Before long his eyes were closed.

The clatter of a wheeled cart bearing trays of food woke Coop. He opened an eye and smiled when he saw Annabelle wide awake. "Sorry, I must have nodded off."

"I was happy to see you getting some rest."

"How are you feeling?"

"My head still hurts and I'm tired and sort of feel like I'm in a fog. Ben came by and told me the latest. He wanted to know if I remembered seeing a vehicle at the office and what I could tell him about the shoes."

Coop nodded. "I'm so sorry, AB. I never dreamed this stupid case would put you in jeopardy."

"I'll be okay. Alex said I need to take the rest of the week off and see how I'm feeling next week. I think she'll release me tomorrow if nothing changes."

Coop grinned. "Aunt Camille will be thrilled. You take off as much time as you need. We've got things covered."

The nurse brought in a tray for Annabelle and Coop kissed her on the forehead. "I'll stop by and see you tomorrow. We're going to take our shifts at the office, so I'll be there tonight starting at ten. If you get bored, call me."

She smiled and said, "Thanks for the gorgeous flowers. Give Gus a hug from me."

Coop sauntered down the hallway and outside where he found Gus asleep in the Jeep. He opened the door and the dog raised his head. "Let's get home, Gus." He nuzzled the dog's neck and said, "AB said to give you a hug. She's doing fine and will see you tomorrow." His fluffy tail thumped as if he understood.

Ben called minutes after he got home and let him know the lab concluded

Annabelle had most likely been struck with a gun and from her description of the shoes it was a male subject. "We didn't get any prints, meaning he probably wore gloves. We also think he used an electronic device to crack the code on the alarm panel."

"When those assholes hurt AB they messed with the wrong guy. I'm more determined than ever to bring them down."

20

After a delicious meal and assuring Aunt Camille the first floor guest room looked perfect for Annabelle, Coop caught a nap for a couple of hours. Aunt Camille sent him off with a fresh batch of cookies and a sandwich, while Gus remained curled up beside her on the chintz sofa.

Coop relieved Ross, who reported both Craig and Meredith had spent the day on the campaign trail in eastern Tennessee and were at a scheduled dinner and fundraiser. "Madison has a friend who knows someone at the Ethics Division. She found out they require request forms, which AB filled out for all those records she retrieved. She listed Harrington and Associates as the requesting party and our address. The friend told Madison the forms are not confidential and many times elected officials or lobbyists will call or stop in and ask to see the requesting party for their records. She suspects when it came to AB's requests, someone in the office notified either Senator Wagner or Baker's firm. She said it's not uncommon for some officials and lobbyists to have a relationship with a staffer who will alert them when requests are filed."

"Sounds ethical, huh?"

Ross nodded. "So, of course we have no proof, but it seems logical the break-in has to be connected to our requests. I'm sure they thought the office would be empty at four in the morning."

Coop locked the door behind Ross and brought up the tracking application on his computer, so he could keep an eye on the screen while he pondered the connections between Senator Wagner and Craig Baker.

A few minutes before eleven, the red and blue dots began moving and Coop saw both of them blinking on Highway 321 outside of Pigeon Forge. They were over three hours from Nashville and were scheduled at another event in Knoxville the next day. Coop assumed they would head for a hotel in Knoxville, so his brows furrowed when he saw the dots continue on the windy route, heading west.

"Where are they going?" he muttered. He continued to stalk the dots across the screen, with Craig in the lead. Coop chewed on his thumb nail while he pondered the route they had chosen. The red dot of Meredith's vehicle stopped moving and the blue dot began going back the way they had come, stopping at the location of the red dot before continuing to backtrack. He watched as the distance between the dots lengthened. "Hmm, her car must have a problem and she's riding back with him."

He continued observing the screen and refreshed the software to make sure the red dot was stationary. An hour later, Craig's vehicle was at the Market Square Garage near The Oliver Hotel and Meredith's dot was still out on Highway 321.

Coop made a note in the surveillance log and went back to studying the records Annabelle had picked up on Tuesday. He spent the remaining hours of his shift researching some of the leading clients of Whitehead, Baker, and McCord. They ran the gamut from automotive and manufacturing to fulfillment centers and semiconductor companies. Many of them had one thing in common: they had all received huge—as in hundreds of

millions of dollars—tax incentives to locate their business in
Tennessee.

Coop used the legislative website to trace some of the legislation related to the tax incentives and filled a page of his legal
pad with bills and information, all of it leading back to sponsor-
ship by Senator Wagner. Not that it was surprising, since he was
considered the champion of economic growth. Most of his
campaign contributions came from the same large companies
on the client roster for Craig Baker.

In between charting things on the wall he checked the screen
for the tracking results, but nothing had changed. He was still
working on the summary of his findings when Madison arrived
at six in the morning, bearing fresh donuts and coffee. "Morning, Coop," she said, setting a cup in front of him as she studied
the new sticky notes on the wall. "Y'all been a busy bee."

Coop took a sip of the warm liquid and sighed. "Just what I
needed." He showed her the log from last night and explained
the connections he was recording, so she could continue the
work. He promised to be in by noon, after some rest and a
shower.

When he got home, overcome with both physical and
emotional fatigue, he collapsed in bed. At nine his cell phone
rang and woke him from a deep sleep. The screen showed Ben
was calling.

"Coop, sorry to bother you, but I was talking to Madison.
She says you show Meredith's car on 321 in the middle of
nowhere and we received word from the police in Knoxville
that they're trying to find Meredith. She didn't report to an
eight o'clock meeting with Senator Wagner and isn't in her
room at The Oliver Hotel."

"I assumed she had car trouble and rode back with Craig.
You'll need to send someone to check on her car. Madison gave
you the coordinates, right?"

"Yeah, I'm talking to my counterpart in Knoxville. I haven't divulged everything, but told him we're in the middle of a high-profile investigation involving Meredith. The vehicle is in Blount County, so he's getting them to check it out and sending one of his men down from Knoxville. He'll let me know as soon as they get a report. Should be less than thirty minutes. I'll call you back."

Coop was wide awake and rushed to shower while he waited for the call back. He was gobbling down a hearty breakfast when his phone rang again. He saw it was Ben and answered. "Did you find her?"

"Yeah, her car had gone off the road and hit a tree. She's hurt and they're airlifting her to UT Medical Center now. Do you want to take a road trip with me to Knoxville?"

"I would, but I need to get AB out of the hospital. What time are you heading over?"

"I can give you an hour or so. I'm not sure she'll be up to talking to us anytime soon. Just depends on the severity of her injuries."

Coop hung up and made a call to Dr. Weston, explaining his predicament. She hesitated and said she couldn't make it happen that quickly, but would be happy to take care of getting Annabelle settled at Aunt Camille's when she was discharged.

"Thanks, Alex. That would take a load off my mind. I'll stop by and tell AB the latest and let her know the plan. Aunt Camille will be ready and waiting for her patient," he said with a laugh.

While he was on the phone, his aunt had packed up a cooler with sandwiches, cookies, and fruit, plus bottles of water and sweet tea. He gave her a hug and told her to call him when Annabelle arrived. He bent down and gave Gus a good rubbing, getting several licks in return. "I'll see y'all soon."

He made a stop at the hospital and brought Annabelle up to speed and told her Alex would make sure she got settled once she was released. He called Madison on the way to Ben's office and told her he'd be gone for the day. She told him they would handle keeping watch on Craig's transmitter and call him if there was any suspicious activity.

Ben was ready to go when Coop arrived. They loaded overnight bags into the Crown Victoria, ready for the three hour road trip. On the way, Coop went over his progress on the lobbying and campaign records. "This is all tied together, I know it."

"I'm hoping Meredith will talk now. From what you saw on the tracking software, Craig left her out there on purpose. I have a strong suspicion it was no accident she went off the road. I worked with Chief Mobley and the administrator at the hospital to hide Meredith the best we can. I don't want to compromise our only chance to get to her before Craig."

"We can confront him based on what I saw, but I agree it'd be better if she came clean with what she knows." Coop broke out the provisions Aunt Camille had packed and they ate on the road.

As he took his last bite of cookie, Coop's eyes sparkled with enthusiasm. He thumbed the screen of his cell phone and held it to his ear as he rifled through the notebook he carried. "Hey, Madison, do me a favor and find the spouses of a couple of accident victims from a few years ago. I'll text you the names. We need to find out if they remember any issues at work that were bothering the victims before the accidents. Don't raise too many flags, try to keep it low key." He hung up and sent the names and dates from his notebook.

Ben said, "Meredith's accident made you think of the others, huh?"

"Yep, I don't believe in coincidences and all three accidents sound way too similar to me."

They parked at the hospital and in checking with Chief Mobley's men found Meredith was still in the trauma unit undergoing treatment and tests. She hadn't yet been questioned and Chief Mobley agreed to let Ben conduct the interview. Blount County was still on scene investigating the accident, but their preliminary conclusions were loss of control due to speed. The airbags had done their job, but one of the large limbs from the tree she collided with went through the windshield. Her car was older and not equipped with the modern emergency GPS crash systems that would have alerted law enforcement immediately.

Chief Mobley said they interviewed Craig before they found Meredith and he said they left the event around the same time, but he didn't notice if she went directly to the hotel. They had no plans together until the morning meeting, which is when they realized she was missing.

"He assumed she was dead or would be by the time they found her. There would be no reason to take the route to get to Knoxville," said Coop.

"The way you described the screen he was in front of her, right? So, there could have been another vehicle involved if she was run off the road."

Coop nodded. "I don't think they were close enough for him to have slammed on his brakes or something like that to cause the accident. It looked like he was always in front of her, with a short distance between the two of them. Then when she stopped, he turned around and came back."

"Let's keep that to ourselves for right now," said Ben.

Coop consulted his phone and saw the Knoxville campaign event was in full swing and wasn't scheduled to end until later in the evening. He suspected Senator Wagner or Craig may come by the hospital to check on Meredith after the event. He confirmed with Ross that Craig's car was still at the hotel and hadn't moved, which made sense since the venue was within walking distance.

Ben kept in contact with Chief Mobley, who made sure the hospital staff understood Ben and Coop were to be admitted into Meredith's room. Shortly before five, a nurse escorted them upstairs. They checked in at the nurse's station right outside her unit and were reminded she would be tired from the surgery procedures, so their visit would need to be brief.

They saw an unrecognizable woman in bed, with her head bandaged and face slashed with cuts and burned from the air bags. Both of her eyes were blackened, one arm was in a cast, and so was one of her legs. The battered husk before them looked nothing like the commanding and uptight woman they had spoken with earlier in the week.

She cracked open her eyes when they shuffled into the room. She squinted as she looked at both of them and silent tears rolled down her face. "Ms. Stevens," said Ben. "We're sorry to disturb you. We have some questions about the accident last night." He hesitated and looked at Coop. "Are you up to talking with us for a few minutes?"

She studied them both and Coop plucked a tissue from the box and put it in her good hand. She dabbed her eyes and in a small and hoarse voice said, "Yes."

"Let me start by saying the reason we found you was because of Mr. Harrington."

Meredith's forehead puckered and her eyes clouded with uncertainty. Coop began, "This won't make you happy, but I slipped a tracking device on your car when you were at Silverwood on Monday. I recognize you know a lot more than you're telling us and I wanted to keep an eye on you." Her black rimmed eyes hardened as he continued. "So, my firm has been monitoring your activity, which led us to your location after your accident."

Ben added, "Mr. Harrington also monitored Craig Baker's vehicle and saw it travelling with you on the evening of the accident." Her eyes widened. "As he watched, he thought your car broke down and you rode back to Knoxville with Craig, but that's not at all what happened is it?"

She shifted her eyes back and forth and sighed. "It wasn't an accident," she said, her voice raspy. Coop reached for the glass of water on her tray and held the straw to her mouth. She sipped and swallowed. "I was run off the road."

"Why were you on that stretch of road?" asked Ben.

"Craig said we needed to talk privately and asked me to follow him. He didn't want anyone to see us."

"Did you have that conversation?"

"No. The plan was he would pull over at a good spot." She swallowed hard. "This big pickup truck, I think, was behind me, practically pushing me along those curves and I kept speeding up to get away from it. I remember screaming when I saw I was headed off the road and then I was in the air and don't remember much after that."

"Can you identify the truck? Color, license plate, anything?"

"No, it was too dark, I just saw lights and they were high."

"Do you know if Craig came back to check on you?"

"I don't know." Her eyes filled with tears again. "If he did, he didn't bother to get me any help."

Coop looked at Ben and got a nod. "I hate to be blunt, Ms. Stevens, but I think you know who killed Grayson Taylor and that knowledge has put you in jeopardy. I hope you realize how important it is for you to be truthful."

She stared at the television screen, but didn't speak, lips pursed.

Ben added, "I've arranged to have you kept here under a different name. You'll also be listed as a patient under your name, but we have a decoy in that bed. I'm concerned once it's known you're alive, the person responsible for your accident may try again."

She turned her head and sucked in her breath, the consternation on her face turning to fear. "I hadn't thought of that."

"You're listed as in a coma, unresponsive, not expected to live, with no visitors allowed. We've got an undercover officer dressed up in bandages, in your hospital bed, in case somebody gets in to try something. You'll be registered as Cybil Reynolds and kept here on a different floor. I'm not requesting guards because that would only serve to alert someone to your where-abouts. We're going to pretend we think it was an accident and you're not awake."

She moved her head a fraction of an inch, indicating her agreement. "Is there anyone we can call for you?" asked Coop.

"My sister in California. Her number's in my purse and my cell phone if they've found it."

"We'll call her and get her on her way. If you were in a coma, she'd be here right?"

Meredith exhaled and winced when she tried to shrug. "I think so." She repositioned herself and added, "I'm not close to my family."

They continued talking and determined Senator Wagner had met her sister years ago, but Craig had not. Meredith declined an attorney, saying she couldn't trust any she knew, and agreed to a videotaped interview in her hospital bed. She would share what she knew about Grayson Taylor's death and any other crimes in exchange for immunity from prosecution. Meredith grew weary as the conversation continued, her eyes fluttering to stay open. They arranged to come back in the morning with the video technician and the legal agreement.

Ben booked a hotel room near the hospital while Coop updated his office on the unfolding events. They didn't want to run into Craig or Senator Wagner at the hospital and made sure they were out well before the fundraising event ended. They opted for take-out food on their way to the hotel. Once they checked in Ben spent hours on the phone perfecting the legal logistics for Meredith's interview.

Coop hit an icon on his cell phone as he wolfed down some fries. "Hey, Aunt Camille, how's AB?"

His aunt reported the patient was doing well and was

ensconced in the guest room with Gus lounging atop her bed, keeping watch. Annabelle was tired and had been sleeping off and on since she had been discharged. Mrs. Henderson worked her magic with some homemade soup and biscuits and brownie sundaes for dessert.

Coop updated her on the happenings in Knoxville and while he was promising to be home soon, his cell beeped indicating another call. "I've gotta run, but will see you tomorrow. Give Gus and AB a hug from me."

He connected the second call from Ross. "Hey, Coop, I wasn't sure if you were in a position to monitor the tracking software. Wanted you to know Craig's car is on the move from his hotel. Looks like he's heading in the direction of the hospital."

"We're at our hotel, so I'll pull it up now. Keep watching though and I'll be in touch." Ross let him know Madison was talking to the family members of the two accident victims and would have something to report soon. Coop watched the dot on his phone and fifteen minutes later saw it stop at the hospital parking area. Ben was on his phone, but Coop showed him the screen.

Ben made another call and informed the Knoxville detectives disguised as hospital employees of Craig's movements. When he hung up, he said, "They're ready and will call back with an update."

They paired their greasy burgers and fries with some of the leftover cookies from Aunt Camille and waited by their phones. Ben had talked to Meredith's sister and filled her in on the fact that Meredith was in a serious accident. She was making plans to fly to Tennessee in the coming days. For now, she was told the coma story.

Coop got a text from Madison letting him know the spouses of the two victims remembered them both being stressed about things at work, but neither of them divulged specifics. She ended it with *Nothing definitive, but both of them swear they were careful drivers, not speeders. Let me know if you find something to tie them together and I'll keep digging.*

Less than half an hour later, Craig's dot was on the move. Ben's phone rang and after a short conversation he disconnected. "Craig and Senator Wagner went to the hospital and asked to see Meredith. They were told no visitors and that she was not conscious yet. Senator Wagner stressed how important she was to him and appeared to be concerned about her well-being. He wanted Meredith's doctor to call him and left his private cell number."

"They didn't try the room?"

Ben shook his head. "They were given the room number, but didn't make any attempt. We're going to have the doctor call with the coma story, saying he shouldn't say, but due to the fact that it's Senator Wagner and she's his longtime staffer, he'll bend the rules."

"According to the campaign website, they have another luncheon tomorrow in Clarksville, so they need to be on the road in the morning. Craig, of course, has no obligation to be at the event, so he may stick around."

"We'll keep our eye on him," said Coop, tapping the screen of his phone to view Craig's car back at The Oliver Hotel.

~

In the hours before dawn, Ben's cell rang out. He fumbled with the items on the nightstand and gripped the phone. "Mason," he answered, followed by a brief conversation and ended with, "I'll be there in less than an hour."

"What's up?"

"A guy came to the hospital and was lurking in the hallway outside of the decoy's room. He probably wouldn't have been caught, but the crew we have in there is watching everything like hawks. Our faux nurse ran him off, but the cameras got some good photos of him. They followed him on the security cameras and got his plate number. Comes back as a rental, but they're running it down."

They rushed to get ready and were out the door in less than thirty minutes. It was almost five in the morning, cool, with a clear sky the color of ink. Ben steered the Crown Victoria to a Dunkin' Donuts and picked up five dozen donuts and a couple of boxes of their coffee. Coop snagged a cup of decaf and helped carry the load to the car.

"Just how much is your donut budget?"

Ben laughed as he shut the back door. "Unlimited, if I can get this case closed." He drove to the Knoxville Police Department, where armed with the signature boxes, they developed instant camaraderie. Chief Mobley met them and brought up the video images of the hospital visitor.

"The rental car comes back to a corporation based out of the Cayman Islands, White Sands Development, Inc. We don't have facial recognition software, so there's no quick way to identify our friend," said Chief Mobley. "Do either of you recognize him?"

Coop and Ben shook their heads as they studied the video of a tall, dark-haired man, with a trimmed beard and mustache. He looked to be in his early thirties, strong and athletic. Coop pulled out his cell phone and took a picture of the man and sent a text.

Ben asked that the video be emailed to his department, so they could assist in the identification. "Was he cooperative when he was told to leave last night?"

Chief Mobley nodded. "Polite, didn't say much, just that he was a friend from out of town, but understood and would try again tomorrow." He added the undercover officer didn't notice anything that would be helpful about his speech patterns, except she didn't think he was from the area, noting he lacked a drawl or southern accent.

Chief Mobley and Ben reviewed the legal documents that had been drawn up by the Nashville District Attorney with the blessing of the locals in Knoxville. "Our video guy will be here at eight to pick up his equipment and will meet you in Meredith's room at nine," said Chief Mobley. "You two are welcome to use a spare office while you wait. There's a phone and computer in it, if you need to use either."

As soon as they sat, Coop's phone pinged with a text. "It's from AB. She says she feels good enough to do some research. She's going to start looking into White Sands Development and Madison and Ross are going to concentrate on our guy."

Coop's phone rang. Madison reported Craig's car was on the move. He consulted the screen and followed the dot as it travelled on I-40 out of town. "Craig's heading back. I wonder if the good senator is with him."

"Even if he's not with him, he's got to head out soon to make the luncheon," replied Ben. They both busied themselves with email correspondence while they waited to leave for the hospital.

When they arrived at Meredith's door, they caught a glimpse of a number of scrub clad nurses and doctors surrounding Meredith's bed. The nurse at the station hollered out, "You can't go in there."

21

The nurse came from behind the counter and lowered her voice. "She had a bad night and there are some complications. Her doctor doesn't want any visitors or anything that could cause her any stress, until he's got her stabilized again." She pointed to a small room behind the nursing desk. "You two are welcome to wait it out in our conference room. Not sure how long it'll be."

Both of their shoulders sagged as they spotted the video technician with his cases rounding the desk. Ben intercepted him and shared the news. They exchanged cards and the young man left.

Ben slumped into a chair and said, "I know you're used to no sleep, but I'm exhausted. I'm losing my patience."

Coop shut the door after the nurse promised to alert them the moment the patient was cleared for visitors. "Maybe we should spend our time waiting figuring out a strategy for taking Craig down once we have her statement."

They tinkered with ideas, wondering still how anything in Craig's world was connected to Grayson. While Ben went

downstairs to pick up lunch from the food court, Annabelle
called.

"How are you feeling, AB?"

"Better today. I'm bored stiff, so glad you have something for
me to do. Gus is camped out right next to me and Aunt Camille
is feeding me nonstop." She laughed and then added, "I called
because I have a line on White Sands."

"I always said you are the best researcher I know."

"Well, it's a shell corporation, as I'm sure you guessed. I dug
around and found out it's linked to several of the main clients
on Craig's lobbying list. Our initial look at the companies on the
list didn't go far enough. Several of the companies are actually
owned by parent corporations. All of the clients linked to White
Sands are through a parent corporation called HIP Development, Inc."

"What do we know about HIP?"

"HIP is Harold and Isabelle Palmer, as in Emily Taylor's
sister and her rich husband."

"So, the guy who came to visit Meredith, most likely to
finish the job, works for Emily's brother-in-law?"

"It's convoluted, but yes, White Sands is definitely Harold
and Isabelle. They have a mass of companies, corporations and
partnerships here and I'm guessing more than one off-shore
shell company, but that's what I know at this point."

"Is the manufacturing company and semi-conductor firm
where the other accident victims worked part of HIP?"

"You are quick, Coop. Yep, HIP is the parent company of
both of them."

"Give Madison a call and fill her in, so she can try to connect
those other accidents. We're still waiting to interview
Meredith."

"Okay, Coop. I'll keep digging and see what else I can learn.
Keep me posted."

"Don't overdo it, AB. You need your rest."

"I'm fine. I'll see you tonight."

Ben returned with bags of food and Coop filled him in on Annabelle's findings. His eyes twinkled with excitement as he put in a call to Kate and said, "If AB ever tires of working for you, she's got a job on my team."

It was after one o'clock when the nurse escorted them to Meredith's room and the video technician set up his camera. Meredith confirmed she was ready and feeling better. She read over the legal agreement and signed it with a shaking hand, waiving her right to an attorney.

Ben eased into the interview with benign questions about her place of residence, employment history, and other basic questions. He then moved into more difficult terrain and asked Meredith to describe the event she attended at Silverwood on the evening of Grayson Taylor's death.

Meredith took a deep breath and began, "I attended with Senator Wagner, as I always did. It was another campaign opportunity in his run for governor as well as a legislative event. He had business to discuss about the budget bills with several of the lobbyists and did that after we met with constituents. Everything about those activities I said in my first interview with you was truthful, with the exception of being on the terrace and witnessing...an incident with Grayson Taylor. I didn't know him before that night."

She paused and Coop held the glass of water for her. She took a long sip and swallowed, resting against her pillows. "Craig and I were in the garden area after he met with Senator Wagner. We were talking about a...situation. We heard someone on the terrace and Craig was concerned we had been overheard. Then Beau busted through the doors and began yelling at Grayson. After their scuffle we watched through the bushes and saw Grayson return to the terrace and before I knew what was happening, Craig shot through the shrubbery and grabbed the top off the ledge and hit him in the head. He toppled over the edge and I heard an awful thud. I hurried and stepped through to the ledge. Craig told me to stay there and watch for anyone. He ran to his car and got a pair of gloves, while I stood there looking down on the poor man." She reached for another drink of water and a noisy gulp followed. "He returned and dragged Grayson to the bushes along the wall. It was dark and once he hauled him away from the stone below, I couldn't see much."

Ben asked, "What was the situation you and Craig were discussing?"

She gripped a tissue and took a long slow breath. "Senator Wagner's campaign. Craig told me there was a problem with one of his clients in that someone in the accounting office had begun asking too many questions. He was afraid it could lead to a problem with the senator's campaign for governor."

"Enlighten us on what exactly would be the problem?"

"Kickbacks," she said, with a firm gaze. "Senator Wagner dedicated his career to increasing development in the state and several of the large corporations that benefited from some of his legal expertise and legislative support, wanted to reward him with payments. They couldn't do so directly, so some of those payments were routed through Craig's law firm and paid to Senator Wagner in his 'of counsel' role."

Ben continued the questions and they discovered Meredith was aware of several offshore accounts Senator Wagner held and that money was routinely wired into those accounts. She didn't know how Craig intended to deal with the possible problem related to the accounting questions and told them Senator Wagner had absolute trust in Craig and he handled everything associated with the kickback operation. "I heard the term 'plausible deniability' more than once and know Senator Wagner didn't want to be involved in anything that would implicate him in wrongdoing." She paused and added, "Craig did not want me to talk about what happened at Silverwood with Senator Wagner."

Ben asked Meredith about the people who had died in the car accidents who worked for Craig's clients. She didn't recognize the names and had no knowledge of the accidents. When Ben described the details, her lips quivered and fresh tears sprang to her eyes. He showed her the picture from the video at the hospital and asked if she recognized the man. She studied it and said, "I'm not sure. He looks a bit familiar, but I'm not sure why or where I've seen him."

Ben continued and asked, "What do you know about HIP Development or White Sands Development?"

"White Sands is familiar. There have been several deposits into Senator Wagner's accounts in the Caymans from White Sands. I know HIP Development is Harold Palmer's company. He's the leading developer in the state and involved in several corporations. He's a huge fan of Senator Wagner and a large contributor to his campaign." She confirmed she had account numbers in the diary in her purse and turned it over to them. She studied the rumpled tissue in her hand. "What's going to happen to Grant?"

"I'm not sure at this point. Once I have all the facts, it will be up to the District Attorney and other agencies to figure it out." He looked at the clock and asked, "Do you need a break, Ms. Stevens?"

"No, go ahead, I'd like to get this over with."

He inquired about Senator Wagner's similar special counsel position at Peter Collins' firm and the nature of the payments. "He consults on a few special projects for some of the lawyers in Peter's firm, but as far as I know, he's only paid for the advice and consulting, nothing to do with kickbacks."

He probed into the phone calls she had made to Craig on the night of the murder and the communications she had with Craig since they interviewed her. "I, uh, I couldn't deal with what I witnessed on the terrace. Craig killing Grayson Taylor. I was in a panic and told him we needed to tell the police that it was an accident. He told me not to worry about it, that he would handle it and to keep my mouth shut." She shut her eyes and licked her lips. "He tried to reassure me at first, but then became angrier and told me if I wanted to keep my job and lifestyle, I would shut up and let him manage things. He didn't want me to discuss it with Senator Wagner and told me I could ruin his run for governor if I didn't go along. He reminded me I would have a cushy position once Grant won."

She explained Craig's idea about telling the police she had been drunk and she had called to proposition him. "He said we had to have our stories straight." After the questions about the phone calls, he furnished her with a burner phone and gave her a number to use to reach him.

"Did Craig know you lost your earring?"

Her eyes widened in horror. "No, I was afraid to tell him." She sighed and added, "I guess I shouldn't have called to see if it had been found, but they were a gift from Grant and I wanted to locate it."

"But you called him on the burner phone after we interviewed you at Silverwood?"

"I was scared out of my mind. I told him both of you had been to see me again and were questioning me about the murder. I never mentioned the earring. He told me to pull myself together. I told him I couldn't take it anymore and thought we should tell Senator Wagner what had happened."

"We're almost wrapped up here, Ms. Stevens. To summarize, you have direct knowledge of Craig Baker killing Grayson Taylor with a blow to the head and further concealing his body in the shrubbery below the terrace wall. You also have knowledge of Craig Baker orchestrating and handling the operation of routing money from his clients to Senator Grant Wagner through a position at his law firm designed to funnel these illegal kickbacks to the senator. You further have knowledge of offshore accounts owned by Senator Wagner and know some of the deposits in those accounts came from White Sands Development, Inc. Do you have knowledge of any other crimes perpetrated by Mr. Baker or his associates or Senator Wagner or his associates?"

She squeezed her eyes as tears fell down her battered face. "I don't know of any other crimes and I never thought of the money and deposits as real crimes, just politics and business. I knew it could be bad for Senator Wagner's campaign and position, but none of it seemed important, until Craig killed Mr. Taylor."

"After you expressed your concern about the murder to Mr. Baker, were you ever in fear for your life?"

Panic shot through her bloodshot eyes. "Not until after the accident. Now I'm convinced Craig wanted to get rid of me. If it were an accident, he should have stopped to help me, but I've had lots of time to think and realize I was making him nervous the more I balked at the incident at Silverwood. I was jeopardizing everything."

For the benefit of the video, Ben stated the date, time, and place, before ending the interview. "Your sister should be here tonight and after you talk with her, give me a call. I'm happy to help arrange a transfer to a new hospital for you. Someplace where nobody will know you, so you can recuperate without concern for your safety. Once they know you've spoken with us, they may try to silence you again. We've still got undercover police in the hospital, but I think if would be a good idea to move you."

She gave a slight nod and promised to get in touch with him after her sister arrived. "I'm grateful for your help, Chief Mason and yours, Mr. Harrington. I regret lying to you initially and realize all of this could have been prevented if I had told you the truth months ago."

They left her sobbing quietly with a fresh box of tissues and a warm copy of the immunity agreement she had signed.

Ben and Coop stopped by the Knoxville Police Department to email the video file to the District Attorney and retrieve a copy to take with them. They thanked Chief Mobley and promised to be in touch concerning Meredith's transport out of Knoxville. On their way out of town, they stopped at a market for drinks and a few snacks and Coop called Aunt Camille to check in and let her know he'd be home for a late supper.

As soon as they hit the interstate, Ben received a call from Kate, whose normally calm voice was excited. She was on speaker when she said, "Madison and I staked out HIP all day and finally hit pay dirt on our mysterious man in the rental car. He's part of the security team at HIP."

"How'd y'all manage that?" asked Ben, with admiration in his voice.

"We can't reveal all our secrets," she said, with a chuckle. "Suffice it to say Madison plays an excellent part as a jilted girl-friend and we found a sympathetic secretary in the building who confirmed the guy's identity as Leonard Hall. He lives in an apartment in East Nashville." She summarized Leonard's history, growing up in Nebraska and getting into trouble as a juvenile and young adult for burglary, stealing cars, and assaults. He'd been living in Nashville for the last seven years, working for Harold Palmer.

Kate and Jimmy were planning to pay Leonard a visit as soon as he went home and Ben wanted him in an interrogation room by the time he and Coop returned to Nashville. Kate was working the old accident cases and trying to link them to Leonard via HIP or White Sands or any of the other myriad of companies in the tangled web of businesses.

Ben spoke with the District Attorney and the FBI while they travelled. Ben flung his phone on the seat after disconnecting. "I knew we'd have to get the Feds involved with the level of corruption we're dealing with and Senator Wagner's position. I don't want to give up the case. I want Craig for murder. They can have the good senator."

"Will they give you some time to wrap up the investigation?"

"That's what I'm trying to buy right now. The Special Agent in Charge is a good guy and he's trying, but sometimes things get out of control fast. They're notorious for swooping in and taking over a case after we've done all the hard work. They want the glory that comes with a press conference. The U.S. Attorney is talking to the District Attorney."

"We need to break Leonard and get him to roll on his chain of command," said Coop. "They need to give us some time."

Ben nodded as he drove faster. "They're doing their financial thing with the banks in the Caymans, so that will keep them busy, but I agree, we need to get everything we can to lock up Craig. The senator is going down for the fraud and bribery stuff no matter what, once they get the records sorted out, but I don't want to give Craig any warning."

"Emily's brother-in-law is going to be swept up with all the other rubbish. It will be interesting to see her reaction."

Ben steered his Crown Victoria into his parking spot at headquarters, thirty minutes ahead of schedule. Coop sent a text to Annabelle letting her know he'd be tied up and to eat without him.

They found Kate and Jimmy, along with Ross and Madison in the conference room. Notes were scrawled on all the whiteboards, with lines and circles connecting items. "Hey, boss and Coop," said Jimmy, when he looked up and saw them.

"Did you guys get Leonard?"

A smug smile blossomed on Kate's face. "Sure did, he's in the box, waiting."

"With all of us working and the help of our bedridden researcher," Madison raised her eyebrows at Coop, "we've got some links you can use during your interrogation to rattle his cage with regard to the two other so-called accidents."

Ben took some time to get organized and jotted down notes pertaining to the vehicles they had linked to HIP, credit card receipts for fuel, a ticket for a burned out headlight, and bill for new tires. They also had Leonard's cell phone records striped with yellow highlights. Ben smiled as he studied the evidence. "Terrific work, all of you."

He handed his notes to Kate and motioned with his head for her and Jimmy to conduct the interview. They both smiled, while he led Coop and the others to the observation room. Jimmy read Leonard his rights and watched his eyes narrow in defiance. "I don't want to talk to you without my lawyer."

Kate said, "No problem, Leonard. You don't have to talk to us, but I think you may want to listen." Behind the mirror, they watched as the partners began the dance, first a slow waltz around the suspect and then the staccato and snap of a tango, as they jabbed him with pieces of evidence. They were both masters and enjoyed the back and forth as they followed each other nailing down facts and embellishing less concrete details to convince Leonard he was looking at two murder charges and if Meredith didn't pull through, three. They threw in the assault and break-in at Coop's office, suspecting he'd been the perpetrator.

"Here's the deal, we don't think it's fair for you to burn on these charges, when we know you were just doing your job. You were doing what you were told, right?" said Kate, looking at Leonard and then turning her attention to Jimmy.

"Yeah, but once he gets an attorney, there won't be any deals for him. He'll take the rap, since his lawyer won't really be working for him now, will he? Not to mention his history of criminal activity from Nebraska." said Jimmy.

"Right, right," said Kate, nodding her head. "Probably Craig's the lawyer Harold would send, right?" she continued, with a grin. They were ignoring Leonard, carrying on a conversation without him.

The group behind the mirror saw Leonard's bravado begin to crumble at the mention of his boss and Craig.

"They'll leave him hanging in the wind. That's how those types always get away with screwing everyone else," added Jimmy. "Then who knows how long before they pay somebody off in prison to get rid of him altogether. He ought to know they always remove any obstacles or threats."

"You're right. Even if he shuts up and takes it, in the end he'll be dead, shanked in the shower at Riverbend. We know the law, so if you want an attorney, that's fine, we'll get you a phone, Leonard," said Kate, closing the cover on the thick file she held.

"So, you guys can get me protection and a deal if I talk?" asked Leonard, in a voice lacking the courage of his earlier comments.

"Sure thing, Leonard. We'll get the District Attorney in here and make you a deal," said Jimmy.

"Okay, okay, let's do that," said Leonard, stretching his back and letting out his breath. "Do they know I'm here?"

Ben pulled his cell phone and made a quick call. Deputy District Attorney Marvin Clark was waiting in another room watching the proceedings, waiting for the green light.

"Who?" asked Kate.

"Craig or Harold or anyone at HIP."

"No, that's why we went to your house, Leonard," she smiled. Marvin tapped on the door and opened it. "Leonard Hall, meet DDA Clark. He'll work up the paperwork with you and then we'll need you to write down everything you know about Craig Baker, Senator Grant Wagner, HIP, White Sands, and the many other companies under their umbrella. I'll bring you some food when we come back."

Leonard nodded and Jimmy and Kate left Mr. Clark to his legal maneuvers and exited the room. They joined Ben and the others in the conference room and were surprised to find Aunt Camille and Annabelle with a huge basket of wonderful smelling food.

They commandeered one of the tables and set up a buffet of fried chicken, potato salad, coleslaw, biscuits, mashed potatoes and gravy, and plates of cookies and brownies. "AB and I decided since Coop was goin' to miss supper, we'd bring it down here and treat y'all to a good meal," said Aunt Camille, as she finished stacking the plates and silverware.

They wasted no time forming a line and loading their plates. Between bites, they regaled both of them with the latest developments and praised Annabelle for her research that helped them nail Leonard. An hour later, they helped pack up the catered picnic and Mr. Clark appeared with a wide smile. "He's all yours, detectives."

Kate and Jimmy went back with a plate from Aunt Camille's basket and a soda for Leonard and continued the interview. They obtained a ten page written account of the accidents he had arranged on behalf of Craig Baker, including the break-in and assault on Annabelle, and his knowledge of HIP and White Sands Development, Inc. He had been offered a much lesser charge than murder for hire or vehicular homicide in exchange for his testimony. He agreed to forgo a telephone call, so as not to alert anyone he was in custody and would be spending the night in a holding cell.

While Kate and Jimmy were busy in the interrogation room, Ben received a call from Meredith and put the transfer plan in motion. She was being transported to a hospital in Texas, with the help of Chief Mobley and his department. She was expected to remain there for several weeks and he assured her she would be afforded protection as long as necessary.

As the night lingered on, the adrenaline responsible for

energizing the group for the past several days waned. Ben spoke with the FBI and the U.S. Attorney several times and during his last conference call with them, they agreed to meet in the morning to discuss the execution of their plan to snare Senator Wagner and Harold Palmer, while leaving Craig Baker for Ben and his team.

22

Coop crept through the quiet house, careful not to disturb his aunt or Annabelle. He stole a look in the guest room and saw Gus sprawled across the foot of her bed. The dog raised his head for a moment before snuggling back in with his new roommate. Coop shook his head and suppressed a laugh as he wandered to his wing.

The excitement of the day, combined with his usual lack of sleep had worn him out. He slumped into bed, feeling some of the burden of Gray's case lift, as the realization of telling Taylor they had caught his father's killer struck him. The harsh reality that Gray had been in the wrong place at the wrong time would be something he could never justify.

Coop was up early, feeling less tired, but anxious about the day ahead. He found Gus and Annabelle in the breakfast room. "Hey, AB, how ya feeling? I never got a chance to talk to you much at the precinct."

She smiled, the morning sun accentuating the highlights in her hair. "I'm feeling so much better. I'm trying to convince Aunt Camille I'm ready to go home." She rolled her eyes. "You can imagine my success."

He grinned. "She loves to dote on you and have your company. You need to be pampered after what happened. Leonard confessed last night to the three 'accidents,' plus some other errands he'd run for Craig, including breaking into the office and assaulting you. He was taking photos of the evidence we had amassed and you surprised him." He paused as he put jam on his toast. "I'd like to get him alone in a room and beat him for what he did to you, AB."

She nodded. "I get to hit him first," she said with a smile. "I'm okay and lucky. He could have killed me with the gun instead of just whacking me on the head."

"He took the deal, of course, and will get a few years, but he's a small fish compared to Craig, Senator Wagner, and Harold Palmer."

"He's a tool," she said with a snicker. "In more ways than one. I understand the way it works and to get the big ones, sometimes you have to let the little fish swim away. It'll work out in the end."

They finished breakfast and Coop cleared the dishes. "I hope today goes well. I cringe when the Feds are involved. I want to go talk with Taylor and his grandparents as soon as we get things wrapped up on this one. Then I'll be home." He gave Gus a pat. "Gus will be sad when you go. I see he's taken to sleeping on your bed with you."

She laughed and said, "He's good company and keeps my feet warm."

"Tell Aunt Camille I'll be home for supper," said Coop, as he went through the door.

Coop walked through the precinct, feeling the buzz of excitement and anticipation in the air. When he rounded the corner, he saw the entire detective division had been infiltrated with agents and officers from a variety of the alphabet soup agencies. Ben was in his office surrounded by suits and Coop slipped into a vacant chair next to Kate and Jimmy, feeling a bit underdressed in his jeans and red t-shirt, stating "There. Their. They're Not the Same."

Jimmy slid a box of donuts over and said, "At least the Feds know to bring goodies." Coop waved it away, full from breakfast and too on edge to eat. Soon Ben emerged from his office and stood between two somber men, each sporting the lapel pin of their agency—FBI and DOJ. Ben introduced them as Special Agent in Charge Mark Walton and U.S. Attorney Trevor McDonald.

"Operational plans are being distributed now and I'll be reviewing the main points. This will be a three-pronged joint operation, with teams assigned to each target. We will be executing synchronized search warrants at a number of offices and homes related to our suspects. We will also be executing arrest warrants simultaneously on our three targets—Baker, Wagner, and Palmer. Nashville will be taking the lead on Baker, while the FBI will be in charge of both Wagner and Palmer. Each team is comprised of personnel from all three agencies."

Ben flipped through the pages of the plan and called on the team leaders to review the strategy for each location. Several vans and box trucks were ready to roll to collect the electronic and paper evidence expected from the search warrants. "Nobody speaks to the media. Once the operation is over, we will have a news conference and statements from each agency. The Department of Justice has the lead on press relations."

After a few questions, Ben dismissed the group and each team leader took over loading personnel and organizing vehicles. Ben tossed Coop a Nashville Police sweatshirt to put on and he rode with Ben and a team of agents and officers who swarmed the office of Whitehead, Baker, and McCord. To the astonishment of the receptionist, an officer removed her headset and detained her at her desk, while a line of armed agents and officers continued down the hall, fortified with warrants. They peeled off the main hall and covered all the offices, including the data center. Ben and Coop, along with half a dozen other officers, didn't bother to knock on their way through Craig's door.

"Mr. Craig Baker," said Ben, in a thunderous voice, "You are under arrest for the murder of Grayson Taylor, the attempted murder of Meredith Stevens, the murder of Sally Cartwright, and the murder of Richard Bradley. Additional charges will be forthcoming from the Department of Justice."

"You're making a career ending mistake, Chief Mason," said Craig. "I want an attorney and I'm not saying a word."

"Pick a good one," said Ben, as he cuffed Craig's hands behind his back. He read him his rights as he escorted him down the hall. Attorneys and staff members lurked in doorways and lined the hall, some crying, all dumbfounded at the efficiency of the mass of law enforcement officers flooding their workplace, loading boxes and computers into the elevator.

The same thing was happening in Grant Wagner's campaign office, legislative office, and home. He was telling his wife to call Craig, which she would soon learn would be futile. Harold Palmer was at his home and taken into custody, while his offices were stripped of records and electronic data and equipment. His assets had been frozen and he also asked his wife to call Craig.

Craig's assistant was busy trying to portray a professional image when she received the frantic calls from the wives. Her hands trembled as she logged the messages into the software system. She was practiced at lying about her boss's whereabouts, but unnerved at the sight of him being paraded through the corridors in handcuffs. She knew the walls were crumbling as she promised to have one of the other partners get in touch with the women without delay.

As soon as she got her wits about her, she pulled up her resume and polished it before sending it off to competing firms, hoping to get out before the whole place imploded.

Coop left Ben to his interrogation duties. Craig, unlike his errand boy, Leonard, proved to be a skillful opponent and was saying nothing until he spoke with an attorney. The Department of Justice was experiencing a similar stalemate with Senator Wagner and Harold Palmer. They both demanded Craig Baker be called but the wind went out of their sails when they were informed he was in custody and not available.

While the three of them were still locked in interrogation rooms, all vying to the be the first throw the others to the wolves to save their own skin, the Department of Justice called a press conference.

U.S. Attorney Trevor McDonald explained Senator Wagner and Harold Palmer were in custody on federal arrest warrants. He read off a litany of charges, including conspiracy, wire fraud, mail fraud, and extortion. He outlined the bribery and kickback scheme Senator Wagner had concocted, using his position to grant favors to companies with business before the State of Tennessee. He read from the complaint, "In truth and in fact, Wagner has obtained millions of dollars in outside income as a direct result of his corrupt use of his official position to obtain money in the form of bribes and kickbacks, including from clients with substantial business before the State, and not as a result of legitimate outside income Wagner earned as a private attorney."

He further enlightened the throng of focused reporters to the facts implicating Craig Baker as a party to the corrupt scheme of routing bribes and extorted funds through the law firm of Whitehead, Baker, and McCord to Senator Wagner via his 'of counsel' position, which was largely fictitious and set up only as a method to launder the money.

He did an effective job of burying the lead and when he announced Craig Baker was being held by the Nashville Police Department for the murder of Grayson Taylor and two others, plus the attempted murder of Meredith Stevens, the intensity of the camera flashes blinded him. All the reporters began to speak at once, intent on asking questions. The attorney held up his hand, both to block out the glaring light and to quiet the rowdy group.

He delineated Harold Palmer's relationship by marriage to Grayson Taylor and a collective gasp reverberated through the room. He continued to outline the conspiracy, whereby Mr. Palmer received substantial benefits from governmental entities, arranged by Senator Wagner, using his powerful position in the legislature. He also implicated Mr. Palmer in the murder of the two employees who worked for subsidiaries of his parent company, whereby Mr. Palmer supplied one of his own security people to carry out the vehicular homicides.

"I will not be taking questions at this time, but will be updating you as soon as we have any new or significant information. I want to thank Chief of Detectives Ben Mason and the Nashville Police Department for their outstanding work on these cases and the Federal Bureau of Investigation, who together with the Department of Justice were able to send a strong message to those involved in corruption, especially those who are stewards of tax dollars and elected to public service."

They posed for more pictures and then walked away, leaving the reporters chanting for more, as they exited the room. Ben met Coop in the hallway and pulled him to the side. "As soon as we had them all in custody, I had Kate contact Emily Taylor to tell her the news. She found out Emily was in Kentucky, since her father died last week. I knew she'd hear it on the news tonight and might have already gotten a call from her sister, but I wanted to give Kate the satisfaction of telling her in person so she and Jimmy drove up there." He wiggled his cell phone in his hand. "I got a call from her saying they're on their way home. She said Emily was her usual arrogant self, until they told her the specifics and related the three arrests, including her brother-in-law's. Kate said she went pale and crumpled to the floor. Jimmy helped her into a chair and they left her in a catatonic state, after seeking out her mother to sit with her. Seems both of them were quite concerned with what people would think when they heard the news."

"It's a damn shame Gray didn't marry Abby in high school and make a life with her and Taylor. I think the three of them would have been happy," said Coop.

"Kate made sure she told Emily you were instrumental in the apprehension of Gray's killer and had never quit working the case, even after she terminated your contract. Kate said Emily didn't say a word, but she could see she was stunned."

"Well, I wasn't doing it for her. I did it for Taylor...and for Gray."

The agents shook hands with Ben and Coop said his goodbyes. Knowing Taylor was out of school early as a senior, he called his cell phone on the way to the Jeep. He told him he had news about his father and asked if he could meet him with his grandparents.

Taylor called him back within minutes and told Coop he'd talked with his mom and grandparents and he invited Coop to meet at their new house at three o'clock. Coop decided to swing by his house and pick up Annabelle, so she could participate in the closing of the case.

She was eager to get out of the house and Gus followed them to the Jeep, delighted to give up his front seat to Annabelle. They drove the short distance to Abby's neighborhood and before Coop shut off the engine, Taylor opened the door and welcomed them. Abby insisted Gus accompany them into the house. They gathered in the cheerful living room where Coop revealed the entire sordid account of the corruption and greed that had led to the murder of the Taylors' only son and the father young Taylor had never had the chance to know.

He held nothing back and told them how they had tracked Craig and Meredith, weaving in the prior deaths attributed to traffic accidents, and Annabelle's unfortunate assault at the office. Tears and shock spread across their faces as they listened to the story unfold. He warned them the press conference would be aired on the news and the story was already trending on social media and online news sites.

"The earring really was the most important piece of evidence?" asked Taylor, tears dotting his face.

"Yes, that was the tipping point, but Craig trying to kill Meredith on the road was what made her tell her story. Once we had her knowledge, everything fell into place."

Taylor hung his head. "I'm so sorry I didn't tell the truth when you first talked to me. Luckily, Chief Mason accepted my community service idea and Sarah was nice enough to give me a second chance at Silverwood. I'll never make that mistake again."

"Annabelle, I'm so very sorry you were injured because of all of this," said Lila Rose, gripping her hand.

Annabelle squeezed back. "I'm fine. It's just one of the hazards of working with this guy," she said, giving Coop an elbow.

"I know Gray's death was senseless and random in that he was targeted because Craig *thought* Gray overheard them talking about the kickback scheme. I hope having the whole story and the why behind his murder, will help you move on with your lives," said Coop. "It's been a privilege to know all of you. I only wish we hadn't met under such heart wrenching circumstances."

Lila Rose and Abby served tea and cookies while they continued talking. Coop steered the conversation to Taylor's college plans. The young man's face lit up when he talked about Vanderbilt and flashed with worry when he discussed waiting to hear about his acceptance. Coop and Annabelle assured him he would be accepted and wanted to be on the list to be notified when he received the happy news.

As Coop and Annabelle prepared to leave, the family thanked them with hugs and handclasps and made them promise to keep in touch. Chase slipped a folded paper into Coop's hand when he shook it. Annabelle shot him a questioning look when she saw the paper and he gave her a small shrug in return. Abby succeeded in getting both of them to agree to dinner at her house the following weekend.

Taylor walked them to the Jeep and gave Gus a thorough petting before the dog jumped into the back. He continued to wave until they rounded the corner with Gus giving a quick bark goodbye.

"What did Chase give you?"

"Oh, I put it in my pocket." He reached in and pulled it out, unfolding a check. Both of their eyes widened when they saw the amount and the simple "Thank you" he had written on the memo line.

"Holy cow," said Annabelle.

"Everyone gets a bonus, courtesy of Chase and Lila Rose," said Coop.

"I'm so glad they have Taylor in their lives," she said, as a tear slid down her cheek.

He reached across and squeezed her knee. "How about we stop for some ice cream on the way home?" asked Coop, wiggling his eyebrows at Annabelle.

"We'll spoil our supper."

"Don't tell Aunt Camille," he said, with a laugh and pointed the Jeep for Steve's Ice Cream Shop. He treated Annabelle to a chocolate waffle cone and Gus got a lick from his. They chose a double rocker on the patio, swinging as they listened to a Beau Branson tune, content to savor the beauty of a perfect fall day in Music City.

EPILOGUE

K*iller Music* is the first book in the Cooper Harrington Detective Novels. You'll discover a new case in each book in the series, but the characters you've come to know will continue throughout the series.

If you've missed reading any, here are the links to the entire series, in order.

Killer Music
Deadly Connection
Dead Wrong
Cold Killer
Deadly Deception

The books don't have to be read in order, but are more enjoyable when you do, since you'll learn more about Coop's backstory as the series unfolds. Continue reading to discover more whodunits that keep readers guessing until the end. If you're a new reader to Coop's books, you won't want to miss the other novels in the series.

ACKNOWLEDGMENTS

Writing *Killer Music* was challenging, but rewarding. The inspiration for this book came from a trip I took to Nashville. I loved the area, especially the history and the beauty of the old plantations and gardens, which I wanted to weave into a story.

I retired from the legislative branch of another state government and used my knowledge and experience plus my love of capital cities while formulating this novel. I spent some time at the Legislative Plaza and the Tennessee Capitol Building and connected with some former colleagues for technical questions related to the buildings. My thanks go out to these hardworking staffers who are always willing to impart their expertise and knowledge. The liberties I took with the process and entities were all my own.

The best part of writing is the freedom to invent people and situations. I enjoy utilizing my knowledge, in this case of the legislative process, as a backdrop for a wild and fictional story full of created characters, some lovable, and others detestable. This book is a departure from my other three Hometown Harbor novels in the women's fiction genre, but it was fun to write and I anticipate continuing with more Cooper Harrington mysteries.

As always I'm thankful for my early readers, who are diligent when it comes to reading my manuscripts. Theresa, Ruth, and Dana are always willing to read my rough drafts and give me valuable feedback and ideas. I relied on my dad's expertise and over three decades in the law enforcement field for many of the technical details in *Killer Music*.

I love my new cover branding from Elizabeth Mackey, who always does an excellent job.

I'm grateful for the support and encouragement of my friends and family as I continue to pursue my dream of writing. I appreciate all of the readers who have taken the time to provide a review on Amazon or Goodreads. These reviews are especially important in promoting future books, so if you enjoy my novels, please consider leaving a positive review.

Remember to visit my website at www.tammylgrace.com or Facebook to keep in touch—I'd love to hear from you.

FROM THE AUTHOR

Thank you for reading KILLER MUSIC. There are more books in the series and I hope to continue writing new cases for Coop for many years. Each book features a new case, with the characters you've come to know.

For readers who enjoy women's fiction, you'll want to check out my Hometown Harbor Series. There are six books in the series, set in the picturesque San Juan Islands in Washington. Be sure and download the free novella, HOMETOWN HARBOR: THE BEGINNING. It's a prequel to FINDING HOME that I know you'll enjoy.

My new GLASS BEACH COTTAGE SERIES is also loved by readers. It is a heartwarming story of a woman's resilience buoyed by the bonds of friendship, an unexpected gift, and the joy she finds in helping others. As with all my books, the furry four-legged characters play a prominent role. BEACH HAVEN and MOONLIGHT BEACH are both available in this series.

If you're a fan of sweet Christmas stories, you'll want to check out A SEASON FOR HOPE and THE MAGIC OF THE SEASON, in my Christmas in Silver Falls Series. CHRISTMAS IN SNOW VALLEY is another stand-alone Christmas novella set in a cute small town. I've also written a connected series with five other authors, SOUL SISTERS AT CEDAR MOUNTAIN LODGE, and you'll want to check out all of those books.

I'm excited about my new releases for Bookouture, writing as Casey Wilson. A DOG'S HOPE and A DOG'S CHANCE are two emotional, but heartwarming books about the connection we have with dogs.

Speaking of dogs, I'd love to send you my exclusive interview with the canine companions in the Hometown Harbor Series as a thank-you for joining my exclusive group of readers. You can sign up here at my website.

MORE FROM TAMMY L. GRACE

GLASS BEACH COTTAGE SERIES

Beach Haven

Moonlight Beach

Beach Dreams

WRITING AS CASEY WILSON

A Dog's Hope

A Dog's Chance

WISHING TREE SERIES

The Wishing Tree

Wish Again

Overdue Wishes

SISTERS OF THE HEART SERIES

Greetings from Lavender Valley

Pathway to Lavender Valley

Sanctuary at Lavender Valley

Blossoms at Lavender Valley

Comfort in Lavender Valley

Reunion in Lavender Valley

Remember to subscribe to Tammy's exclusive group of readers for your gift, only available to readers on her mailing list. **Sign up at www. tammylgrace.com. Follow this link to subscribe at https://wp.me/ P9umIy-e** and you'll receive the exclusive interview she did with all the canine characters in her Hometown Harbor Series.

Follow Tammy on Facebook by liking her page. You may also follow Tammy on book retailers or at BookBub by clicking on the follow button.

ABOUT THE AUTHOR

Tammy L. Grace is the *USA Today* bestselling and award-winning author of the Cooper Harrington Detective Novels, the best-selling Hometown Harbor Series, and the Glass Beach Cottage Series, along with several sweet Christmas novellas. Tammy also writes under the pen name of Casey Wilson for Bookouture and Grand Central Publishing. You'll find Tammy online at www.tammylgrace.com where you can join her mailing list and be part of her exclusive group of readers. Connect with Tammy on social media by clicking on the icons below and liking her author pages on major book retailers.

facebook.com/tammylgrace.books

twitter.com/TammyLGrace

instagram.com/authortammylgrace

bookbub.com/authors/tammy-l-grace

goodreads.com/tammylgrace

pinterest.com/tammylgrace

Made in the USA
Coppell, TX
07 June 2024

33235021R00144